T

ACCLAIM FOR COLLEEN COBLE

"As always, Colleen Coble never disappoints. *Strands of Truth* is no exception. I was hooked from the first page. Trying to read this story slowly is impossible. Don't be surprised when you find yourself flipping the pages in a hurry to find out what happens next! This one is for your keeper shelf."

—Lynette Eason, bestselling and award-winning author of the Blue Justice series

"Just when I think Colleen Coble's stories can't get any better, she proves me wrong. In *Strands of Truth*, I couldn't turn the pages fast enough. The characterization of Ridge and Harper and their relationship pulled me immediately into the story. Fast paced, with so many unexpected twists and turns, I read this book in one sitting. Coble has pushed the bar higher than I'd imagined. This book is one not to be missed. Highly recommend!"

—Robin Caroll, bestselling author of the Darkwater Inn series

"Free-dive into a romantic suspense that will leave you breathless and craving for more."

—DiAnn Mills, bestselling author

"Colleen Coble's latest book, *Strands of Truth*, grips you on page one with a heart-pounding opening and doesn't let go until the last satisfying word. I love her skill in pulling the reader in with believable, likable characters, interesting locations, and a mystery just waiting to be untangled. Highly recommended."

—Carrie Stuart Parks, author of *Fragments of Fear*

"It's in her blood! Colleen Coble once again shows her suspense prowess with a thriller as intricate and beautiful as a strand of DNA. *Strands of Truth* dives into an unusual profession involving mollusks and shell beds that weaves a unique, silky thread throughout the story. So fascinating I couldn't stop reading!"

—Ronie Kendig, bestselling author of The Tox Files

"Once again, Colleen Coble delivers an intriguing, suspenseful tale in *Strands of Truth*. The mystery and tension mount toward an explosive and satisfying finish. Well done."

—Creston Mapes, bestselling author

"*Secrets at Cedar Cabin* is filled with twists and turns that will keep readers turning the pages as they plunge into the horrific world of sex trafficking where they come face to face with evil. Colleen Coble delivers a fast-paced story with a strong, lovable ensemble cast and a sweet heaping helping of romance."

—Kelly Irvin, author of *Tell Her No Lies*

"Once again Colleen Coble has delivered a page-turning, can't-put-down suspense thriller with *Secrets at Cedar Cabin*! I vowed I'd read it slowly over several nights before going to bed. The story wouldn't wait—I HAD to finish it!"

—Carrie Stuart Parks, author of *Formula of Deception*

"This is an engrossing historical story with plenty of romance and danger for readers to get hooked by."

—*The Parkersburg News and Sentinel* on *Freedom's Light*

"Coble . . . weaves a suspense-filled romance set during the Revolutionary War. Coble's fine historical novel introduces a strong heroine—both in faith and character—that will appeal deeply to readers."

—*Publishers Weekly* on *Freedom's Light*

"This follow-up to *The View from Rainshadow Bay* features delightful characters and an evocative, atmospheric setting. Ideal for fans of romantic suspense and authors Dani Pettrey, Dee Henderson, and Brandilyn Collins."

—*Library Journal* for *The House at Saltwater Point*

"*The View from Rainshadow Bay* opens with a heart-pounding, run-for-your-life chase. This book will stay with you for a long time, long after you flip to the last page."

—*RT Book Reviews*, 4 stars

"Set on Washington State's Olympic Peninsula, this first volume of Coble's new suspense series is a tensely plotted and harrowing tale of murder, corporate greed, and family secrets. Devotees of Dani Pettrey, Brenda Novak, and Allison Brennan will find a new favorite here."

—*Library Journal* on *The View from Rainshadow Bay*

"Coble (*Twilight at Blueberry Barrens*) keeps the tension tight and the action moving in this gripping tale, the first in her Lavender Tides series set in the Pacific Northwest."

—*Publishers Weekly* on *The View from Rainshadow Bay*

"Filled with the suspense for which Coble is known, the novel is rich in detail with a healthy dose of romance, allowing readers to bask in the beauty of Washington State's lavender fields, lush forests and jagged coastline."

—*BookPage* on *The View from Rainshadow Bay*

"Prepare to stay up all night with Colleen Coble. Coble's beautiful, emotional prose coupled with her keen sense of pacing, escalating danger, and very real characters place her firmly at the top of the suspense genre. I could not put this book down."

—Allison Brennan, *New York Times* bestselling author of *Shattered*, on *The View from Rainshadow Bay*

"I loved returning to Rock Harbor and you will too. *Beneath Copper Falls* is Colleen at her best!"

—Dani Pettrey, bestselling author of the Alaskan Courage and Chesapeake Valor series

"Return to Rock Harbor for Colleen Coble's best story to date. *Beneath Copper Falls* is a twisting, turning thrill ride from page one that drops you headfirst into danger that will leave you breathless, sleep deprived, and eager for more! I couldn't turn the pages fast enough!"

—Lynette Eason, award-winning, bestselling
author of the Elite Guardians series

"The tension, both suspenseful and romantic, is gripping, reflecting Coble's prowess with the genre."

—*Publishers Weekly*, starred review for
Twilight at Blueberry Barrens

"Incredible storytelling and intricately drawn characters. You won't want to miss *Twilight at Blueberry Barrens*!"

—Brenda Novak, *New York Times* and
USA TODAY bestselling author

"Coble has a gift for making a setting come to life. After reading *Twilight at Blueberry Barrens*, I feel like I've lived in Maine all my life. This plot kept me guessing until the end, and her characters seem like my friends. I don't want to let them go!"

—Terri Blackstock, *USA TODAY* bestselling author of *If I Run*

"I'm a longtime fan of Colleen Coble, and *Twilight at Blueberry Barrens* is the perfect example of why. Coble delivers riveting suspense, delicious romance, and carefully crafted characters, all with the deft hand of a veteran writer. If you love romantic suspense, pick this one up. You won't be disappointed!"

—Denise Hunter, author of *The Goodbye Bride*

"Colleen Coble, the queen of Christian romantic mysteries, is back with her best book yet. Filled with familiar characters, plot twists, and a confusion of antagonists, I couldn't keep the pages of this novel set in Maine turning fast enough. I reconnected with characters I love while taking a journey filled with murder, suspense, and the prospect of love. This truly is her best book to date, and perfect for readers who adore a page-turner laced with romance."

—Cara Putman, award-winning author of *Shadowed by Grace* and *Where Treetops Glisten*, on *Twilight at Blueberry Barrens*

"Gripping! Colleen Coble has again written a page-turning romantic suspense with *Twilight at Blueberry Barrens*! Not only did she keep me up nights racing through the pages to see what would happen next, I genuinely cared for her characters. Colleen sets the bar high for romantic suspense!"

—Carrie Stuart Parks, author of *A Cry from the Dust* and *When Death Draws Near*

"Colleen Coble thrills readers again with her newest novel, an addictive suspense trenched in family, betrayal, and . . . murder."

—DiAnn Mills, author of *Deadly Encounter*, on *Twilight at Blueberry Barrens*

"Coble's latest, *Twilight at Blueberry Barrens*, is one of her best yet! With characters you want to know in person, a perfect setting, and a plot that had me holding my breath, laughing, and crying, this story will stay with the reader long after the book is closed. My highest recommendation."

—Robin Caroll, bestselling novelist

"Colleen's *Twilight at Blueberry Barrens* is filled with a bevy of twists and surprises, a wonderful romance, and the warmth of family love. I couldn't have asked for more. This author has always been a five-star novelist, but I think it's time to up the ante with this book. It's on my keeping shelf!"

—Hannah Alexander, author of the Hallowed Halls series

"Second chances, old flames, and startling new revelations combine to form a story filled with faith, trial, forgiveness, and redemption.

Crack the cover and step in, but beware—*Mermaid Moon* is harboring secrets that will keep you guessing."

—Lisa Wingate, *New York Times* bestselling
author of *Before We Were Yours*

"I burned through *The Inn at Ocean's Edge* in one sitting. An intricate plot by a master storyteller. Colleen Coble has done it again with this gripping opening to a new series. I can't wait to spend more time at Sunset Cove."

—Heather Burch, bestselling author of *One Lavender Ribbon*

"Coble doesn't disappoint with her custom blend of suspense and romance."

—*Publishers Weekly* on *The Inn at Ocean's Edge*

"Veteran author Coble has penned another winner. Filled with mystery and romance that are unpredictable until the last page, this novel will grip readers long past when they should put their books down. Recommended to readers of contemporary mysteries."

—*CBA Retailers + Resources* review of
The Inn at Ocean's Edge

"Coble truly shines when she's penning a mystery, and this tale will really keep the reader guessing . . . Mystery lovers will definitely want to put this book on their purchase list."

—*RT Book Reviews* on *The Inn at Ocean's Edge*

"Master storyteller Colleen Coble has done it again. *The Inn at Ocean's Edge* is an intricately woven, well-crafted story of romance, suspense, family secrets, and a decades-old mystery. Needless to say, it had me hooked from page one. I simply couldn't stop turning the pages. This one's going on my keeper shelf."

—Lynette Eason, award-winning, bestselling
author of the Hidden Identity series

"Evocative and gripping, *The Inn at Ocean's Edge* will keep you flipping pages long into the night."

—Dani Pettrey, bestselling author of the Alaskan Courage series

"Coble's atmospheric and suspenseful series launch should appeal to fans of Tracie Peterson and other authors of Christian romantic suspense."

—*Library Journal* review of *Tidewater Inn*

"Romantically tense, but with just the right touch of danger, this cowboy love story is surprisingly clever—and pleasingly sweet."

—USAToday.com review of *Blue Moon Promise*

"[An] outstanding, completely engaging tale that will have you on the edge of your seat . . . A must-have for all fans of romantic suspense!"

—TheRomanceReadersConnection.com review of *Anathema*

"Colleen Coble lays an intricate trail in *Without a Trace* and draws the reader on like a hound with a scent."

—*Romantic Times*, 4 1/2 stars

"Coble's historical series just keeps getting better with each entry."

—*Library Journal* starred review of *The Lightkeeper's Ball*

"Don't ever mistake [Coble's] for the fluffy romances with a little bit of suspense. She writes solid suspense, and she ties it all together beautifully with a wonderful message."

—LifeinReviewBlog.com review of *Lonestar Angel*

"Colleen is a master storyteller."

—Karen Kingsbury, bestselling author of *Unlocked* and *Learning*

STRANDS
OF TRUTH

ALSO BY COLLEEN COBLE

LAVENDER TIDES NOVELS
The View from Rainshadow Bay
Leaving Lavender Tides Novella
The House at Saltwater Point
Secrets at Cedar Cabin

SUNSET COVE NOVELS
The Inn at Ocean's Edge
Mermaid Moon
Twilight at Blueberry Barrens

HOPE BEACH NOVELS
Tidewater Inn
Rosemary Cottage
Seagrass Pier
All Is Bright: A Hope Beach
Christmas Novella (e-book only)

ROCK HARBOR NOVELS
Without a Trace
Beyond a Doubt
Into the Deep
Cry in the Night
Haven of Swans (formerly
titled *Abomination*)
Silent Night: A Rock Harbor
Christmas Novella (e-book only)
Beneath Copper Falls

YA/MIDDLE GRADE ROCK HARBOR BOOKS
Rock Harbor Search and Rescue
Rock Harbor Lost and Found

CHILDREN'S ROCK HARBOR BOOK
The Blessings Jar

UNDER TEXAS STARS NOVELS
Blue Moon Promise
Safe in His Arms
Bluebonnet Bride Novella (e-book only)

THE ALOHA REEF NOVELS
Distant Echoes
Black Sands
Dangerous Depths
Midnight Sea
Holy Night: An Aloha Reef
Christmas Novella (e-book only)

THE MERCY FALLS SERIES
The Lightkeeper's Daughter
The Lightkeeper's Bride
The Lightkeeper's Ball

JOURNEY OF THE HEART SERIES
A Heart's Disguise
A Heart's Obsession
A Heart's Danger
A Heart's Betrayal
A Heart's Promise
A Heart's Home

LONESTAR NOVELS
Lonestar Sanctuary
Lonestar Secrets
Lonestar Homecoming
Lonestar Angel
All Is Calm: A Lonestar Christmas
Novella (e-book only)

Freedom's Light
Alaska Twilight
Fire Dancer
Where Shadows Meet (formerly
titled *Anathema*)
Butterfly Palace

STRANDS
OF TRUTH

A NOVEL

COLLEEN COBLE

THOMAS NELSON
Since 1798

Strands of Truth

© 2019 by Colleen Coble

Published in Nashville, Tennessee, by Thomas Nelson. Thomas Nelson is a registered trademark of HarperCollins Christian Publishing, Inc.

Thomas Nelson titles may be purchased in bulk for educational, business, fund-raising, or sales promotional use. For information, please email SpecialMarkets@ ThomasNelson.com.

Publisher's Note: This novel is a work of fiction. Names, characters, places, and incidents are either products of the author's imagination or used fictitiously. All characters are fictional, and any similarity to people living or dead is purely coincidental.

ISBN 978-0-7180-8590-2 (library edition)

Library of Congress Cataloging-in-Publication Data

Names: Coble, Colleen, author.
Title: Strands of truth.
Description: Nashville, Tennessee : Thomas Nelson, 2019.
Identifiers: LCCN 2019007770| ISBN 9780718085889 (paperback) | ISBN 9780718085896 (epub)
Subjects: | GSAFD: Romantic suspense fiction.
Classification: LCC PS3553.O2285 S77 2019 | DDC 813/.54--dc23 LC record available at https://lccn.loc.gov/2019007770

Printed in the United States of America

19 20 21 22 23 LSC 5 4 3 2 1

For my dear daughter-in-love
Donna Coble
whose DNA interest propelled the idea for this novel.
Thanks so much, honey!

Prologue

Lisa ran to her Datsun Bluebird and jerked open the yellow door. Her pulse strummed in her neck, and she glanced behind her to make sure she wasn't being followed. She'd tried not to show fear during the confrontation, but it was all she could do not to cry. She couldn't face life without him.

She'd been on edge ever since yesterday.

Twilight backlit the treetops and highlighted the hanging moss. Instead of finding it beautiful, she saw frightening shadows and shuddered. She slid under the wheel and started the engine, then pulled out of her driveway onto the road.

She turned toward the Gulf. The water always calmed her when she was upset—and she had crossed upset moments ago and swerved into the scared zone.

Her belly barely fit under the wheel, but this baby would be born soon, and then she'd have her figure back. She accelerated away from her home, a dilapidated one-story house with peeling white paint, and switched on her headlights.

The radio blared full of the news about the Berlin Wall

coming down, but Lisa didn't care about that, not now. She switched channels until she found Tom Petty's "Free Fallin'" playing, but even her favorite tune failed to sooth her shattered nerves. Could she seriously be murdered over this? She'd glimpsed madness in those eyes.

She pressed the brakes as she came to a four-way stop, but the brake pedal went clear to the floor. She gasped and pumped the pedal again. No response. The car shot through the intersection, barely missing the tail end of another vehicle that had entered it before her.

Hands gripping the steering wheel, she struggled to keep the car on the road as she frantically thought of a way to bring it to a stop that didn't involve hitting another car or a tree. The baby in her belly kicked as if he or she knew their lives hung suspended in time.

"We're going to make it, little one. We have to. I can't leave you alone." No one would love her baby if she died. Her mother couldn't care for her child. She cared more about her drugs than anything else.

Lisa tried to tamp down her rising emotions, but she'd never been so frightened. The car fishtailed on the sandy road as she forced it back from the shoulder. Huge trees lined the pavement in a dense formation. Where could she drive off into relative safety? A field sprawled over on the right, just past the four-way stop ahead. If she made it through, it seemed the only place where they might survive.

Had the brakes been cut? What else could it be? She'd just had the car serviced.

Lisa approached the stop sign much too fast. The slight downhill slope had only accelerated the speed that hovered at nearly seventy. Her mouth went bone dry.

Her future with her child and the love of her life depended on the next few moments.

She could do it—she had to.

The tires squealed as the car barely held on to the road through the slight turn at high speed. Before Lisa could breathe a sigh of relief, a lumbering truck approached from the right side, and she laid on her horn with all her strength. She unleashed a scream as the car hurtled toward the big dump truck.

The violent impact robbed her lungs of air, and she blacked out. When she came to, she was in an ambulance. She fought back the darkness long enough to tell the paramedic, "Save my baby. Please . . ."

She whispered a final prayer for God to take care of her child before a darker night claimed her.

1

The examination table was cold and hard under her back as Harper Taylor looked around the room. She focused on the picture of a familiar Florida beach, which helped block out the doctor's movements and the smell of antiseptic. She'd been on the beach at Honeymoon Island yesterday, and she could still smell the briny scent of the bay and hear the call of the gulls. The ocean always sang a siren song she found impossible to resist.

Calm. Peace. The smell of a newborn baby's head.

"All done." Dr. Cox's face came to her side, and she was smiling. "Lie here for about fifteen minutes, and then you can get dressed and go home." She tugged the paper sheet down over Harper's legs.

"How soon will I know if the embryo transfer was successful?" Though she'd researched the process to death, she wanted some assurance.

"Two weeks. I know right now it seems like an eternity, but those days will pass before you know it. I've already submitted the lab requisition for a beta-HCG test. If we get a positive, we'll track the counts every few days to make sure they are increasing properly." Dr. Cox patted her hand. "Hang in there." She exited the room, leaving Harper alone to stare at the ceiling.

Her longing for a child brought tears to her eyes. She'd felt empty for so long. Alone. And she'd be a good mom—she knew she would. All the kids in the church nursery loved her, and she babysat for friends every chance she got. She had a wealth of patience, and she'd do everything in her power to make sure her child knew she or he was wanted.

She slipped her hand to her stomach. The gender didn't matter to her at all. She could love either a boy or a girl. It didn't matter that this baby wasn't her own blood. The little one would grow inside her, and the two of them would be inseparable.

Once the fifteen minutes were up, she was finally able to go to the bathroom and get dressed. She already felt different. Was that a good sign, or was it all in her head? She slipped her feet into flip-flops, then headed toward the reception area.

The tension she'd held inside melted when she saw her business partner, Oliver Jackson, in the waiting room, engrossed in conversation with an attractive woman in her fifties. She hadn't been sure he'd be here. He'd dropped her off, then gone to practice his bagpipes with the band for the Scottish Highland Games in April. He said he'd be back, but he often got caught up in what he was doing and lost track of time. It wouldn't have been the first time he'd stood her up.

Oliver was a big man, well over six feet tall, with broad shoulders and a firm stomach from the hours spent in his elaborate home gym. She'd always wondered if he colored his still-dark hair or if he was one of those lucky people who didn't gray early.

Even here in a fertility clinic, this man in his sixties turned women's heads. She'd watched them fawn over him for years, and he'd had his share of relationships over the fifteen years since his divorce. But Oliver never stuck with one woman for long. Was there even such a thing as a forever love? She hadn't seen any evidence of it, and it felt much safer to build her life without expecting that kind of faithfulness from any man. Having a child could fill that hole in her heart without the need to be on her guard around a man.

He saw her and ended his conversation, then joined her at the door. His dark-brown eyes held concern. "You changed your mind?"

She shook her head. "Not a chance."

"It seems an extreme way to go about having a family. You're only thirty. There's plenty of time to have children in the traditional way."

"Only thirty? There's not even a boyfriend in the wings. Besides, you don't know what it's like to long for a family all your life and never even have so much as a cousin to turn to." She knew better than to try to explain her reasons. No one could understand the guard she'd placed around her heart unless they'd lived her life.

His brow creased in a frown. "I tried to find your family."

"I know you did."

All he'd discovered was her mother, Lisa Taylor, had died moments after Harper's birth. Oliver had never been able to discover her father's name. Harper still had unpleasant memories of her grandmother, who had cared for Harper until she was eight before dying of a drug overdose at fifty. Hard as those years were, her grandmother's neglect had been better than the foster homes where Harper had landed.

This embryo adoption was going to change her life.

"I'll get the car."

She nodded and stepped outside into a beautiful February day that lacked the usual Florida humidity. Oliver drove under the porte cochere, and she climbed into his white Mercedes convertible. He'd put the top down, and the sound of the wind deterred further conversation as he drove her home.

He parked along the road by the inlet where she'd anchored her houseboat. "Want me to stay awhile?"

She shook her head. "I'm going to lie on the top deck in the sunshine and read a book. I'll think happy thoughts and try not to worry."

His white teeth flashed in an approving smile. "Sounds like a great idea."

She held his gaze. "You've always been there for me, Oliver. From the first moment Ridge dragged me out of the garage with his new sleeping bag in my hands. How did you see past the angry kid I was at fifteen?"

He shrugged and stared at the ground. "I'd just given my kids everything they could possibly want for Christmas, and they'd looked at the gifts with a cursory thank-you that didn't feel genuine. Willow was pouting about not getting a car. Then there you were. I looked in your eyes and saw the determination I'd felt myself when I was growing up poor in Alabama. I knew in that moment I had to help you or regret it for the rest of my life."

Tears burned her eyes. "You've done so much—making sure I had counseling, tutoring, a job, college. All of it would have been out of reach if not for you."

He touched her cheek. "You did me proud, Harper. Now go rest. Call me if you need me."

She blinked back the tears and waggled her fingers at him in a cheery good-bye, then got out and walked down the pier to where the *Sea Silk* bobbed in the waves. A pelican tipped its head to gawk at her, then flapped off on big wings. When she got closer to her houseboat, she slowed to a stop. The door to the cabin had been wrenched off. Someone had broken in.

She opened her purse to grab her phone to call the police, and then her gut clenched. She'd left her phone in the boat cabin. She'd have to go aboard to report the break-in. Could the intruder still be there?

She looked around and listened to the wind through the mangroves. There was no other sound, but she felt an ominous presence, and fear rippled down her back. She reversed course and went to her SUV parked in a small pull-off nearby. She'd drive into Dunedin and report it.

———

Ridge Jackson drove through downtown Dunedin at twilight to meet his father. His dad was usually straightforward and direct, but when Dad had called for a meeting, he'd been vague and distracted. Ridge couldn't still a niggle of uneasiness—it was as if Dad knew Ridge would be a hard sell on whatever new idea he'd come up with.

He had no doubt it was a new business scheme. Oliver Jackson had his finger in more pies of business enterprises than Ridge could count, but his dad's main company was Jackson Pharmaceuticals. The juggernaut business had grown immensely in the last ten years. He had the Midas touch. Everyone expected Ridge to be like his dad—charismatic and business oriented—but what Ridge wanted to do was pursue his work of studying mollusks in peace.

He smiled at the thought of telling his dad the great news about his new job. The offer had come through yesterday, and he still couldn't take it all in. Dad's distraction couldn't have come at a worse time. Ridge had to sell his place in Gainesville and find somewhere to live on Sanibel Island.

He parked and exited, ready to be out of the vehicle after the long drive from Gainesville. He went into The Dunedin Smokehouse, his favorite restaurant. The tangy aroma of beef brisket teased his nose and made his mouth water. They had the best brisket and pecan pie in the state.

He wound his way around the wooden tables until he found Dad chatting up a server in the back corner. He had never figured out how his dad could uncover someone's life story in thirty seconds flat. Ridge liked people, but he felt intrusive when he asked someone how their day was going.

Dad's grin split his genial face. "There you are, Ridge. I've already ordered our usual brisket nachos to share. How was your trip?"

"Good. Ran into some traffic in Tampa, but it wasn't too bad."

"Uh-huh." His dad stared off into the distance. "I've got a new project for you, son."

Ridge squared his shoulders and steeled himself for the coming battle. "Before you even get started, Dad, I've got a new job. I'm leaving the Florida Museum, and I'll be working at Bailey-Matthews Shell Museum on Sanibel Island. I'll get to work with one of the best malacologists in the country. I'm pretty stoked about it."

Most people heard the term *malacologist* and their eyes

glazed over. He'd been fascinated with mollusks ever since he found his first shell at age two. It was a dream come true to work for the shell museum. He'd be in charge of shell exhibits from around the world.

His dad's mouth grew pinched. "I, ah, I'm sure it's a good job, son, but I've got something bigger in mind for you. It's a chance to use your knowledge of mollusks for something to benefit mankind. This isn't just growing collections, but something really valuable."

Dad always managed to get in his jabs. Preserving mollusks had its own kind of nobility. Ridge narrowed his eyes at his dad and shut up for a moment as the server brought their drinks. When she left, he leaned forward. "Okay, what is it?"

"I've bought a lab for you. You'll be able to study mollusks and snails to see if they hold any promise for medicinal uses. I'd like you to concentrate on curing dementia first. I don't want you or Willow to end up like my dad."

Ridge's grandfather had died of Alzheimer's last year, and it hit Dad hard.

Ridge held back his flicker of interest. His dad knew exactly which buttons to push, and Ridge didn't want to encourage him. Ridge had long believed the sea held treasures that would help mankind. Researchers thought mollusks might contain major neurological and antibiotic uses. "That sounds— interesting."

"I've already put out the call for lab assistants and researchers. You'll just oversee it and direct the research. I've even created a collection room for you to fully explore the different mollusks." His dad took a sip of his tea. "It will be a few weeks before we're up and running, but in the meantime, you can comb through research and see where you want to start."

"You're just now telling me about it?"

His dad shrugged. "I wanted you to see the lab in all its glory first. We can go take a look when we leave here. There's only one caveat."

Ah, finally the truth. Story of his life. Dad always held back the full truth about anything. He should be called the master manipulator.

Ridge took a swig of his drink. "What is it?"

"I want you to start with pen shells. They're already so versatile, and I believe there's more of their magic yet to be discovered."

White-hot anger shot up Ridge's spine. "This is about Harper instead of me, isn't it? It's been that way since you first saw her camping out in our backyard as a teenager. You're such a sucker for a sob story. I overheard you on the phone the other day, you know. You were telling her you'd be there for her and the baby. She used to get into trouble wherever she went, and I doubt that's changed. And you're still the same patsy." He spat out the last words with a sneer.

Dad's brows drew together in a dark frown. "I've never understood your hostility toward her. And she's long outgrown any kind of reckless behavior."

They'd had this discussion on many occasions, and he wasn't going to change his dad's mind about her. From the moment she'd shown up in Dad's life, Ridge had resented her and the way his father catered to her. Ridge had gone off to his freshman year of college when Dad took Harper under his wing. She'd been a runaway from the foster care system, and he'd done more for her than for his own kids. He'd gotten his secretary to agree to foster the girl. She hadn't had to work during her high school years like he and Willow had. Dad had hired tutors to help her catch up while they'd been expected to figure out their studies by themselves.

The woman had been a thorn in his side for fifteen years. No part of him wanted to have anything to do with her. "What's Harper have to say about it?"

"I haven't told her yet."

Ridge stared at his dad. Typical. Only reveal half of what you know and keep the other half for negotiation. He was sick of his father's half-truths.

But what if in working with Harper, he was able to find definitive proof that she was only hanging around Dad because of his money? Ridge knew it was true. His dad hated being used, and it wasn't often someone managed to get the best of him. Harper was that one exception.

He wanted to get to the bottom of whatever clever plan she'd hatched.

He reached for a nacho laden with smoked brisket and jalapeños. "Tell me more about the lab."

His resolve helped him walk through the lab after dinner. He would enjoy working with the impressive equipment and facilities, and it almost superseded his goal of bringing down Harper. Almost.

2

It should be easy to swim out there, grab her, and haul her back here to his vehicle. While there were several boats out there, he thought she was the only one diving. He swiped his wet hair off his forehead and reached for his mask. Diving was his passion, and he relished any chance he got to exercise his expertise.

He checked his dive computer. Plenty of air. In and out in twenty minutes. He adjusted his mask over his eyes, then slipped his mouthpiece into place before wading out into the water and plunging into the waves.

Visibility was about thirty feet with all the sand in the water, but he knew where he was headed and struck out for the mollusk beds north of Dunedin, about a hundred feet off-shore and below twelve feet of water. Seaweed tried to snag his ankles as he swam through, and he spotted a bull shark off to his right. His hand went to the knife at his waist, but he hoped not to have to use it.

A diver off to his left snared his attention, and he paused. Where'd he come from? The older guy with dark hair was big. Not good. He would have to either wait until the guy was done here or take him out.

He didn't have time to waste waiting around. The Taylor woman was likely to finish her work on the mollusk beds soon.

Decision made, he pulled out his knife and swam quickly to the diver examining the cage over the mollusk beds. He didn't seem to notice anyone else was in the water, and by the time his head came up and his eyes widened behind his mask, the knife sliced his air hose.

Bubbles rose in the water as the older man fought hard to break free, but he didn't let him go until the diver's eyes rolled back in his head and his mouth slackened. He hauled him to the unidentified boat and shoved him onto the dive platform, then hauled up the anchor. The tide would carry it out to sea. He didn't want the guy's murder on his hands.

Perfect. Now to grab the woman, deliver her, and collect his money. His son's life was riding on his success. It was the only way to pay for Alex's surgery, so he had to do whatever was necessary, no matter how repugnant.

The warm Gulf water embraced her like a hug. Harper paused as a playful manatee came close enough to touch. The sea mammal she'd named Cyrus swam past her before perching on the sandy sea floor to scratch his bottom. Manatees were related to elephants, and Harper could spend time with one for hours.

She grinned and swam over to him. Today had been a fine day snorkeling above her pen shells, a bed of bivalve mollusks. The shells were about six inches tall and tapered to a sharp point. The fibers protruding from the pointed end helped anchor them into the beds. Their growth was progressing

nicely. The netting designed to protect the beds from preda-
tors seemed to be in good shape, and she'd watched her best
friend, Sara Kavanagh, dive down to secure one edge of a cage.

The first harvest would be in two weeks, and she was
eager to see what kind of black pearls she'd find. A special file
in her computer holding recipes for pen shell meat was growing as well, and with the new harvest, she'd have byssus. The
filament produced by the shells to keep them in place in the
sand would be ready for use.

Sara surfaced beside her and pushed up her mask. "Out of
air and I'm beat. Let's head back to the boat."

"In just a minute. I can't just leave this handsome fellow
floating by himself." She waggled her fingers at the manatee.
"Have you seen Oliver?"

Sara shook her head. "He's the worst diving partner in the
world. He never stays within eyesight."

"He thinks it's not necessary since the beds are so shallow."

"People have drowned in less water than this," Sara grumb-
led. As an EMT for the Coast Guard, she'd seen more than her
fair share of drownings.

Sara shaded her eyes with her hand. "Looks like his boat is
gone. The least he could have done was tell us he was leaving.
Don't stay out too long without a rest." She struck out in strong
strokes for their boat.

Sara was right. It wasn't like Oliver to be so thoughtless.

Harper frowned and swam nearer the manatee. She
laughed out loud as the large creature floated on the waves
as if he were body surfing. The minutes slipped away as she
frolicked with the manatee. She glanced at her watch. Sara
had left over forty-five minutes ago. Harper blew the manatee
a kiss and headed for the boat.

A shadowy figure exploded from the murky water to her right and swam toward her. She flinched as she caught sight of the silvery flash from a knife in the man's hand. What was happening? He waggled the knife in front of her mask as if he thought the sight would paralyze her, but it galvanized her into action.

Adrenaline kicked in, and her hand went for her own knife at her waist, but she couldn't unsheathe it before the guy reached her.

His hand clamped down in a painful grip on her arm, and he jerked her under the waves. She tried to pry his fingers loose but couldn't get him to release her.

A flurry of bubbles obscured his face, but she got an impression of dark hair and flinty eyes. He grabbed her hand to drag her toward the shore.

With renewed desperation she fought against him, and his grip slackened enough for her to swim from him. Panic gave strength to her long legs, and she kicked as hard as she could for the safety of her boat. If she could beat him there, she had flares and other things she could use as a weapon. Her lungs burned with the need to breathe, but she flutter-kicked her fins furiously and finally grabbed ahold of the ladder.

Her head broke the surface, and she dragged gulps of air into her lungs. She hauled herself up the ladder as fast as she could.

A hand seized her ankle as she scrambled for the last rung, and she kicked the guy in the face, then flung herself to the deck of the boat. Her little black schipperke, Bear, barked and leaped past her to snap at the man as he came after her.

"Get him, Bear!" She dove for the storage box where she kept the flare gun and grabbed it, then turned to see Bear sink his teeth into the man's hand as the guy hung on to the top rung.

The man yowled and let go of the ladder, then fell back into the water. Bear put his paws atop the railing and continued to bark. Her hair still damp, Sara came out of the wheelhouse with wide eyes.

"Start the engine!" Harper flung her five-eleven length toward Sara, who didn't ask any questions as she turned and switched on the engine.

In moments Sara had the boat speeding out to sea. The trembling started in Harper's arms and spread to her legs. She sank onto the deck as she stared out over the waves toward where they'd fled. There was no sign of another boat or of her attacker.

Sara flung her honey-colored hair out of her eyes and glanced back at her. "You okay? What happened?"

Harper swallowed hard and nodded. "There was a-a man. I don't know if he was trying to kill me or kidnap me."

The speed and silence of the attack had been unnerving and surreal. She told Sara what had happened, and her expression grew more somber. "Someone broke into my houseboat yesterday while I was gone. I reported it to the police, but they didn't find anything."

"It might be related." Sara reached for her phone. "Thank goodness Bear was there. We'd better call this in."

"I suppose so, but I don't have a good description. His wet hair could have been brown or light blond, and I didn't see his eye color. It happened so fast." Harper's voice wobbled. "And we have to call Oliver. His boat is gone, but I want to make sure he's okay."

"We'll head back in a minute. You're as white as sea foam."

Sara rummaged for a bottle of water and handed it to her. "Take a drink and a few deep breaths. Did he cut you anywhere?"

Harper shook her head and tried to stop the trembling in her limbs. She took a swig of water. "I'm okay. It's just the adrenaline. I've never been attacked before. It seemed so random and senseless."

Sara and her fiancé, Josh Holman, were with the Coast Guard. They'd both transferred here after Josh had returned from a year's temporary assignment on the West Coast. Harper listened with half an ear as her friend called Josh and filled him in.

"Josh will be here in half an hour. Try calling Oliver."

"I didn't bring my phone with me."

"Of course you didn't." Sara handed hers over. The two of them had met their first year at Duke University when Harper needed to borrow Sara's cell phone outside Duke Gardens, and they had been fast friends for twelve years now.

Harper placed the call, but it went to voice mail. "He's not answering. Let's get back and make sure he hasn't been hurt."

She sipped her water, then scooped up her dog and cuddled him close. The warmth of his fur began to calm the nerves jittering up her spine.

"Could this be a warning to move my pen shell beds? I got a call two days ago about this being an ancient Native American burial site. Maybe Eric doesn't want to wait for me to figure out what to do."

"Seems extreme, but I suppose it's possible. I'll mention it to Josh." Sara waved. "Here he comes now."

3

What had happened to his dad? Standing in the bow of his boat, Ridge peered past the mangroves near the shore and watched for Dad's boat. A manatee skimmed by, and he normally would have stopped the boat to watch, but an inner urgency drove him on.

He'd been at lunch with Jamal, a fatherless boy from church he'd taken under his wing, when Harper called. He'd let it go to voice mail, then listened to the message. She'd been panicked about not being able to track down his dad, and at first Ridge had discounted her fear. Until he hadn't been able to raise his dad himself. *Wind Dancer* wasn't docked at Dad's house or at the boat slip in the marina.

The Coast Guard was out searching for Dad, too, but Ridge hadn't been able to wait at home. He knew his dad's favorite fishing spots and the best places to dock and eat. He might just be chatting with another server or a guy mowing a lawn. It was likely nothing. His dad's phone probably had gone dead, or he'd forgotten it in the boat.

But as much as he tried to rationalize the situation, an inner voice whispered something was wrong.

The late-afternoon sun glinted off the waves, and the

channel began to narrow. Dad wouldn't have been able to get any farther inland, so Ridge backed up until the channel widened enough to turn around. The Coast Guard would have checked the area where Dad had disappeared, but what if he'd run out of fuel and was at the mercy of the current and winds? He could have been pushed out to sea.

But why didn't he call for help?

Ridge set his jaw and decided to head out to sea a bit. He reached for his phone to make another call to his dad. The phone rang several times, then went to voice mail again. He started to put his phone away, then smacked himself in the forehead.

They had the GPS phone tracker on each other. Why hadn't he thought of it before? He activated the program and waited for it to search. When the location dot popped up, he frowned. Dad was way out to sea, farther than he would have thought the wind and waves could drive him. Ridge put a call in to the Coast Guard with the location, then increased his speed and went to find his father.

The wind freshened, and he put on more speed. He had a feeling his dad needed him.

Half an hour later, he spotted a boat bobbing in the waves. A Coast Guard cutter approached from the opposite direction, and he waved at them. Though it was nearly dark, he could make out *Wind Dancer*'s familiar lines. But there was no sign of his father's brawny body.

He reached the Grady-White before the cutter and secured his line to the *Wind Dancer*, then clambered aboard. "Dad?"

He went to the cockpit, but no one answered him. The Coast Guard cutter secured their lines just off the bow of the Grady-White as he went to check out the cabin. As he descended the steps in the darkness, he heard a distant groan.

"Dad?" He reached over and flipped on the lights.

His father lay in a crumpled heap on the deck. "Dad!" Ridge raced to crouch by his dad and pressed his fingertips against his neck. Pulse thready and uneven. "I'll get help!"

He rushed up the steps and waved to the Coast Guard. "Help! I need a medic."

In minutes someone was tending to his dad. Someone else called for a chopper to transport him to the hospital as quickly as possible.

"Hang on, Dad. Don't you leave me."

His dad's hand twitched in his, and he squeezed back. "You're going to be all right. We're heading to the hospital."

Did his dad even hear him? His chest barely moved, and Ridge feared he was watching his father slip away from him.

"Don't die, Dad, please don't die." He held his father's hand and prayed until the helicopter came, and then he prayed all the way back to the hospital in his boat.

When he finally arrived, he was told his dad was in a coma. The doctors weren't yet sure if he'd had a heart attack or a stroke, but he was in a bad way. Ridge stood and looked down at his father, so still and lifeless. The only sound was the beeping of the machines hooked to him.

He would have to tell his sister. And Harper. Neither meeting would be pleasant.

⌒

The waves lapped at the *Sea Silk*'s hull. Harper sat on the dock with her bare feet dangling a few inches above the water. She'd anchored her boat at the marina opposite Edgewater Park in Dunedin. She loved sitting on her boat with the beach town in view. Trees framed the brick shops and the brightly painted clapboard structures. Visitors came just to view the murals of oranges painted on the sides of the shops. The hum of Jet Skis and the sight of windsurfers added to her sense of contentment in her hometown.

The scent of seafood from Dunedin Fish Market wafted to her, but she wasn't hungry. After the grilling by the Coast Guard about the attack, she was exhausted and even more upset. It hadn't made any sense, but she was mostly worried about Oliver.

He was nowhere to be found. Ridge had never returned her frantic phone call, but maybe he was with his dad now. No one had seen Oliver's boat since they'd gone diving.

She desperately wanted to hear his voice. She was sure he'd call any minute.

Her gaze strayed to Oliver's vacant spot in the marina. He sometimes took his boat to his dock in Clearwater. Surely that's what had happened this time.

The mystical, golden quality of light hid the bay's secrets, and she tried to push away the worry. Oliver had to be fine. Bear sat beside her with his alert gaze watching silver fish dart among the rocks on the bottom. The little dog looked like a miniature black bear and had a huge heart.

Someone called her name, and Sara came toward her carrying her laptop. She dropped down beside Harper and opened the lid. "Look! You have a close family match."

With her worry about Oliver it took a few seconds for Harper to track what Sara meant. "You mean the DNA test?"

Sara nodded. "I checked out the match, and I think she's a half sibling. There are some more distant ones, too, but let's start with her first. If she doesn't lead anywhere, we can take a look at the others. Those matches appear to be on your mother's side."

Half sister. Was it possible she wasn't alone?

Harper hadn't given much credence to the DNA program's ability to help her find a living relative, but Sara hadn't taken no for an answer. She'd bought it for Harper's birthday a month ago and had checked it religiously for her ever since.

Harper's hand strayed to her belly. Maybe she wouldn't be alone for long even if the DNA thing didn't pan out. Should she tell Sara what she'd done? Only Oliver knew she planned to have a baby. But no. Not until Harper knew she was pregnant.

Sara plopped the laptop onto Harper's thighs. "Have a look."

A ripple of excitement ran up her spine, and Harper opened the link. She blinked at the cM number that indicated how close of a relationship existed in the DNA. It *did* seem likely the woman was a half sibling.

The shared contact details listed the relative, and Harper lingered over the name: Annabelle Rice. Her chest compressed, and her pulse stammered in her throat. At last she might learn the name of her father.

"Email her now and set up a time to meet."

"I don't know, Sara. I need to think about what to say. I can't just waltz in and ask who her father is."

"Why not? You've been searching for him a long time."

Like all her life. "Did you talk to your mom today?"

Sara and her mother talked several times a week. Harper couldn't even imagine how great it must be to have a mom to talk to so intimately like that. She wanted to be that kind of mom herself. Someday she wanted her son or daughter to know he or she could call her about every little detail.

"Just briefly." Sara rose and touched Harper's shoulder.

"I'll let you think about how to word it. I've got to get back to Clearwater."

"You're a good friend, Sara."

"Friends help friends. Let me know what you hear." She went back down the dock and disappeared into the shadows.

That was one of the many lovely things about Sara—she only pushed so far, then backed off to let Harper deal with the problem her way.

She stared at the link to email Annabelle. Maybe it would be best to just request a meeting without asking any questions yet. She typed out the request before she could chicken out and hit Send.

Her stomach rumbled, and Bear gave her a hopeful look. "Yeah, we'll go eat dinner." She closed the laptop and stood, brushing dirt and debris from her shorts.

The sunset outlined a man on a small trawler motoring her way. The figure on deck waved to her. "Harper! Don't you ever answer your phone?"

She looked around for her phone but it was missing, though she'd sworn she'd brought it out here to await news of Oliver. "Ridge?" She waited for him to dock in Oliver's mooring, and then he stepped onto the dock and came toward her.

About thirty-three, Ridge Jackson always had a take-no-prisoners air about him. His piercing dark eyes warned the onlooker that he suffered no fools around him—and he'd never hidden his disdain for Harper's influence on his father. It used to bother her that he held her teenage rebellion against her, but she was never going to change his mind, so she just had to show him that girl was long gone.

He had Oliver's thick, nearly black hair, sculpted nose, and lips. Ridge's good looks and family money greased the way to many dinner invitations from hostesses eager to introduce him to available daughters or nieces.

He would have played the *Jane Eyre* character Edward Rochester to perfection. They'd been around each other a lot over the years—holidays, Oliver's birthdays, and various family functions. He might have disliked her then, but she'd been fascinated by him. She never had to guess at his intentions or worry that he might slip into her room on the nights she stayed with the family. He made no secret of his dislike, and that was the way she liked it. No games, no hidden agenda behind an insincere smile.

And he was so *smart.* She used to listen to him talk to his sister about his love of sea life, and his love of mollusks had fueled her own decision to study marine biology. Not that she'd ever dare tell him.

"Have you found Oliver?"

His eyes pinned her in place, and he crossed muscular arms over his chest. "He's in the hospital."

She gasped and clutched her hands together. "What happened? I-Is he going to be okay?"

"We're not sure yet. Maybe a stroke or a heart attack, but who knows. I found his boat out at sea, and I thought he was going down with you today."

"He did." She told him about the attack on her and how his father's boat was missing when they surfaced. "We searched for him but couldn't find it."

"So, did he dive today?"

"Yes. He seemed fine when he got there."

Ridge frowned. "Could he have had a stroke from the bends?"

"I don't see how. The beds are only twelve feet deep."

"I need to tell the doctors though, just in case."

"I'll go see him now. Which hospital?"

Ridge glanced up as an eagle squawked overhead. "He is in critical condition. No visitors but family."

Well, that got Ridge's point across. No matter how much she and Oliver cared about each other, she'd never matter to his real family.

"Thanks for coming out here to tell me." She wanted to tell him he'd delivered his message so please leave, but Harper's southern manners prevented her from such rudeness. She laced her fingers together and slid him a wary look as he surveyed her aging houseboat.

Why wasn't he leaving? He stepped closer to her and farther away from his trawler. He must have some other agenda for coming. Her mouth went dry. If he took over his father's affairs, Ridge would probably withdraw the funding for her pen shell beds.

Which would be a disaster of epic proportions. Oliver was her only investor, but it wasn't just the money—it was his belief in her work. She wasn't sure she'd be able to overcome her own inner qualms about her ability without Oliver there to bolster her.

Ridge squatted and rubbed Bear's ears. "I should have brought you a treat, buddy."

The dog's ears perked up and he whined, then licked Ridge's fingers. Traitor dog. To be fair, Ridge was the one who had gotten Bear for Oliver two years ago as a puppy. Two days later, after Bear chewed up Oliver's Salvatore Ferragamo loafers, Oliver had told Harper if she didn't take him, he'd drown the puppy. She'd taken him even though she knew Oliver's bark was worse than his bite.

"He didn't tell you?" Ridge stared down at her. "It appears we're going to work together."

"What are you talking about?"

"Dad bought a lab he wants me to run. He thinks the pen shells may have some medicinal benefit, and I'm supposed to do what I can to find it."

She took a step back. "You don't even believe in the project."

"For Pete's sake, quit acting like I'm going to take the whole thing away from you. I'll meet you at the pen shell beds in the morning, and we'll discuss what to do next."

Her mouth agape, she watched him step back into his trawler and motor away. Dismay didn't begin to cover how she felt about this turn of events.

4

He could have handled last night better. Ridge eyed the curves and planes of Harper's face as she sat in the bow of her boat on Sunday afternoon, staring into the glowering clouds. She'd scraped her thick red hair back into a ponytail, but the starkness suited her high cheekbones and expressive turquoise eyes, which let him know the full extent of her contempt.

The animosity between them was her fault, not his.

Ridge would never forget that first meeting. He'd found her in the garage stealing his new sleeping bag and had called his dad. She'd been defiant and angry instead of shamed by her behavior. Over the next couple of years, whenever she'd been in the house, he caught her with her sticky fingers in everything from his dad's desk to his sister's purse. And she was always trying to pit Willow and him against their dad.

Why Dad continued to help her was beyond Ridge.

She finally glanced his way. "How's Oliver?" Her gaze flickered to Bear, who sat adoringly at his feet, and her frown deepened.

"Still in a coma." Did he tell her the doctors thought Dad might have been oxygen starved? He didn't understand how that could have happened though. The mollusk beds were in shallow water and his dad was an expert diver. He planned to examine his dad's dive equipment. "I'm going to take a look at the beds."

A flush ran up the pale skin of her neck and lodged in her cheeks. "I think you'll agree they look healthy. I have our first restaurant order for the pen shell meat too." She squinted in the sunshine and stared out at a boat bobbing in the distance. "I'm not sure how much I'll have to spare for lab testing. I wish Oliver would have talked to me about that."

He frowned and bent over to pull on his fins. Did he want the venture to fail? At least it might get her out of Dad's life.

He didn't look at her but moved instead to the back of the boat. "I'll be the judge of the health of the beds." He fell backward into the ocean, and the clear blue water closed over his head in a warm embrace.

What was wrong with him? No matter how much he lectured himself to at least be polite, the moment he got around Harper he turned into a snarling jerk.

He kicked furiously down to the pen shell beds. Taking his time, he checked out the way they were anchored and the general health of the mollusks. She was right. They were in excellent shape.

Her harebrained scheme might not be so wild after all.

He left the beds behind and kicked for the surface. As he reached the boat's hull, he heard the throb of an engine in the distance. He quickly climbed the ladder to the deck.

Her eyes were wide as she stared over his shoulder at the approaching craft. Bear growled and moved in front of her, and she wrinkled her nose.

"What's wrong?" He faced the boat drawing near enough to dock with them.

The man at the helm looked vaguely familiar. His smooth

head was tanned, and what remained of his hair was a rim of brown from ear to ear around the back. He appeared to be in his forties. He cut the engine but made no move to come aboard *Sea Silk II*.

The guy balled his hand into a fist. "I asked you to stay away from the burial site."

Harper lifted her chin and took a step toward him. "Did you attack me yesterday and try to force me to swim with you to the shore?"

"I have no idea what you're talking about."

Ridge stared at the man and remembered where he'd seen him. "You're running for city council." His mind groped for the man's name. "Eric Kennedy."

"That's right. And I've already warned Ms. Taylor of the likely illegality of the location of those mollusk beds. We've discovered an ancient Native American burial site just yards past the beds."

"A hundred yards away!" She scooped up Bear. "I'm not disturbing any bones, nor am I breaking any laws. No one but you is saying I need to move the beds."

"I thought the burial grounds were down near Venice," Ridge said. "And even down there, no one is cordoning off the area or restricting access."

"We don't know what we have here yet. I don't want it disturbed until the archaeologists have a chance to evaluate it. I explained all this to Ms. Taylor already. Who are you?"

The man's imperious tone rubbed Ridge the wrong way. Typical politician trying to catapult himself into the limelight with some hot topic that might make the news. "Her business partner. You have a court order about this or anything to back up your claim?"

Kennedy reddened. "No, but I know I'm right."

Ridge crossed his arms over his chest. "Find a judge who believes you and come talk to us then."

Kennedy glared but said nothing. His boat roared away in a wash of motor-generated waves and stinking fuel.

Ridge glanced at Harper as she sank onto a seat and hugged Bear to her chest. He could have sworn he saw her swaying before she sat. "You okay? You're pale."

"I'm fine." But her wobbly voice betrayed her agitation.

"You didn't tell me the details last night. What happened?"

He listened with mounting concern to the details of the attack and the break-in the night before that. "You don't have any idea who it was?"

"I just got an impression of a muscular guy. It all happened so fast. Kennedy was the first person I thought of, but that's not really his style."

"It still might have been related to this Native American burial ground. Do you know how far away they found bones?"

"Their site is a hundred yards away. I've seen no evidence of any archaeological finds in my beds, and I have to dig them up and replant the shells on occasion. I think this is just a political stunt he's trying to pull." Her voice was stronger now, and her color had returned.

But that didn't explain the attack on her or the break-in.

Harper's life might change on this bright Monday morning. She parked in the drive and got out, ready to stretch after the nearly two-hour drive from Dunedin. She'd been lucky the person she'd been matched with in the DNA program wasn't halfway across the country with the way people moved around.

Sara had offered to come with her to meet Annabelle Rice, but Harper wanted to do this by herself. If today ended in crushing disappointment, she didn't want any witnesses. She could tell Sara about it this afternoon at the bivalve beds.

The single-story house on Brindle Street was typical of Orlando. A raised portico over the entry accented the cream stucco home. Carefully tended flower beds spilled fragrance into the air along a winding sidewalk. More flowers filled window boxes and added bright color and character to the home.

Annabelle's email had been welcoming enough, but Harper had given herself a stern talking to about having reasonable expectations. She'd spent most of her life yearning to learn about her father, and it would be easy to pin all her hopes on this one meeting. She fully expected to find the woman wasn't really her half sister.

As she approached the arched front door, she wished she hadn't left Bear at home. His warm, wiggly body would have brought comfort now. Inhaling the aroma of chocolate chip cookies wafting from somewhere, she pressed the doorbell.

"Coming!" Almost immediately the door opened. "You must be Harper." The woman motioned her in. "I've got fresh coffee brewing, and the cinnamon rolls are still warm. I'm so excited to meet you. I'm Annabelle, of course."

She embraced Harper in a quick hug that surrounded her in the scent of sugar and chocolate, then stepped away before it got awkward.

Annabelle had soft pink skin and bright-blue eyes under gray-and-blonde hair cut into a stylish bob. She wore designer jeans and a lacy top that showed off toned arms, though she had to be around fifty—much older than Harper had been expecting. The words she had practiced evaporated on her tongue, but she forced herself to smile and follow Annabelle inside though tension coiled in Harper's belly.

Nearly twenty years' difference existed between them, so this "match" didn't seem likely.

Sunlight bounced off the light oak floors and streamed through the front windows. The ceiling in the open floor plan soared at least sixteen feet above their heads. The sofa and chairs were a pale gray, and yellow accent pillows gave them a pop of color. The area rug was a gray abstract print splashed with more cheery yellow.

Harper instantly felt at home in the space. "You have a lovely home."

"Thanks. I'm an interior decorator and change it up every year or so, just to try something new." Annabelle gestured to the sofa. "Have a seat." She bent over a stainless-steel serving cart and poured two cups of coffee. "Cream or sugar?"

"Just black." Harper smiled and wrapped her fingers around the bright-red stoneware mug. "I'm not sure what questions I'm supposed to ask or even how to feel. Have you had other matches to your DNA?"

Annabelle took a sip of her coffee, then settled into the overstuffed chair opposite Harper. She curled her legs under her and shook her head. "I didn't expect to, not really. My mother died when I was a baby, and I have no idea who my father is. I was hoping you could tell me. And let's get the truth out right now. With as high as we are on the match scale, our father has to be the same man. I've done a lot of research, and we are definitely half sisters."

Harper caught her breath and set her mug on the side table.

The parallels between their circumstances seemed surreal. She wanted to ask more questions about how Annabelle's mother died, but it felt too intrusive until they became better acquainted. "My mother died when I was an infant, too, and no one has been able to name my father. You don't know anything at all?"

That part was disappointing. She'd hoped to discover her father's identity.

Annabelle's smile turned wistful. "My mother was an only child, so I don't even have any first cousins. My family consists of my two sons and my dead husband's relatives. Jim died of a brain aneurism when the boys were five and three. I had just finished getting my degree, so at least I was able to support us. I sometimes thought about my ancestry, but until my boys got out on their own, there was never time to pursue it."

Her blue eyes clouded. "I was recently diagnosed with lymphoma, and that made me think more about discovering health problems in my genetic line. For my boys' sakes especially."

Harper's chest squeezed. "I'm so sorry. Have the treatments been rough?"

"I haven't started them yet. I'm scheduled to start chemo next week. I'm sure I'll be all right. It won't be fun, but I've been through worse."

Annabelle's optimistic outlook was endearing, and Harper liked her more and more. "I'll be praying for you."

"Thank you. I'll take all the prayers I can get. So tell me about you."

Harper took a sip of coffee, but there was no delaying the inevitable. "My mom died when she was almost due with me. The brakes failed on her car, and it slammed into a big dump truck. She was still alive when she arrived at the hospital, and they were able to deliver me, but my mother died hours later. I lived with my grandmother until she died. After that, I went into foster care."

Annabelle's eyes filled with tears, but she touched Harper's hand without saying anything.

Harper took another sip of coffee. "I ran away when I was fifteen. I ended up sleeping in the backyard of a man who became my mentor. He found me a good foster home with his secretary, then made sure I graduated and got to college. He dug into my background as much as he could, but even his money hasn't been able to find out anything more than my mother died."

"I'm so sorry."

"What happened to your mom?"

Annabelle passed a plate of rolls to Harper. "She was murdered. The murder was never solved. My oldest son is a police officer now, and I've asked him so many times to take a fresh look at the evidence, but he says it's too late to learn much. She was bludgeoned with an unknown object."

Harper took a cinnamon roll and passed the plate back, though it seemed wrong to be nibbling on a warm roll when discussing such a horrible event. "I'm so sorry. How old were you?"

"About five months old. I was adopted by a very sweet family who couldn't have kids."

"You had no family?"

"My mom's dad and stepmother refused to take me. My adoptive parents kept all the newspaper clippings about the murder and gave me everything they knew about my mother when I was fifteen. That's why I know so much about her."

At least Annabelle never had to worry about locking her

bedroom door at night. "It's odd that both of our mothers died when we were so young." Harper's thoughts raced, and she blurted out what she'd been stewing about for a long time. "Oliver wondered if someone tampered with my mother's brakes."

Annabelle touched her hand to her throat. "Did you ever talk to the detective in charge of the investigation?"

"No. He's retired now."

Annabelle's expression turned thoughtful. "You could look him up and ask questions. Did Oliver say why he wondered about the brake tampering?"

"He said the car had just been serviced, so it was odd the brakes would fail like that."

Could Oliver be right?

Had both their mothers been murdered?

5

Judy Russo barely contained the exuberance rippling up her bell bottom jeans and right through the back of her blue baby doll top. She'd had a good feeling when she left Woodstock a few days ago that her life was about to change, but it was up to her to get what she wanted.

She turned off her Camaro in the middle of "Born to Be Wild," squared her shoulders in the shimmering heat of the Weeki Wachee parking lot, then marched to the office door to stand in line with other mermaid applicants. The humidity was like a physical presence that pressed against her so tightly it was hard to draw a breath. She was used to the dry air of West Texas, and this Florida weather would take some getting used to. She dug a rubber band out of her bag, then lifted her long hair off her neck and put it in a ponytail.

"Good call," the woman in charge of hiring said. Her thick brown hair was up in a stylish bouffant with a ponytail hanging down the back.

Judy felt positively dowdy next to her. "Judy Russo from

38

Abilene. I heard y'all are hiring mermaids? I was part of a swim team back home and have plenty of experience."

The woman looked about five years older than Judy, maybe · twenty-three or four. "You just get here?"

Judy nodded. "I haven't even found a hotel yet."

"You won't need one if you're as good as you say. You're pretty, and our visitors will like your curly red hair. Get suited up and let me see you swim. I'm Grace Beck, by the way."

Judy's lungs filled with a joyous gasp of air. "Where do I change?"

Grace pointed out a door. "Back there. Use one of our swimsuits." She stood and surveyed the remaining four applicants. "I think I have all I'm looking for right now. Thanks for your time." She opened the door for Judy.

In less than ten minutes Judy was suited up and in the crystal-clear water of the springs. She performed some of the moves she'd seen here last summer with her parents, and Grace nodded with approval through the glass into the auditorium. When Judy exited the building, she had a job.

Her new life was about to start, and she was so ready to put her backwater life in Texas behind her. Weeki Wachee was now owned by ABC, and there was always the chance someone important would spot her and give her a shot at an acting career.

Her smile was bright as she rushed toward her car to drive around to one of the mermaid cottages in the back.

A screech of brakes brought her head up, and she stared through the windshield into the warm brown eyes of the most handsome man she'd ever seen. He managed to stop his Mustang a couple of inches from her hips.

His face was white when he got out. "I nearly hit you."

"It was my fault. I wasn't watching where I was going."

She looked him over, this gorgeous guy in his navy uniform. She knew enough about the military to recognize his officer insignia. "I'm sorry if I scared you. I'm Judy Russo, the newest mermaid here."

A grin as adorable as Elvis's lifted his lips, and she was lost. She imagined introducing him to her friends back home and could see the approval in her dad's eyes if she brought home a navy man. Not that she cared about her dad's opinion, of course. He didn't deserve any consideration after he'd left her with his shrewish second wife.

He took a step toward her. "You have lunch yet, Judy Russo? Even mermaids have to eat."

"I'm starving."

He went around to the passenger side of his car and opened the door. "Let me whisk you off for some sustenance then. I've got a boat with some beer chilling and some food in the cooler. How does that sound?"

She smiled and sashayed toward the open car door. "Like heaven."

This visit was not turning out as Harper had envisioned. Instead of discussing connections and discovering her father's identity, she was knee deep in talking about murder.

She took the last sip of her lukewarm coffee. "What can you tell me about your mother?"

"What do you know about the Weeki Wachee mermaids?"

"One of my foster mothers took me there when I was ten. It was magical." The beautiful, smiling women floating in the clear spring had mesmerized her.

"My mother was one of the early mermaids. Let me show you." Annabelle turned on the television and started the DVD player. "I have it all queued up."

The screen flickered to life and began to play. The young women swam in perfect synchronization under the water. From the modest one-piece bathing suits, Harper guessed the video was taken in the late sixties. They didn't wear fish tails in the video like she'd seen when she went.

The recording seemed to be a promo and was dubbed with a man's voice. "The great conch shell at the canyon's rim is actually an air lock where the mermaids await their cue, breathing air until they emerge to perform their excitingly beautiful routines." He droned on about how the spring poured forth 117 million gallons of water a day at a perfect temperature of seventy-four degrees.

Harper couldn't take her eyes off the women performing on the screen. It was like peeking back into a long-forgotten era to the old kitschy Florida. A beautiful redhead swam closer to the auditorium's window and smiled as she began to peel and eat a banana.

"That's my mother," Annabelle said. "Judy Russo."

"She's lovely."

"I was sorry I didn't inherit her coloring." Annabelle sent a speculative glance Harper's direction. "Did your mother have red hair like you?"

"Yes."

Their father must have liked redheads. Harper felt a little nauseated, but she couldn't look away from the flickering screen.

"Newton Perry was the mastermind behind the mermaids. He used to train navy frogmen and got the bright idea about a tourist attraction featuring beautiful girls. In the early days the girls didn't even get paid—they just got room and board. Highway 19 was a two-lane road without much traffic, and when the girls heard a car, they'd run out to the road in their bathing suits and flag down passing motorists. The original theater only seated eighteen."

"When was this film made?"

Her expression wistful, Annabelle stared at the television. "It was in 1969. ABC had bought it by then, in 1959, and had expanded the theater to seat four hundred. My mom lived in one of the mermaid cottages out back."

A mermaid cottage sounded almost too charming for words, and Harper's imagination was fired by the images Annabelle's history brought to life.

The film ended, and Annabelle clicked off the TV. "She was found in her cottage. They were never able to determine what object pierced her temple and killed her. I was staying with her best friend, who found her a couple of hours after Mom was killed."

Harper's chest squeezed at the thought of a baby being left in such tragic circumstances. "Is her best friend still alive? Have you spoken with her?"

"I've never tracked her down. I don't even know if she's still alive. If you're interested, I have a shoebox full of newspaper clippings and other information my parents gave me."

"I'd love to see them. I'll take good care of them and bring them back to you."

"They're just copies. I have the originals in a safe place."

Harper frowned. "You have them hidden?"

Annabelle bit her lip. "This is going to sound crazy. I just had them in a shoebox in my closet, but lately I've felt like some-one is following me." She shrugged. "Probably paranoia from being sick, but the other day I got home, and the back door was standing open. I don't always lock the doors—it's not usually necessary around here—but I *know* I shut the door. And the house felt violated somehow." She gave a shaky laugh. "My son Scott checked out the house, but he couldn't find any evidence of a break-in."

"But you still felt you should make copies and hide the originals?"

Annabelle nodded. "Let me get them for you. I have them in my office." She rose and went down the hall, then reappeared a few moments later with a cardboard box.

Harper took it and stuffed it into her big bag. "I'll look at them right away. As soon as I talk to the detective who investigated my mother's death, I'll come back and we can discuss it. Should I wait a few weeks until you adjust to your chemo schedule?"

"No. I want to know immediately. I need something else to think about other than what's facing me."

Harper didn't want to lose her sister now that she'd found her. She touched Annabelle's hand. "I'll see what I can find out and come back on Saturday."

She normally wasn't the hugging sort, but she found herself clinging tightly to Annabelle at the door when they said good-bye. She slid under the wheel and headed out to meet Sara at the bivalve beds. Wait until she heard all this.

6

His dad still clung to life. The afternoon sun glared into his eyes as Ridge, dressed in a shortie wetsuit, walked from his dad's house down to the dock where he'd anchored the boat last night. He'd gotten a frantic call from Jamal's mom after her mother had had a heart attack. He'd agreed to take him until her mom was stable.

It couldn't have come at a worse time, but he had to be there for the boy. Jamal needed him.

"So what are we looking for?" Jamal had the rangy lope of a typical fifteen-year-old, and he'd shaved his head since Ridge saw him last. All that was left was a two-inch strip of black hair running down the center of his head.

"Anything that seems out of place." Ridge motioned for Jamal to precede him aboard the vessel.

The boat, a brand-new Grady-White Freedom, was his dad's pride and joy. He could afford something bigger, but he'd wanted a smaller, nimble boat to get closer to shore for fishing and for access to the pen shell beds. He found Dad's dive equipment in a heap back by the swim platform. He stooped and picked up the air gauge. Empty. His dad couldn't have been down long enough to have used up his air—at least not according to Harper.

Ridge began to go over everything—the BCD and regulator as well as the octopus and hoses. When he ran his hands over the hoses, he felt something. He turned into full sunlight and examined the hose. It had a slice in it. The air would have leaked out fairly quickly with a cut this size in the rubber.

Someone with a knife had come at Harper. Had the same man cut his dad's air hose—maybe to eliminate him from seeing her attack?

Ridge went belowdecks and checked out the other dive equipment, which was in good working order. He went back up topside and found Jamal. "You game to ride out to the mollusk beds?"

"Sure." The teenager sprawled into the seat with the controls. "Can I act as captain?"

"Sure. You know how to handle a boat?"

"I can learn."

He couldn't resist the boy's pleading expression and showed him how to start the engine and steer. They motored out to the location of the mollusk beds, and then Ridge dropped anchor and got ready. Harper had pointed out where his dad had been the day before, and he thought he was as close as possible.

"I'm going to dive down. You can keep an eye on the boat." He planned to teach Jamal to dive one of these days.

A pelican flapped overhead, and two gulls landed on the boat to observe him with beady eyes. They were probably hoping for a handout. He went to the stern and fell backward into the water. The water temperature was near seventy, warm for February, but still cold enough to make him wish he'd donned a full wetsuit.

He kicked down to the mollusk beds and swam over the top of the wire cages. They appeared to be the same as yesterday. Controlling his breathing to get the maximum time out of his air, he swam west past the beds and down to the sandy bottom. He took his time cruising over the area even though he had no idea what he might be looking for. Anything that might explain what had happened to his father.

After an hour he was ready to give up and head back to the boat when he spotted something half buried in the sand in about twenty feet of water. He kicked down at the glint of metal and found a knife. With a gloved hand he picked it up and clipped it carefully to his belt. It was unlikely there would be a way to find out who this had belonged to, but it might be the knife used to cut his dad's air hose. He'd turn it over to law enforcement.

He only had a few minutes of air left, so he began his ascent. When his head broke the surface, he looked around. Where was the boat? He turned 180 degrees and spied the boat drifting away from him.

"Jamal!" When there was no answer, he swam toward the boat and reached it after several minutes of hard work. He slapped a hand on the lower rung of the ladder and hauled himself up. "Jamal?"

His chest was tight as he went to the helm where he found the boy sprawled on the floor. Was he asleep or injured? Ridge knelt beside him and touched his shoulder. "Jamal?"

The boy's head rolled to one side, and Ridge saw a goose egg on the back of his head. Blood oozed from the spot.

Jamal's eyelids fluttered, and he groaned. "Ridge? What happened?"

Ridge helped him sit up. "Do you remember anything?"

Jamal frowned. "Some guy came aboard. A big white dude wearing a mask. I couldn't tell much more than that. He hit me with his air tank." He fingered the lump on his head. "He took your dad's tank and hose with him."

The intruder had taken the evidence. Ridge got Jamal seated in a chair and went to start the engine. "Let's run you by the ER and make sure you don't have a concussion."

Had someone recognized him as Oliver's son and decided to try to derail any investigation into what happened? It would be the only reason to take the cut hose.

Which meant there was something very sinister about his dad's condition.

He reached for his phone as he headed to Dunedin, then called the Coast Guard to report what he'd found. After he took care of Jamal, Ridge would confirm with the doctors that oxygen deprivation was almost certainly the underlying cause of his dad's condition. It might affect his treatment.

———

The salt-laden air whipped Harper's ponytail as she sat on the boat and watched Sara shrugging on her tanks and getting ready for the dive. Harper had rushed back from Orlando, eager to tell her friend about the visit, and Sara had been as awestruck as Harper at the news.

Sara glanced her way with a question in her eyes. "You're not suited up."

Harper would have to tell Sara she couldn't dive. An excuse wouldn't work—it had to be the truth. She didn't expect her friend to understand her desire for a baby at all costs.

"Um, Sara, do you think you can handle the planting of

more pen shells for me? I'm not going to be able to dive. I might be pregnant." Sara would know what that meant—she was a health technician with the Coast Guard.

Sara's gray eyes widened. "B-But who? How?"

She should have launched into this in a different way. "You know how much I want family. I know this is a shock. I normally would have talked this over with you before I did it, but it all happened so fast, and you were gone the week I got the call."

Harper drew in a deep breath. "I decided to adopt an embryo. I talked about it with my doctor a few months ago, and he called me when he heard about a single mom who'd gone through IVF before her husband left her. She had an embryo left. She's very pro-life and wanted the babies to have a chance at life. She was open to another single mom."

Sara held up her hand. "Wait, I don't think I'm following you. People can adopt other people's embryos?"

Harper nodded. "I could have used my own eggs and donor sperm, but then I've got a child who doesn't know where they came from—just like me. This way my child will know who his or her birth parents are. I received the embryo last week. I won't know for a couple of weeks if it implanted, but I don't want to risk harming the baby by diving."

"Of course you don't." Sara gave her a curious look. "You've thought all this through?"

"You think I'm crazy, don't you? Oliver did, too, but I'm giving life to a baby that would normally be thrown away. And I'll finally have a family of my own."

Sara lifted a brow. "Being a single mom is hard."

"I don't deny that, but I think I can handle it. I've got tons of patience, and I love kids."

"I know you do." Tanks clanking, Sara rose and bent over to hug her. "I'll be there for you. So what do you need me to do?"

That had gone better than Harper had hoped. "Just plant the pen shells in bare spaces. I'll snorkel along above you and make sure you're doing okay."

"You got it." Sara hopped over the side of the *Sea Silk II* and into the water.

With her mask and snorkel in place, Harper handed down the bucket of pen shells, then jumped in herself. The warm water closed over her head, and she surfaced and adjusted her mask. She kicked past a school of silvery fish and swam over to the pen shell beds. She stopped and stared below her. One of the cages had been torn off. That area of her pen shell farm had been ravaged. All the shells were missing, leaving gaping holes.

Who would have done this? Some random fisherman who felt he was entitled to her shells? Or was it something much more sinister? Ridge hadn't thought the attacks had anything to do with the shell beds, but this might change his mind.

Sara began to plant the shells into the ravaged beds. When she was done, she joined Harper and they swam back to the boat. Harper climbed the ladder, then reached down to lift up the tanks Sara had shed.

Sara tossed her mask to Harper. "Any idea what happened down there?"

Harper pulled off her mask and snorkel. "Someone harvested my shells. The cages are posted as belonging to me, so they had to know they were stealing. I lost a lot of money. Maybe I should put out a few cameras."

"Could it have been deliberate destruction?"

"It's possible. Eric Kennedy has been badgering me about moving the beds, but it's a massive undertaking. They aren't hurting anything where they are, and he's just playing a political game, so I don't know what to do. The bigger question is, does the damage have anything to do with the attacks on Oliver and me?"

Sara toweled off her hair. "Maybe a camera would be the thing to do. At least you could determine the culprit and maybe get to the bottom of all this."

"It could just be a fisherman who wanted them. It's still not right since they belong to me, but it might not be anything sinister."

She was grasping at straws, and from the look Sara threw her, Sara knew it too.

"Josh said the Coast Guard struck out on finding that guy who attacked you. They stopped several boats and questioned a few people, but no one stood out as a possible suspect. So we're at a dead end."

Harper hadn't expected any real results. She hadn't even gotten a good look at the guy. "I appreciate the effort. We're so close to shore, the attacker might have entered the water from there. Maybe it's someone hired by Kennedy. He showed up here right after the attack."

"You have to admit that seems a little extreme for a politician. I've been thinking about it ever since it happened. The guy could have killed you."

"But he didn't use the knife on me. I don't know what he wanted."

Sara pulled on board shorts and a shirt. "Everything was quiet overnight?"

"As a clam. Bear didn't make a peep." At the sound of his name, the dog picked up his head and woofed at her, then settled back down and closed his eyes.

"I don't like you staying alone on that boat with no one around to hear if you scream."

"I have Bear. He'll warn me if there's an intruder." The word *scream* brought an unpleasant word picture to mind, and she shivered. She pulled a sweatshirt over her wet bathing suit and moved to the controls. "We might as well head for home."

"Let's go to my place. I'll fix you a late lunch."

Her stomach rumbled. "I wouldn't say no to food." She reached for bottles of water from the cooler and tossed one to Sara.

The company would be good too. After the past twenty-four hours and two strange occurrences back to back, Harper wasn't eager to go to the deserted houseboat. She started the motor and headed for the dock.

Harper slowed the boat while Sara hopped out the bow and grabbed a post at the dock to secure the boat. She'd have lunch with Sara and forget all about these attacks for a while.

7

The night breeze held a bit of a chill, but Ridge was too white hot with outrage to shiver as he walked from the parking lot to the marina. He'd taken Jamal to Dad's house with instructions to call if he needed him. At least Jamal didn't have a concussion.

Ridge passed the park with its painted dolphin and walked past the signs along the dock for dolphin sightseeing tours. Dunedin held on to that laid-back beach town vibe he'd always loved. He'd often come here to enjoy the town's Scottish celebrations, and he was particularly fond of bagpipes.

He spied the *Sea Silk*'s lights almost at once. Harper was home. He skirted a couple strolling along the pier and reached her houseboat.

Though it looked old, it seemed sturdy. Harper never took it out into open water but stayed either docked here or in some small mangrove inlet along the coast.

Proper etiquette demanded he ask for permission to board, but he didn't think she'd hear him from inside, so he stepped aboard and went to the door and knocked. No one answered, so he knocked again. Not even Bear barked. Maybe she'd gone to get food from the Fish Market.

He retraced his steps back to the pier. He'd try calling her later. He was halfway down the pier when he heard a familiar bark, and Bear rushed toward him. The dog leaped on his leg, and he picked him up as Harper reached them. "I wondered if you'd gone after food."

Her hair was still up in a ponytail, and she carried a take-out box. "I just picked up some quesadillas from Olde Bay Café, and I'm happy to share."

He started to turn down her offer, but his stomach growled. "Well, now that you mention it, I haven't eaten since breakfast, so I'll take you up on the offer."

"Let's sit out here. It's a beautiful night." Without waiting for an answer, she settled onto the pier and dropped her legs over the side, then opened the box of food.

The tantalizing aroma of seafood and cheese wafted to his nose. He settled down beside her with Bear, who lay down on Ridge's lap. "Smells like the shrimp and blue crab quesadillas."

"You nailed it." She held out the box to him.

He selected a piece and bit into it. The peppers, sour cream, black beans, and seafood hit his tongue, and he gobbled it down like a starving man. "Man, these are good."

"My favorite too." She chewed a moment, then fixed him with a questioning gaze. "So what's going on? How's your dad?"

"His condition is the same, but I told the doctors I'm pretty sure he was attacked." He told her about what he'd found aboard his dad's boat as well as the knife in the sand. "And someone hit Jamal—a kid! What kind of maniac are we dealing with?"

"Is Jamal okay?"

"Yeah, he's fine. Resting. I'll go check on him soon."

Her eyes got bigger as he spoke, and she shivered. "I'll bet it was the same assailant. It's so weird. My mollusk beds aren't worth this kind of attention. I don't get it. Someone dug up most of my pen shells today."

"I think Dad was in the wrong place at the wrong time. The guy who attacked Jamal took Dad's air tank and sliced hose." He'd been thinking about this all afternoon. "Maybe there's something important out there someone doesn't want you to find."

She blinked. "Like what?"

"Treasure? Illegal activity? Drug smuggling? The list could go on and on."

"But the guy who grabbed me wasn't trying to hurt me. He was trying to take me with him."

That fact hadn't registered with him. "You said the guy had a knife."

"But he didn't try to use it on me—it was a warning not to resist. I escaped anyway, of course, but he came after me. Bear bit him."

Bear lifted his head at the mention of his name, then lay back down on Ridge's lap. Ridge frowned as he thought about the attack, but she was right—the fact the man chased her indicated it wasn't someone trying to warn her off the area. "This is very odd. Have you had any other kinds of attacks?"

She shook her head. "Just the break-in I already told you about. Did the information help the doctors?"

"Not really. They still think the lack of oxygen brought on a stroke or a heart attack. His heart enzymes are elevated, and the CT scan indicates he's had at least a mini stroke at some point, though it might not have been on Saturday. Even though he's still in a coma, his doctors are cautiously optimistic."

"I've been praying for him constantly. Oliver's been my rock for a lot of years."

And no one else in Dad's family had liked it. Ridge had always wondered if she only saw Dad as a meal ticket, but the moisture in her eyes and the quiver in her voice seemed sincere.

He reached for another slice of quesadilla. "I talked to the police and asked for an officer to guard Dad, but since I have no proof he is in danger, I got shot down. So I hired a security guard to hang out by the ICU door. I also alerted hospital security, and they said they'd keep an eye on his room."

"You really think Oliver might be in danger?"

He shrugged. "The thug was persistent with you, so it's possible Dad's a target too. We don't know what this is all about."

"I'll rip up the beds. I'm not risking Oliver's life. I'll start over somewhere else."

He thought about her offer for a long moment. "I'm not convinced this has anything to do with the beds yet. You might be sacrificing a lot of Dad's money for no good reason."

In the twilight her cheeks went pink, and he knew his well-aimed barb about Dad's money had struck home. Good. Maybe she'd realize what a mooch she'd been for years.

He set Bear aside and got up. "I've gotta go check on Jamal. Let me know if you see or hear anything."

He should have been happy she'd heard his displeasure, but he felt only a stab of shame as he walked to his truck.

Ridge could hear his dad's voice booming down the hallway of the cardiac floor as he approached the door. On his way back from Gainesville this morning, the hospital had called to let him know Dad was awake, and Ridge had barely managed to hope for a weak hello. His dad's voice was the sweetest sound he'd heard in his life.

Even from here, he heard Dad drawing out the nurse and asking her questions about herself. She was telling him how excited she was to be on the dayshift now and that her husband finally found a job after being unemployed for three months.

He paused in the doorway and saw the nurse giving Dad a sip of water. Her dark eyes were bright and she was smiling as she brushed past Ridge. "You've got a nice father," she whispered.

He smiled and nodded. The hospital was fairly new, and his dad's room held several blue leather recliners and a sofa. The sleek gray cabinets contained plenty of space for belongings, and it was a more welcoming space than most hospital rooms.

Ridge pulled a chair beside the bed. "You are already sweet-talking the nurses. I thought that last nurse was going to kiss you on her way out."

Dad's black hair was combed, and he wore the pajamas Ridge had brought from home so he didn't have to wear a hospital gown. The oxygen cannula still snaked around his head, but some of the other monitoring equipment had been removed. Sunlight streamed in the big window on the other side of the bed. A breakfast tray sat on the bedside table, but Dad hadn't touched much of the food.

His dad plucked at the crisp white sheet. "How long have I been here? I don't remember much."

"Since Saturday, and it's Tuesday now. You were in a coma. Do you remember what happened?"

"The last thing I remember was talking to Harper for a few minutes before I dove. Then I woke up here. What do you know?"

Should he tell his dad about the assaults? It might agitate him and cause another heart attack. "The doctor thinks you had a heart attack. You've also had a mini stroke, though they are unsure if it occurred on Saturday or at some previous time."

The color washed out of his dad's face. "Heart attacks and strokes are for old people. I'm not going down without a fight. Get me released so I can get home."

"You need to cool your jets for a few days. You're not getting out until the doctor is sure you're stabilized. In the meantime I'll arrange for a nurse when you get home as well as any equipment you might need."

His dad's black brows drew together in a thunderous scowl. "I don't need a nurse."

"Oh? You're able to get to the bathroom by yourself now?"

"Well, no, but it won't be long."

It was going to be a long convalescence. "We'll see how you do."

Dad pressed the button on the side rail and lifted the head of the bed. "Did you tell Harper about the new lab?"

"I didn't have a choice since you hadn't told her."

His dad reached for the glass of water on his stand and took a sip from the straw. "She was okay with it?"

"I don't think she liked the idea of working with me any more than I like the idea of working with her, but we'll manage. I examined the setup, and the bivalve beds look good. We might have problems though. You hear anything about a Native American burial ground being found offshore near the beds?"

Dad shook his head. "What's going on?"

Ridge told him about the politician showing up, but he withheld the news of Harper's attack. The last thing he needed was for Dad to get in a tizzy about her safety. He'd be calling for his Glock and go rushing off without being formally released.

"Let me check into it. If there truly is a burial ground there, we may need to move the beds. What did Harper think of the research lab?"

"She isn't sure she'll have enough pen shells to share for research. She has already seeded them for black pearls, and she's sold some of the meat to restaurants to try to build a market for it." And he still wasn't sure he wanted to give up his new job for this either.

"The research is a priority. I'll make sure she understands that."

Like his dad would insist on his own way with Harper. He never had in the past. Anything she wanted, Dad had provided.

"Why, Dad?" The burning question had never been answered.

Harper always got priority over Willow and him. Growing up, all he'd wanted to do was spend time with his dad. He wanted Dad at his football games and his science award ceremonies, but Dad was always off on this business trip and that business trip. He had barely hidden his disappointment when Ridge told him he wanted to study mollusks instead of join the family businesses.

Ridge stepped away. "Never mind. I need to go."

The last thing he wanted to do was upset his dad and cause another episode. After all this time, what did it matter?

8

Harper had to force herself to concentrate on the road as she drove from Tampa to Dunedin with the top down on her Jeep Wrangler. The glowering sky flickered with lightning, and she smelled rain. Motor homes and cars clogged I-275 as she left the city behind, and there was no good place to stop so she took the next exit and pulled into a deserted lot. She got out and secured the cloth top of her Jeep. The first fat raindrops began to fall before she finished, and she was soaked by the time she slid back under the steering wheel.

Lightning flashed overhead again, and the thunder rumbled through her bones as twilight fell. Her cell played the beginning chords of Jack Johnson's "Only the Ocean" and she gasped and pressed the answer icon. "Oliver, you're awake! I've been so worried."

"I was beginning to think I'd get your voice mail."

"I was out of the Jeep putting up the top. It's storming here."

"Where are you?"

"Just outside Tampa. I had to get some supplies."

His answer was garbled. Lightning flickered again, and she had trouble hearing his answer over the sound of lashing rain, wind, and thunder. "Say again? The storm drowned you out."

"Ridge told me about the nosy politician. I'll take care of it."

"I'd rather you weren't worrying about anything like that while you're still recovering."

"I'm going crazy here in the hospital. It will help to think about something else."

"You mean you have to keep your fingers in the pie." She chuckled, but Oliver's need to be in charge had caused more than one argument between them. He had a big heart but a big personality as well.

"That too."

A long pause followed, and she looked at her phone to make sure they were still connected. Why had he called? She knew better than to think it was to chitchat. Oliver always had an agenda. "You still there, Oliver?"

"Yes, I'm here. Listen, would you go past the house and talk to Ridge? This feud between the two of you has to stop." His voice wobbled.

Harper clenched the phone. She'd never heard his voice shake like that. "Sure, I can try." She'd do anything for him, but she doubted Ridge would let go of his animosity just because she asked.

The pounding of the rain lightened, and she started the Jeep and turned on the windshield wipers. "I'll do what I can, but don't expect too much, okay? You know he doesn't like me. I'll turn around and head for his place."

"He's staying at my house while I'm in here to make sure no one breaks in."

Oliver was paranoid about security, and more than once Harper had waited in the rain while he removed all the security and locks to let her in. "I'm about ten minutes from your place. I'll stop by."

He grunted. "So how are you feeling?"

"Okay. It's too soon to be feeling pregnant or anything."

"Well, call me when you get to the house. If he doesn't answer the door, I'll text you the codes to get in."

"Sounds good." She ended the call and pulled out of the lot. Ridge's reaction wouldn't be good if he didn't want to open the door to her and she forced her way in.

Her stomach was in knots as she merged into traffic on the bridge and drove over Old Tampa Bay with the black night pressing in. Whitecaps churned in the bay's gunmetal-gray water, but she kept her gaze on the cars ahead of her. During a storm the Courtney Campbell Causeway was downright terrifying, and she wanted to get across before the wind picked up any more.

When she pulled into the circle drive in front of Oliver's palatial home, she didn't see Ridge's truck in the wash of light from the security lamp, but he could have parked in one of the four garage bays. The rain had stopped, and stars began to peek through the dark clouds as she went to the door.

She pressed the doorbell and heard it echo from inside. *Please don't be here.* A quick stop, and she could be on her way home. There was no sound from inside, and she eased out a relieved breath. She'd just go now.

She turned toward her Jeep, then forced herself to swing back and press the doorbell again. If she was going to comply with Oliver's request, she needed to do it right. Her hands curled into fists when she heard footsteps from inside.

The door opened and Ridge peered out at her. His thick black hair stood up on end, and his button-down collared shirt was wrinkled. He looked pale and drawn.

He stared at her for a long moment. "What are you doing here?"

"Your dad said you haven't answered his texts or calls." She refrained from reminding him he'd jumped all over her for that very thing just days ago.

He frowned and bit his lip. "I fell asleep, I guess. It's been a rough few days."

She allowed herself a shaft of compassion. He loved his dad, and this had to have been hard. "I'd rather not discuss this on the porch. Can I come in and talk to you?"

"Sure." He stepped aside to allow her to enter.

How was she even going to bring up the topic?

———

As twilight fell Annabelle switched on the lights in the living room and curled up on the sofa with a homemade chicken potpie. The cancer treatments were scheduled to start next week, but even the thought of the side effects of chemo couldn't dim her exuberance at finding her sister. Since yesterday their conversation had been all she'd thought about. She'd been shocked to discover Harper was so young though. Their father must be quite the ladies' man. He must have gotten Harper's mother pregnant when he was in his forties at least.

She spooned a mouthful of potpie onto her tongue and let the flavor of sage and chicken linger. The cat squirreled around her ankles meowing for her dinner, and Annabelle finished her meal, then got up to spoon the canned food into Rico's bowl.

The light on the back deck was out, and she stepped to the switch plate to flip it on. Nothing. The bulb must be out, and she'd need a ladder to reach it. Scott wouldn't mind coming over to do it. She shot him a text and told him she'd tell him about her visit with Harper yesterday when he got there.

See you in fifteen.

Since Scott's father died, he was quick to come help her. At twenty-five Scott was one of the youngest detectives on the Orlando police force. In spite of his tough job, he was a marshmallow inside when it came to her. He had worried Harper would take advantage of her, but that was his law enforcement background talking.

She heard a sound in the backyard and frowned. Another raccoon had probably gotten into the trash can. The animals had been such a nuisance lately. She grabbed a BB pistol Scott had brought her and a flashlight, then advanced to the door. She opened it with as little noise as possible and stepped out onto the deck. The flashlight hadn't worked last time she tried it either, and she'd forgotten to change the batteries.

She squinted in the darkness but didn't see anything moving around the garbage cans. The moon hid behind the clouds, and it was as dark as a cave out in the yard. Whatever sound she'd heard didn't repeat, so she turned to go back into the house. Her hand touched the door, and the echo of a footfall sounded behind her.

Whirling, she brought up the BB gun and flicked off the safety, but before her forefinger found the trigger, a hand clapped over her mouth and something stabbed her arm. A needle? The man was at least six feet, with bulky muscles. It was too dark to see his face as he dragged her deeper into the shadows. She fought with renewed strength and bit savagely at the fingers clasping her mouth.

He muttered an oath and let go. She whirled to run away, but her legs felt like she was trying to swim in quicksand.

"No, no," she moaned. Her arms pinwheeled as she tried to maintain her balance on feet that felt as big as pontoons.

Her knees buckled, and she dropped onto the deck. Her lids fluttered, but she wouldn't be able to fight the blackness floating at the edges of her sight. The darkness that claimed her was as black as the water in a mangrove alley.

"Bite me, will you?" The man's gruff voice was the last thing she heard.

When she blinked away the confusion, Annabelle heard the hum of tires on a wet road. She reached up and touched something metallic over her head. She was in a coffin? She curled her hands into fists and tapped at the lid overhead, but her cries were barely more than a whisper.

Wait, it wasn't a coffin. She was in a trunk. Her hands were free though and so were her feet. She swiveled around and kicked at the lock. To her amazement the lid sprang free and she smelled the fresh scent of rain. She lifted the trunk lid a few inches to peer out and try to figure out her location. Her head cleared more by the moment, and she saw headlights following along the highway.

If she could get out of the trunk, she could find help. The car slowed as if to make a turn, and now was likely her only chance. She heaved the lid up as high as it would go, then rolled out of the trunk. Her right shoulder hit the pavement first and pain exploded down her back and arm. She tumbled toward the ditch and came to rest with a mouthful of gravel.

The car's brake lights gleamed, and it swerved toward the opposite ditch.

Ignoring the pain radiating all through her body, she staggered to her feet and ran to the center of the road. "Help, help!" She waved her hands over her head, and the approaching truck slowed, then stopped. Her stomach roiled, probably from the drug he'd injected. Her mouth felt like cotton.

A man thrust his head out of the open window. "You need help, ma'am?"

"Please, take me to the hospital and call the police." She collapsed to her knees.

The kidnapper's car squealed away and darkness claimed her again.

9

Stretched out in the sun like a cat, Judy kept her eyes closed and let the heat warm the ocean's chill from her skin. The scent of Coppertone suntan lotion mingled with the salt air in an intoxicating aroma. The big ocean cruiser bobbed in the waves with the shore shimmering in the distance. They'd played and splashed in the water like children, and she felt like she'd known him her whole life.

She could feel his gaze on her like a caress. He'd made no secret of his infatuation with her, and she had never felt a pull like this toward a man. Part of her attraction to him was the way he wore his wealth like a second skin. It was in the fit of his uniform and the scent of his Aramis cologne. It was in this expensive new boat and the items scattered around it. She wanted more out of her future than the secondhand clothes she was used to, and he might be part of that new beginning she'd come here to find.

She felt like a clodhopper around him though, and she would have to get over feeling inferior.

She opened her eyes to lock gazes with him. His blue eyes

were warm and approving. She reached for her top to throw over her wet swimsuit. "I'm fixin' to eat that food you promised."

He opened the cooler and pulled out shrimp cocktail, potato salad, cheese cubes, and fruit skewers. "Your wish is my command."

The shrimps were huge and luscious, and the Camembert cheese practically melted in her mouth. "There's a powerful lot of food. Were you expectin' company?"

A shadow crossed his eyes, but he shook his head. "I brought what I like. I'm glad you approve."

Was he telling her the truth? Could someone have stood him up and he'd picked her up as a replacement? She pushed away the questions. However it had happened that they were here together, it felt right. Like it was written in the stars.

She tried to place his accent. "Are you from Massachusetts?"

He handed her a skewer of pineapple and mango chunks. "I was until I was about ten. I thought I'd lost that accent long ago. You must have a good ear."

She'd tried on a northeastern accent a time or two when she used to pretend to be Jackie Kennedy. It was good practice for an acting career. "I like your boat."

He smiled. "I just got her. Dad let me pick out whichever one I wanted, and her elegant lines spoke to me. Would you like to see belowdecks? It's quite spacious."

"Sure."

What kind of money would it take for him to be able to walk into a marina and pick out a boat? She couldn't begin to imagine how much this sleek vessel had cost. Probably more than she could expect to make in her lifetime.

She followed him down the ladder into the salon that smelled new. The head was small but efficient, and the galley had enough storage to live aboard however long he wanted. She imagined them sailing down the coast to the Keys or the Bahamas. They could stop at ports along the way and dine on caviar and champagne.

He opened a gleaming teak door. "This is the master stateroom."

She followed him into the spacious room with its big bed and built-in drawers. "Lots of room."

He took a step toward her, and she lifted her face to meet his kiss. Her future was in his arms, and they both knew it.

———

Harper's turquoise eyes locked gazes with him. Her dark-red hair was disheveled by the wind. Why did she have to be so beautiful?

The stray thought had to be clamped down and eradicated, but Ridge couldn't look away.

"Your hair's wet." He winced at his stupid remark.

She touched a long, damp lock. "I got caught in the rain. Are you okay?"

He turned away to grab coffee mugs from the cupboard. "Want some coffee?"

"What, you're not shoving me out the door? I'll take that coffee before you change your mind."

He couldn't hold back the grin as he turned to put a full mug in her hands. "Am I that bad?"

Her gaze searched his. "You can't say you've been exactly friendly."

His amusement vanished. "I don't like seeing my dad taken advantage of."

Her eyes studied him over the rim of her mug as she sipped her coffee. She lowered the cup. "Your dad wants us to bury the hatchet." She sidled over to sit on a bar stool at the marble counter.

He rubbed his forehead and took a gulp of coffee. "You think you've got him in your pocket forever now because you're pregnant?"

Color rushed to her cheeks. "P-Pregnant?"

"I saw the papers he signed claiming he'd take financial responsibility for the baby."

She looked away. "It's not what you think."

"So you're not pregnant."

Harper looked away. "He didn't explain?"

"No, he didn't."

The secretive expression had been Dad's only answer when Ridge found the documents on the desk. Dad always protected Harper no matter what, but he rarely explained his actions.

Was it even any of Ridge's business? He was an adult now and had his own life. Why did he care what his dad did with his money? It belonged to Dad, not him. But every time he told himself he needed to give Harper the same grace God gave him, his anger would well up and sweep away all his good intentions. He didn't understand why it mattered to him, but it did.

"Dad said he wanted us to bury the hatchet, huh? What brought that up?"

She sipped her coffee. "I'm not sure. He called me out of the blue. Maybe it was his brush with death." Her gaze swept back to collide with his. "I respect your dad so much—I love him. He's the best mentor anyone could have. He literally saved my life. You've never tried to see it from my point of view. You've never so much as asked why I ran away from the foster home or why your dad rushed in to help."

He kept his tone even. "You want to tell me now?"

"Do you want to hear it?"

He took a drink of coffee to give himself time to think. Did he want to understand her, or did he want to let his anger fester? "If you want to tell me."

She sighed. "I forgot to lock my bedroom door one night, and the only escape was out the window. I knew I didn't dare go back."

His fingers tightened on the cup. "Your foster dad?"

"Yes."

"Did you go to your foster mom for help or DCF?"

"My foster mom yelled at me and told me I'd been tempting her husband. She said if I told DCF, they wouldn't believe it either. Based on past experience, I thought she was probably right."

He heard the ring of truth in her words. "You were always stealing stuff—my favorite thermos, Willow's sweaters. What were we supposed to think about that?"

She set her cup down, and her gaze fell away from his. "I-I thought I'd need them when things got bad at the home your dad found for me. It took a long time to feel safe. Sometimes I still don't."

His disdain for her began to melt. What did he know about living under that kind of constant fear? His own gripes about not spending enough time with his dad were minor compared to this.

"What about the paper I found? You aren't going to explain, are you?"

She caught her full lower lip between her white teeth. "No."

Irritation burned in his chest and pushed away his sympathy. He walked out of the kitchen. He either had to take her at her word or believe the worst.

She brushed past him into the living room. "I'm going home. It's been a long day. Call your dad. He's worried about you. Harvest is tomorrow, and I can't dive. You up to helping?"

She couldn't dive? He bit back the questions. "Of course." He walked her out, and even when he locked the door behind her, he didn't know what to believe.

10

Harper was still shaking from Ridge's inquisition when she kicked off her flip-flops and stepped aboard the boat, docked tonight in a mangrove alley. The night felt darker than eight o'clock, and she switched on generator-powered lights.

She'd felt the need to hide away, though she told Sara where she was anchoring. The moist air enveloped her like a warm hug. The boards creaked under her bare feet, and she felt her tension ebb away with the glitter of moonlight shining on the water and the sound of the waves lapping against the hull of the boat.

Bear whimpered and launched himself at her leg as soon as she opened the cabin door. She picked him up and snuggled him to her chest. "Hungry, boy? I'll get your dinner."

She carried him inside the galley and found the bag of dog food inside a cabinet. Bear barked and wagged his tail when she put him down, and he wolfed down his dinner.

She looked around the galley at the rusty appliances and flaking cabinets. The place was old, but it was hers. A friend of Oliver's had told her she could have it if she hauled it off, and she'd spent all last summer making it seaworthy. It had taken all her money to repair the hull, but with her first bit of income from the pen shell beds, she was going to fix up the interior. The old green and orange color scheme hailed from the seventies, and it was downright depressing.

The small bedroom held a double bed with a sagging mattress. She'd gotten a turquoise Hawaiian print quilt for the bed, but it clashed with the fraying orange shag carpet in the room. The salon was large enough but also depressing in spite of the windows on both sides. She would remove the wall between the kitchen and salon and put down engineered hardwood floors, then paint the wood walls in white. The decor would be turquoise and white with touches of melon. It wouldn't cost that much, and she could handle the work.

She touched her belly. All those plans would have to change if she was pregnant. Living on a boat wouldn't be practical with a toddler.

She opened the tiny refrigerator and peered inside. Some lasagna was still left from the dish Sara had brought over the other day, but Harper wasn't hungry, not after hiding so much from Ridge. Taking the box she'd gotten from Annabelle, she exited to the night air and climbed to the party deck. It was a little cheerier up here. She'd bought a plastic table and had gotten brightly colored deck chairs to lounge in or to pull up to the table to eat.

Lights swept the dock and illuminated her boat as a pickup pulled into the weedy drive. She recognized Josh's Dodge Ram and his wide shoulders as he got out. Sara hopped out the passenger side and waved at her. She carried a casserole dish in her hands, and as they neared the boat, Harper caught a whiff of some kind of chicken dish.

Sara stepped aboard and smiled up at Harper. "I know it's late, but I brought dinner. If you've already eaten, you can save it for tomorrow. Roast chicken and vegetables cooked in my Instant Pot. There's enough for all of us. We haven't eaten yet."

Josh held up a sack. "And I brought utensils."

His blue eyes were striking in his tanned face. A helicopter pilot for the Coast Guard, Josh was the kind of man you wanted around in an emergency.

"Come on up. I'm glad for the company."

Sara was first up top, and she set the casserole on the table, then lifted off the plastic lid. Josh came up with Bear in one arm and the bag in the other. "I found a stowaway wanting to come up." He set Bear down and the dog trotted over to the table and sniffed.

A Dodgers cap covered Josh's light-brown hair, and he wore shorts and a T-shirt. The paper sack rustled as he fished out paper plates and plastic utensils.

"Smells good." Warmth swept up her chest and neck. Friends were what she needed tonight. They could pore through the box of articles and information her new sister had given her as well. They could help her gain perspective on everything that had happened.

Sara ladled up the food and handed plates all around while Harper fished dripping-cold bottles of water from the cooler on the deck.

Sara uncapped her bottle. "Tell Josh what you heard from Annabelle yesterday. I haven't had a chance to bring him up to speed."

Harper filled him in. Josh's eyes widened when she said Annabelle's mother had been murdered. He pulled on his earlobe as he listened intently. Harper wasn't sure she wanted to get into her own mother's situation, but it seemed to be part of the picture, so she needed to.

"Annabelle thinks I should talk to the detective who investigated my mother's death."

Josh frowned. "Your mother was murdered too?"

"Oliver always wondered if her car had been tampered with." Harper reached for the box of clippings. "Here are some news articles about the murder of Annabelle's mom. I haven't had a chance to read them yet."

Josh's frown deepened. "You have the same father, right? Some mystery guy no one knows? It's pretty odd both women died like that. How old was Annabelle when her mother was murdered?"

"Five months old."

"And you were?"

"Not even born yet. The doctor delivered me just minutes before she died."

"Most of the time what seems to be a coincidence has deeper ties," Josh said.

"So do you agree that I should talk to the detective who investigated the accident? I was planning to, then thought it might seem odd for me to be digging into an accident that happened so long ago. Would he even remember?"

Josh and Sara exchanged a long look before he nodded. "It might not hurt, even if it's to set your mind at ease. Maybe it was the accident it appeared to be."

Harper finished the unspoken words lingering in his eyes. "And maybe it wasn't."

Annabelle's knees and right arm felt like a million red ants had feasted on her. The bright lights of the hospital exam room made her wince, and she threw her arm over her eyes. The pungent smell of antiseptic hit her nose as she struggled to come to full consciousness. It felt later than the nine o'clock displayed on the big wall clock. Her ordeal had only lasted a few hours, though it had felt like days.

"Mom?"

She removed her arm and blinked up at Scott. How long had she been out, and how did he know to come here? "Someone called you?"

He was still in his uniform, and his worried hazel eyes held her gaze. His blond hair was soaked from the rain. "I went to your house, and the back door was standing open. When I couldn't find you, I called for backup, and the dispatcher told me you'd been found on the highway. I came straight to the hospital."

Hadn't she closed the door when she went outside? She couldn't remember. "There was a man out on the back deck. He drugged me with some kind of shot." Her tongue still felt thick.

The chair screeched on the tile floor as he pulled it closer to the bed and sat down. "Can you remember anything else? What about his voice?"

"He only growled at me for biting him. His voice was gruff and mad before I passed out. I woke up in the trunk." She told him about her escape and fingered the long road burn on her arm, wincing as her fingers set the area on fire.

He leaned closer. "Did you see what kind of car it was? Any details about the man?"

She tried to think. It was all so fuzzy. "All I can remember is he was muscular and taller than me. I think the car was maybe blue or black? It all happened so fast, and it was dark in the backyard with no light."

Scott stilled. "No light in the back?"

She shook her head. "The bulb must have gone out."

"Or the perp broke it."

She hadn't thought of that. "I'm forty-nine, Scott. It's not like I'm some beautiful young thing. Why would someone try to kidnap me?"

"I don't know, Mom." His square jaw clenched, and he pressed his lips together. "I'm going to find out though. What about the woman who came to see you yesterday? Could she have had anything to do with this?"

She struggled to sit up. "Harper? She's lovely, honey. Pretty, intelligent, and very sweet. She's been trying to find her father and hoped I might have a lead. Here's the funny thing though—her mother died moments after Harper was born. Harper's mentor always thought someone had tampered with her mother's brakes or forced her off the road. I gave her copies of everything I have from my mom's murder."

He lifted a dark-blond brow. "While that's odd, it seems unlikely to have anything to do with your attack."

He was right. She relaxed against the pillow. "I just want to go home. Can you spring me?"

"They want you to stay the night because you were unconscious. The docs are running toxicology, too, to see what the guy injected into your arm. They want to make sure you have no lingering effects—especially with your . . ." He looked away.

"My cancer." She touched his arm. "It's okay to say the word. We're going to be dealing with it for a while."

Her son's eyes filled with moisture, strong cop that he was, and he took her hand. "You'll beat it, Mom."

She clung to his strong fingers. "I'll give it my best shot. Did you call your brother?"

"I called him. He's catching a red-eye."

"He doesn't need to do that!"

Her younger son, Mark, lived in New York and worked on Wall Street. He'd recently gotten engaged, and she didn't see him much, though she knew he loved her. The boys had their own lives, and she never wanted to be a burden.

"He wanted to. You start treatment next week anyway. It would be good if we're both here for support."

Her dear boys. They were always there for her. She'd have this weekend with them before facing chemo.

"Harper is going to come back on Saturday and let me know what she found out from the detective. We'll see if there's any connection between the two cases."

"I intend to be there. I'm sure Mark will feel the same way."

Annabelle suppressed a sigh. The last thing Harper needed was to face her suspicious son, but she bit back the complaint. He was only trying to look out for her.

11

He stroked the scar on his cheek as he stared at the house but couldn't drum up the courage to go in yet. His boss didn't suffer fools gladly, and he *should* have tied the Rice woman up. How did she manage to get out of his trunk? And what did he do now?

He should get out, go to the front door, and admit his failure, but instead he put his car into Drive and headed away from the recriminations he'd be sure to hear. If he failed he'd have to give back the money he'd been paid. Even worse, his son wouldn't get the kidney transplant he desperately needed.

Failure was not an option.

He drove to the spot where he'd lost her and parked at the side of the road. Where would someone have taken her? Back home or to her son's? Or maybe to the hospital? Falling out of the trunk might have injured her. She'd either be taken to Orlando or to Tampa, but since she was from Orlando, he was betting on there. He pulled back onto the highway and made his way to Florida Hospital on Rollins Street.

He went inside, grabbed an orderly's uniform from a supply closet, and found the men's room where he changed and put on a confident smile before he approached the information desk. Armed with Annabelle's room number, he went up to her floor and scurried toward her room. His smile faltered when he saw a police officer standing outside her door. He reversed his direction and went back to the elevator.

He had no choice but to admit his failure to his boss and get new orders. He placed the call he dreaded and winced as he got chewed out. "It wasn't my fault," he managed to slip in.

"You should have restrained her," his boss barked back. "And you said you saw Harper taking a box from Annabelle's house. Do you know what was in it?"

"No."

"Find out. Better yet, destroy it."

"I'll get right on it."

"I need her brought to me as soon as possible."

"Of course." He ended the call and started the car.

It would be easy enough to find her. He'd planted a locator bug on the hull of her houseboat.

⌒

It was a beautiful night under the stars. Harper sat on the top deck after her friends left. She turned off her lights, and the bright canopy of stars soothed her spirits and dispersed the darkness pressing in. A fish splashed in the water near her boat, and Bear lifted his head.

Several times during the evening she'd wished Sara had come alone. She would've liked to have told her about the confrontation with Ridge. Since he was Oliver's son, maybe he deserved to know the truth, though she feared he'd still be upset his father was involved.

She touched her belly. "Are you in there, peanut?"

She didn't dare hope the procedure had worked. Not yet. A pregnancy test sat waiting on her bedside table, but it was too soon to take it. It had only been a week, and she didn't think it would reveal anything yet. Maybe in another two days she'd take the test, even though the doctor had warned her not to do that. She couldn't stand waiting another week to get a peek at what might be happening.

Bear lay snoozing at her feet as she breathed in the salt air mingled with the distant stench of diesel fuel from a passing boat. Six o'clock would come much too early tomorrow, and she needed to get some rest. It would be a hard day opening the bivalves, though she was eager to deliver the meat to the restaurants and see how they did on the menus. Her entire business model was riding on how customers reacted to the new items. Bivalves weren't commonly seen as edible, but she was counting on the customers coming back for more of the sweet meat.

Bear picked up his head and uttered a low growl. He got up and crouched by the ladder. A vehicle hadn't come down the lane but maybe a deer was out there. Harper tipped her head and listened. Was that a twig that snapped? Bear's fur stood on end, and his growl went to a higher decibel.

She slid down and crouched beside him at the ladder. He calmed a bit when she put her hand on his head, but her sense of unease rose when she heard another snap of vegetation. The cupboard on the other side of the deck held a flashlight, and she slinked over there to grab it. Her heart drummed in her ears. She wanted to call out, but her tongue wouldn't move.

Someone was out there. She could feel it like a light breath on her skin. Senses on high alert, she crept down the ladder with Bear under one arm to the main level and peered into the darkness. Maybe she should move away from shore. The menace she felt from the shadows was palpable. Was it her imagination? She wasn't normally the type to conceive of a threat around every corner, but since the attack in the water, she'd been a little skittish.

She put down the dog and headed for the wheelhouse, but a sound behind her made her whirl with the flashlight out in front of her. Before she could click it on, a dark figure lunged from the shore onto the deck. She caught a glimpse of a ski mask above broad shoulders clad in black before a sickly sweet-smelling cloth descended onto her face.

Bear's growl was ferocious, then he yelped. The man must have kicked him.

Her head swam from the scent, and she flung herself back to try to escape the man's iron grip, but he came with her and his weight bore her to the deck. His bulk pressed against her, and no matter how hard she struggled, she couldn't dislodge the cloth from her face.

Her chest burned with the need for air, and involuntarily she drew in a breath. The sweet odor seeped into her lungs, and numbness began to soften the edges of her consciousness.

She tried to keep her eyelids from closing, but reality receded.

⌒

"Harper?"

A voice from the distance tugged her back toward the surface. She coughed and still smelled the odor of the chemical her attacker had used. Bear licked her face and whined.

"Harper, are you all right?"

Ridge. She forced her eyes open and looked up. She was still on the deck with the moonlight streaming onto her face. Ridge crouched over her. He wore a white polo shirt over khaki shorts, so he wasn't her attacker.

A worried frown crouched between his eyes, and he held a bottle of water to her lips. "Drink."

She obeyed and managed a sip of blessedly cool water. With his arm behind her back, she was able to sit up, though her head still swam. "That awful taste is in my mouth."

He held the bottle to her mouth again. "Did you recognize the guy? It was too dark for me to see much."

"You didn't see him?" The cool water began to wash away the chemical taste.

"He was dragging you toward the bushes when I got here. I shouted at him and he ran off. I didn't chase him because I was concerned when you weren't moving. I heard a vehicle start up and tear away from here so I'm sure he's gone."

Shudders rippled in waves down her body. "I think I'm going to be sick."

He helped her to the side of the boat, and she vomited over the edge.

He rubbed her back. "Ether does that. You'll feel better in a few minutes."

"It was ether?"

"Smells like it to me."

She took the bottle of water he offered and rinsed out her mouth, then swallowed another mouthful. "I knew someone was out there, and I was getting ready to move away from shore, but he jumped aboard before I could get out of here."

"Did he say anything?"

"Not a word. He just clapped that cloth over my face." Harper's legs wouldn't support her, and she sank to the deck. Bear crawled into her lap, and she held him to her chest.

Ridge squatted beside her. "We should get you to the ER and make sure you're all right."

"I'm okay. What are you doing here anyway? It's late."

"It's a little after eleven. I came by to see if you were awake. I wanted to apologize. I'm not proud of how I've been acting."

Was that all it was, or did Ridge know more about the attack than she knew? "This makes two attacks, and in both cases, the man seemed to be trying to abduct me not kill me."

"I don't like it." He stood and offered her a hand. "You get to bed. I'm going to move the boat out away from shore while you sleep. I'll stand guard."

But was that safe? She felt too exhausted to argue with him. At least she could lock the door to the living quarters.

12

Was that the smell of bacon? Harper blinked her eyes open, then winced at the sunshine streaming in her window. Her head pounded, and she assumed it was the aftereffects of the ether the night before. She pulled a lightweight robe over her shortie pajamas and went into the salon.

Ridge stood at the stove flipping omelets. He glanced her way. "Hungry?" Her stomach rumbled before she could answer, and he grinned. "I heard that. Breakfast is ready."

She glanced out the windows onto the water but didn't recognize the shoreline. "Where are we?"

"About a quarter of a mile out from Dunedin. No boats approached us in the night, so I think the guy gave up or didn't have access to a boat."

"Thanks." She took the plate he held out and carried the food to the sofa. "Did you stay up all night?"

"Yep. I wasn't sure if the assailant would come after us." He stooped and put Bear's food bowl on the floor and smiled as the dog tore into his breakfast.

"You should have awakened me to take a turn at standing guard."

Ridge carried his plate of food over and sat in a chair facing the sofa. "You needed to sleep off the ether. Headache?"

"Yes." Her stomach roiled, but she forked a bit of omelet anyway. "My stomach isn't too happy either."

"Ether is nasty stuff. It isn't used much outside of laboratories, which might give us a clue to your attacker. I called the sheriff's department and reported the attack. An investigator is supposed to meet us first thing this morning at the marina. I'll eat breakfast, then take the boat in."

Pain throbbed behind her left eye, and she pressed her fingers against the pulsing spot. "I know we needed to report it, but I feel pretty rough this morning. Talking to a detective doesn't sound fun. I'll get through it though."

She forked a bite of food into her mouth. The cheese and bacon felt heavy but she forced herself to chew and swallow. Getting something in her belly should help reduce the nausea. Ridge didn't have much to say as he gulped down his breakfast.

He rose. "I'll get us to the dock." Bear followed him.

She nodded without looking up and continued to try to get down a little food. A few minutes later the engine throbbed to life, and the shoreline moved past as he motored them to the marina. She carried the remains of breakfast to the small galley and dumped the rest of her omelet in the trash, then gulped down three ibuprofens before she dressed in shorts and a T-shirt. She poured two mugs of coffee and carried them out to the wheelhouse.

Ridge glanced up. "Good call. Coffee might help your head." His left hand rested atop Bear, who was on his lap.

She set his mug of coffee down in front of him, then slipped into the seat beside him. "Why are you doing this?"

"What?"

She looked him over, taking note of the fatigue in his eyes and the tired twist of his mouth. "Staying up all night and taking care of me. We've been at loggerheads since the first time we met."

Those dark eyes of his cut sideways at her, then went back to scouring the water ahead as the marina came into view. "Common decency. I wouldn't let Bear be attacked, and he's a dog."

She shouldn't have been disappointed, because she knew how he felt about her, but it still stung to be dismissed like that. "Well, I appreciate it."

"No problem."

He maneuvered the boat into its slip and cut the engine. "I think I see a couple of deputies sitting on the bench there."

She looked in the direction he'd pointed and spied them, too, a man and a woman. "Let's get this over with." After tying off the boat, she stepped onto the pier and approached the deputies. "Are you waiting for me? I'm Harper Taylor."

Ridge came up behind her and stood close as if to offer solidarity.

The female deputy rose and nodded. She was in her thirties with blonde hair and wore no makeup. "We were notified that you were attacked late last night. Ideally, we would like to have interviewed you right after the assault."

"I was knocked out and pretty fuzzy, so I'm not sure I would have been much help."

The woman lifted a brow and introduced them, but Harper's throbbing head couldn't seem to hold on to the names. She described what little she remembered of the man's appearance and how she'd awakened with Ridge helping her.

"And how do you know Mr. Jackson? Are you dating?" the male deputy asked. The officers eyed Ridge.

"I've known him for fifteen years. His dad is my mentor and business partner."

The suspicion on their faces faded, but the woman turned her attention to Ridge. "Why were you arriving at Ms. Taylor's boat at such a late hour?"

"We'd had an argument and I wanted to apologize."

She should have known he'd spill it. Ridge was one of those people who didn't fudge the truth.

"An argument? What about?" the woman probed.

"It was personal and had nothing to do with this incident."

The two deputies glanced at each other, and the man shrugged. "There isn't much we can do without a description, and you say the man wore a ski mask. You didn't see his vehicle, so there's no way to ID him. Did you go to the hospital?"

"No. Ridge wanted me to, but I just wanted to sleep."

The male deputy's jaw hardened. "Well, I think we've done all we can do here. If you remember anything else about your attacker, call it in." He passed a business card to her.

Harper tucked the card in her pocket and watched them walk off. That had been a waste of time.

Ridge hadn't wanted to leave Harper alone so he'd brought her out to the bivalve beds on his dad's boat. The sea breeze ruffled his dark hair as he climbed the *Wind Dancer*'s ladder and tossed down the bag with the last of the pen shell harvest. Gulls squawked overhead, and an osprey dove off the bow and came up with a wriggling croaker. The wind brought the faint scent of sulfur from the mangroves from the inlet to his right. "There was a nosy manatee down there."

"It was probably Cyrus. He hangs out with me all the time."

She was still pale from her ordeal last night. The frown on her beautiful face told him she still suffered from the headache. After he insisted she get checked by a doctor, they'd come out here so he could harvest the mussels.

She wore white shorts and a tank top that showed off tanned, well-shaped arms. Her dark-red hair was tangled from the moisture-laden salt air. "Thanks for handling all the work."

He dumped the big bivalves out of the bag onto the deck. "Your lungs still have traces of ether. It wouldn't be safe. I got it done. How are you feeling?"

"Almost human. The headache is gone and I'm starting to get hungry."

"There's turkey in the cooler. Veggies and fruit too."

"I'll fix us a snack if you're ready."

"Let's finish up here first." He glanced around the deck. She'd cleaned the pen shells and put the meat into coolers. A stack of harvested sea silk was drying in a basket, and he spotted a small container of black pearls. "Looks like you did everything else. We need to deliver the meat to the restaurants and we're done. How was the pearl harvest?"

"Good. The seeding I planted took well. Look at this one." She showed him a large, perfectly shaped black pearl. "This is the most unique one I've ever seen. It should bring a pretty penny. I'll take the pearls around to some jewelry stores next week and see what I can get for them. A runner is coming for the clams in a little while so we'll be done here for the day. I'll save a few pearls and the sea silk for some fiber-art projects."

They worked in silence to clean the last of the pen shells and had them ready in minutes. He kept stealing glances at her bent head and perfect profile. The fishy scent of the mollusks permeated the boat's deck, and when they were finished, he took a bucket of seawater and sluiced off the mess, then rinsed his hands.

Harper leaned over the side of the boat and swished her hands in the sea. Her expression was pensive, and she didn't say anything.

"Is something bugging you? I kept an eye on the surface in case another boat came by, but everything seemed to be safe."

She gave him a long, speculative look. "It's not the attack. It's something personal."

Even though he didn't have the right to probe, he wondered what was going on behind those beautiful turquoise eyes. "Anything I can do?"

"Why are you suddenly so helpful?"

He shrugged. "I told you—common courtesy."

"So you still dislike me?"

How did he answer her? "We're going to have to work together for Dad's sake. The more I thought about it, the more I want to be part of the lab, and I don't want it to fail. So we need to get along as well as we can."

And once he proved to his dad that she was only out to bilk him of his fortune, he'd be rid of her. Having her out of their lives would be a huge relief. His sister, Willow, felt the same way, and she'd be just as relieved when he succeeded in ridding their dad of Harper's influence.

Harper held out her hand. "Provisional friends then?"

He hesitated a moment before he took it. "I guess you could say that."

He wasn't proud of what he was planning to do, but he had to protect his father.

Her hand was small and warm in his, and he found himself

not wanting to let go. Was she deliberately trying to flirt with him? In spite of how easily men had to fall under her spell, he looked down into her eyes for a long moment before he let go of her hand. "So now that we're friends, do you want to tell me what's causing the shadow in your eyes?"

She smiled. "I found a sister."

He listened while she launched into the saga of the DNA test and everything her sister had said. "So now you're wondering if your mother was murdered? Seems a stretch. You'd think the detective would have explored all the evidence."

"But maybe hearing a previous mistress was murdered would make a difference." She hunched her shoulders and stepped back. "It sounds crazy, doesn't it? But it's even crazier they would both die when Annabelle and I were so small. You're probably right about it being meaningless, but I want to at least talk to the detective. I tried calling the police, but they wouldn't give me his address or phone number."

"I have a good friend who's a cop. What's the detective's name?"

"Don Ward."

He pulled out his phone and shot off a text. "I'm sure he'll get it for me."

And if he did her a favor, she might really lower her guard so he could uncover her true nature. It was easy to hide her real motives behind her beautiful face. He was certain she had an agenda he wasn't going to like, and he intended to find it.

13

The *Sea Silk* bobbed in her mooring at the slip, and Harper walked beside Ridge past Edgewater Park toward downtown Dunedin. It wasn't quite five yet, but the commuter traffic in town was already steady. The quaint town was at its best in the twilight. The streetlights and shops cast a spell from yesteryear.

Her stomach rumbled. "I'm starving. That turkey sandwich didn't last long."

Ridge touched her elbow and guided her across the street. "What are you in the mood for?"

She couldn't believe they'd been together this long without a single argument. "Pizza sounds good."

"Tony's? It's only a couple of blocks."

Tony's was small in size but big in flavor. A big guy with a scar on his cheek exited and held open the door for them as they entered. He looked at Harper a little too long for her comfort, and she moved closer to Ridge. The young man smiled and touched his scar as he moved away. The guy creeped her out, and she wasn't quite sure why.

The yeasty aroma of pizza and calzones made her mouth water as they entered and approached the big glass counter that displayed the pizzas. She stifled a giggle as a server carried a pizza bigger than her out to a family at a table. Tony's was famous for their eighteen-inch New York–style pizza.

"I don't think we want one that big. What's your favorite?" She scanned the menu.

"You won't like it. I always get the Philly steak and cheese."

"That's my favorite too." When he grinned, she knew he'd seen straight through her. "Okay, I've never had it, but I'm game to try a slice."

"We can get it by the slice. What do you usually order?"

"Pepperoni." She laughed when his eyes went wide with alarm. "Okay, I'm not adventurous. Get me a slice of your Philly favorite."

"Just one?"

"And a pepperoni slice."

"You've got it." He turned back to the counter.

Good grief, he was handsome. His dark hair was mussed by the wind, and the kiss of the sun had deepened his tan, which made those dark eyes even more attractive in his square-jawed face. She suspected Oliver had looked this devilishly handsome in his younger days.

Her attraction to Ridge was a disastrous turn of events so she backed away. "I'll grab us a table. I'll have sweet tea to drink."

She claimed an empty table and sat watching other patrons. If they'd gotten here even fifteen minutes later, they probably wouldn't have found a table. Her gaze collided with a man who sat in the back corner. Something about him felt familiar. Was it the jut of his jaw or the way he watched her that made her feel suddenly scared? His head was shaved, which made his dark eyes even more piercing.

She glanced around for Ridge and saw him coming her way

with two plates of pizza. Her mouth was dry, but she managed a stiff smile.

He sat across from her and frowned as he slid her plate over to her. "What's wrong?"

"That guy." She jerked her head to the left a bit. "Back there in the corner. He's watching me." She reached across the table and took his hand when his head started to swivel. "No, don't look. Glance that way naturally."

His thumb moved against her palm in a soothing motion. "Do you recognize him?"

"I don't know—maybe something about his shape. He hasn't quit staring at me since I saw him." She darted another glance toward the man. "He's standing up."

She fell silent as the guy came directly to their table. She couldn't bring herself to meet his gaze.

Ridge tipped his head back and looked at the guy, and a smile lit his face. "Dirk." He rose and the two pumped hands. "I thought you moved to the Keys."

"I did, but I'm back in town and searching for a job." The man's voice was deep and melodic. "Someone said your dad was equipping out a new lab. Are there any openings left?"

"We haven't even started hiring." Ridge pulled out a business card. "Shoot me your résumé, but it's just a formality. I'd thought about trying to track you down and see if I could entice you back to the area, and here you are. Seems like fate to me."

Ridge smiled down at Harper. "Harper, this is Dirk Allen, the sharpest researcher I've ever worked with. We roomed together in college too. Dirk, meet Harper Taylor. She's conducting some research with pen shell beds, and she'll be supplying us with some mollusks to examine for possible pharmaceutical uses."

"I thought that was you, Harper. You probably don't remember me, but I dated your roommate in college a few times."

It clicked then. Harper remembered the bad breakup that had happened when he hit on her at a party. And wasn't he married with a kid now?

Harper managed to grab her composure enough to rise and shake his hand. "Nice to see you, Dirk." She'd never liked him, but at least his animosity made sense now.

She pulled her hand back and sat in her chair. What was proper here? Ask him to join them? It's not like she and Ridge were on a date, and he clearly knew this guy well.

Dirk took the question out of the equation. "Well, I have to run. I'm supposed to take a look at an apartment in a few minutes. I'll be in touch, Ridge, and thanks so much." He clapped Ridge on the back, then skirted past several customers coming through the door and exited to the street.

Harper let out her breath. "I was overreacting. Sorry."

"It's understandable. You don't have to worry about Dirk though. He's a good guy."

"That's great." She felt like an idiot. Was she going to be jumping at shadows and perfectly normal men for days?

She ate while Ridge talked about his ideas for the lab. He'd long thought various sea life held possible answers to health problems.

"Asia has used many marine animals for medicinal applications for centuries. There are so many things we haven't examined with clinical trials, though fungi, plants, and bacteria are already treating cancer. You never met my grandpa, but he died of Alzheimer's. My main goal for years has been to see if there's some cure for that disease. We lost him long before he took his last breath. It was painful to watch."

She reached across the table and touched his hand, then withdrew before it got awkward. "I'm sorry." Reaching for her slice of pepperoni pizza, she smiled at him. "That Philly pizza was better than I expected."

"You should never doubt me."

Maybe there was a flip side to not having family. She'd never had to watch a loved one suffer and die.

The morning sun baked against Harper's skin through the open window in Ridge's pickup. "What do you have against air-conditioning?" She handed him a thermos of coffee.

He took it and set it in his cup holder. "You're a mind reader."

He seemed chipper this morning too. He'd only agreed to leave her at her houseboat last night because she was in a slip with other boats around. It had been a peaceful night, and she felt rested. Her headache was finally gone too.

He slowed to turn into a quaint neighborhood of houses built in the sixties. "Fresh air is good for you. And the sunshine on your arms gives you vitamin D."

She swiped a bead of perspiration off her forehead with the back of her hand. "Do you *ever* use AC?"

"Not if I can help it. It has to be really hot and humid for me to breathe in canned air when I can smell the sea."

They drove in companionable silence to Clearwater. She looked out the window at the egrets snatching up bugs in the grass along the road while he turned up Garth Brooks singing on his sound system. He hummed a few bars in a pleasant baritone, then fell silent as red washed up his cheeks.

"Here we are." He braked and pulled into the drive of a neat bungalow.

She eyed the house. Black shutters enhanced the style of the white siding, and the red door seemed freshly painted. The scent of freshly mown grass wafted to her, and the growl of a mower grew louder. A slim man with white hair rode it around the corner of the house. She opened her door and stepped out onto the drive.

He saw them and killed the engine, then dismounted and approached them. The fishing cap he wore had sweat stains and rips in it. His face was brown and leathery from the sun. "Can I help you?"

Ridge got out of the truck and came around the front of it to stand by Harper. "You're Detective Ward?"

The interest in the man's faded blue eyes sharpened. "Well, not a detective any longer. I'm just a normal Joe now. If you need a detective, I can call a friend at the police department."

Harper stepped forward. "We'd like to talk to you about an old case."

A smile lifted his wide mouth. "Come around to the deck in the back. I just made some sun tea, and I'll fix you a glass while you tell me what you're looking for. I'm about to go bat crazy with my own company. I should never have retired. A man can only fish so much."

Harper liked the guy, and she exchanged a grin with Ridge as they followed the detective around the side of the house. The redwood deck was nearly as big as his small house. Turquoise and white patio furniture circled a freestanding fire pit. A massive outdoor kitchen lined the far end of the space on the other side of French doors.

"This is nice."

He shrugged and went to a small refrigerator. "I don't get enough company to fill it. Most of my friends are still working a beat or have families. Since Angela died, the place is too quiet."

Harper settled onto a lounge chair, and Ridge dropped into the one beside her. "Angela was your wife?" she asked.

Ice clinked into glasses, and the detective topped the glasses with tea. "Married thirty-five years. We had plans to travel and see our kids who are spread out all over the West Coast, but cancer got her a year ago."

"I'm sorry, Detective Ward."

He handed her a water-beaded glass of tea. "Call me Don. Now what can I do for the two of you?"

Ridge took the glass Don offered. "You might not remember this case because it was almost thirty years ago. A car accident involving a pregnant woman. She died shortly after giving birth."

Don settled across from them on a chair and set his glass of tea on the table beside him. "The Taylor case?" His gaze probed hers. "You're the kid?"

Harper nodded and leaned forward. "You remember it?"

"It was a hard one to forget."

Ridge wiped the moisture from his glass. "Because of her being pregnant, or was there something more?"

"That made it stand out, of course, but it was what happened afterward that was peculiar. I never swallowed the official decision that it was an accident."

A swell of emotion rose in Harper's throat. She swallowed a mouthful of cold sweet tea to gain her composure. "What happened?"

Don frowned and propped one foot on his other knee. "The

car disappeared from our lot. Just *poof*, gone right out of a fenced-in lot. My partner and I went over to examine it for evidence after your mother died, and when we couldn't find it, I thought it had been moved. But no one in our department knew where it had gone or who had ordered it."

"What made you think it wasn't an accident?"

"No skid marks approaching the intersection. Your mom didn't try to stop the car before it rammed the truck, so that made me wonder if she couldn't brake because the lines were cut. But without the vehicle to examine, I had no proof. Without evidence it was just another accident. I talked to a couple of coworkers and her best friend, but they didn't know anything."

"My mother had a best friend?"

"Sure. Most women do."

"Do you remember her name?"

He shook his head. "I can check my notes though. Give me your phone number, and I'll let you know when I find it."

Ridge dug out a business card. "Here, take mine. She never has her phone on her." He handed it to Don.

"I'd appreciate that. Did my mother say anything?"

Don's brow wrinkled. "Now that you mention it, she said something about mermaids."

Harper clasped her hands together. "Mermaids? Do you remember exactly what she said about them?"

"She said, 'The mermaid was right.'"

"Nothing more?" Harper's thoughts flashed to her new sister. Her mother was a Weeki Wachee mermaid, but Judy Russo had been dead for many years at the time of Mom's accident. There couldn't be any real connection.

They finished their tea and thanked Don, then headed to Ridge's truck.

He pulled out of the drive and glanced at her. "I see the wheels turning. What are you thinking?"

"I was thinking of the Weeki Wachee mermaids. Could the killer have been a mermaid there? Maybe the same person killed my mom and Judy Russo."

He lifted a brow. "That's a stretch, Harper. They have a lot of turnover."

"It might not have been a female mermaid. The attraction hires men too."

"Judy died fifty years ago, right?"

"Something like that. Maybe forty-eight." She slumped in her seat and closed her eyes in the hot rush of wind through the window. "It's not likely anyone's around who was there at that time."

Ridge turned at the corner and then turned the truck around. "Let's find out."

14

Murder was never a pleasant thought. Ridge glanced at Harper, who sat staring out her window. She had to be thinking about what Don had said. Highway workers were mowing the sides of the road, and the stench of gasoline fumes mixed with the scent of grass as he drove along US 19 toward Weeki Wachee.

He decided to try to turn her thoughts to something else. "I called to check on Dad, and my mom and sister were there. I'm glad I wasn't around for the fireworks." He popped in a Tim McGraw CD he'd put together.

She turned a smile his way. "Fireworks, huh? I've felt the sparks of a few of those displays. Oliver and Christina were divorced by the time I met him, but she'd show up on occasion and it was always loud. He never talked about what had happened."

"She divorced Dad when I was fifteen. When I asked why, she said they had different goals in life, whatever that meant. He was away on a business trip, and when he got home, his belongings were on the front porch. She'd changed the locks and her phone number. A letter from her attorney was front and center on top of his clothes."

She winced. "That's harsh."

"That's Mom. She's a shape-up-or-ship-out kind of person. Dad never shaped up to her expectations, so she shipped him out." He pressed his lips together. "And maybe that's why he made so many business trips when I was growing up. It's hard to live under extreme expectations like that."

She eyed him. "You never shaped up either? It has to be hard having a psychologist for a mother."

"I gave up trying to please her a long time ago. I was either too noisy or I didn't share enough. I either had the wrong kinds of friends or I wasn't athletic enough. No one can live up to her high standards except my sister. Willow is Mom's clone. After the divorce, she went with Mom and I stayed with Dad."

"I always tried to stay out of Willow's way on the rare weekends she came to stay with your dad when I was there. I always thought she was jealous of me."

He didn't tell her they'd had many conversations about how much they disliked her.

"Maybe those high expectations from both of my parents are what drove me to follow my own path. Neither one of them thought my career as a malacologist was a worthy one. Mom thought I should be some kind of professional like a lawyer or a doctor, and Dad wanted me to join him in the business."

"Why didn't you?"

He shrugged. "Dad has such a huge personality, and I knew I'd live in his shadow if I wasn't careful."

"That took a lot of discernment. I love your dad, but he can be overwhelming. Do you see your mom and sister much now?"

"Maybe Christmas and Thanksgiving. Mom is wrapped up in her practice. Every time we're together I get the impression she's trying to figure out how I turned out this way. And Willow turns up her perfect nose and tells me I should have done something worthwhile with my education."

"I've always thought your job was interesting. Maybe because I share the same interest in marine life."

He glanced sideways at her as a thought hit him. Had his fascination with sea creatures fueled her own marine biology career? "According to them I wasted my talents."

How had they gotten on this subject? Talking about his mother and sister wasn't something he did—ever. It was like ripping off his fingernail and examining how the rush of pain felt. McGraw began to sing "Live Like You Were Dying," and Ridge started to sing the chorus without thinking. The lyrics stopped him short though he'd heard the song a thousand times. Was he making the most of his life? What if his own death was right around the corner?

She turned down the radio a bit. "Does it hurt to talk about your family? If so, I'm sorry I asked."

All he was thinking began to spill out like a dam breaking. "I can't believe I'm telling you all this. For years I thought things would change. Mom would come back, and our family would be whole again. My sister and I would be best of friends, and my mom would fix Christmas dinner and greet us all with a smile. We'd have family game nights, and we'd be the all-American family. That's never going to happen."

She adjusted the seat belt at her shoulder and looked away. "I know what you mean. I think all of us long for family because it's supposed to be where someone will love us no matter what. That's why I decided . . ."

He glanced at her perfect nose and cheekbones. "Decided what?"

She turned to stare out the window again. "It's not important. Looks like we're at the park. What's our plan of action?"

Regret coiled in his belly. When was the last time he'd actually talked to someone like this? Years. He had a few friends at the museum, but the most they did was shoot hoops and go to football games. Over the years he'd drawn more and more into himself. Maybe it was just as well they couldn't talk about this anymore. It wouldn't do to get too close.

He pulled into the parking lot past the tall white sculpture of two mermaids. "We're here in time for the three o'clock *Little Mermaid* show."

"Do you want to see the show?"

"I've never seen it, but we might not get any questions answered until the show is over. The backstage people will be busy prepping."

"Good point. Sure, let's watch it. I haven't been since I was a little girl."

He bought the tickets, and they joined the line into the four-hundred-seat auditorium. When the doors opened, they found seats in the middle section and only five rows back. The auditorium lights dimmed and the curtains over the observation windows rose. The smiling mermaids swam into view, and Ridge found himself mesmerized by the synchronized swimming and the way the women seemed to enjoy what they were doing. He glanced around at the spellbound viewers and saw little girls on the edges of their seats and parents equally enthralled.

Turtles and fish swam with the mermaids, and the water was incredibly clear. He might have to come back and dive the springs himself. The show was over in what felt like a blink of an eye, and he guided Harper out into the brilliant sunlight. A line of admirers waited to get autographs and talk to the mermaids.

Harper grabbed his forearm. "Look, I think that woman is their handler." She gestured toward a middle-aged woman with faded blonde hair and smile lines around her eyes. She was directing the mermaids into a queue to talk to the children. "Let's see if she remembers Judy Russo."

They threaded their way through the tourists and reached her as she turned to head back inside.

"Excuse me," Ridge said. "Could we have a minute of your time to ask about the history of the mermaids?" He introduced them both.

"I'm Silvia Sully." Her smile brightened. "Are you with the media?"

"No, we're trying to find out information about Judy Russo," Harper said.

Silvia's smile vanished. "What about her?"

"Did you know her?"

"I knew all the girls. Look, I have to get into comfortable clothes and take down my hair. Come with me back to my cottage and I'll try to help you."

Ridge took Harper's arm. "Lead the way."

Silvia's cottage was a charming one bedroom just down the way from Weeki Wachee. The yard was a tangle of wildflowers and ornamental grasses that would have been at home in England. The scent of roses wafted to Ridge's nose, and he shuddered at the overly sweet smell. It reminded him of a funeral home massed with bouquets. Harper wrinkled her nose too.

Silvia gestured to a round iron table and three chairs. "We can sit out here." She plopped into one of the chairs and kicked off her flip-flops as Ridge and Harper joined her. "Judy Russo, now there's a blast from the past. I haven't thought of her in decades. My mother was a friend of hers, and I remember her beautiful red hair." She glanced at Harper. "Her hair was about the same color as yours except maybe lighter."

Ridge's gaze lingered on Harper's fiery hair before he leaned forward. "Maybe you knew Judy's daughter, Annabelle?" The sun revealed all the gray hair in Silvia's hair, and he guessed her to be around fifty just like Annabelle.

"We used to play with our dolls and stuffed animals when she was a baby. I'd line them up and she'd knock them over. I was older than her, six years I think. After Judy died I never saw Annabelle again."

"Over the years did you hear anything about Judy's death?"

Silvia shook her head. "I was so young. Those days are pretty hazy. Mom might remember more."

Harper shifted in her chair. "Is your mother still alive?"

"Sure. She's only in her seventies and in pretty good health. She lives with me, but she's out for her afternoon bike ride. She still does a little mermaid training at Weeki Wachee." Silvia shaded her eyes with her hand. "Here she comes now."

Silvia waved, and Ridge twisted in his chair to see a short woman with dyed red hair lift her hand in response to Silvia's gesture. She wore yoga pants in pink and purple and rode a blue bike. From a distance she looked like a young woman, but as she neared he saw the map of lines around her mouth and eyes. She didn't appear like she was in her seventies though.

The woman put down a foot as the bike rolled to a stop. "It's hot out there today." She wiped the perspiration from her forehead with the back of her hand. "You have guests."

"They want to talk about your old friend Judy Russo." Silvia glanced at them. "I already forgot your names. Sorry."

Ridge rose and held out his hand to the woman dismounting the bike. "Ridge Jackson, and this is Harper Taylor."

The woman briefly touched his fingers. "Grace Beck. Why are you asking about Judy after all this time? She's been dead and buried for decades."

Ridge gestured to the empty seat and stepped back. "Harper is searching for her birth father, and that search led her to discover her half sister, Annabelle Rice, Judy's daughter."

Grace sat in the chair Ridge had vacated. "Sweet Annabelle. I lost track of her when she was adopted. I never knew what happened to her."

"She lives in Orlando," Harper said.

Grace brightened. "Could I get her phone number? I'd love to see how she's doing. She was the sweetest little thing."

"Of course." Harper fished a pen and notepad from her purse and jotted down Annabelle's phone number, then tore out the sheet and passed it to Grace. "Did you ever meet Annabelle's father?"

Grace fanned her red face with her open hand. "She was very secretive about him. All I know is he was a navy man. With the way she held back, I always suspected he was one of those sailors with a girl in every port. She would sneak out to meet him after our shows. I warned her he was up to no good, but she was smitten."

"Any idea of his name?" Harper asked Grace.

"No, I'm sorry. She just referred to him as 'my guy.'"

Ridge sensed Harper's disappointment, and he put his hand on her shoulder. "What about Judy's murder? Did you suspect anyone?"

The woman's hazel eyes narrowed. "I had my suspicions. There was a young man who helped around the place—Joe Mitchell—who was infatuated with Judy. She caught him peeping in her window. Back in those days the mermaids stayed in cottages out back. It was as hot as blazes with no air-conditioning, and our windows were always open. It was either face the heat or face the mosquitoes, so we took the breeze and hoped for the best. He got fired the week before Judy died. I always thought he might have done it. Joe claimed he loved her and would never hurt her, but he had shifty eyes."

Harper leaned back in her chair. "I heard a friend found her. Was that you?"

Grace propped her elbow on the table and rested her cheek on her palm. "It was. Silvia loved little Annabelle, and we kept her often. I ran her home while Silvia stayed with my roommate. I called out to her, then went inside. I found her lying on the floor in a pool of blood." She shuddered. "It was horrible. I grabbed Annabelle and rushed her out of the cottage, then called the sheriff's department."

Ridge didn't think Grace would be able to tell them something they didn't know. "So you weren't in there very long?"

"Just long enough to tell she was dead. Her eyes were open and staring." Grace shuddered again and clasped herself. "I haven't thought of this in a long time. The sea silk she'd been making was heaped on the table behind her, and it looked like she'd been working on it all evening, because there was a big pile."

Harper straightened. "Sea silk? She knew how to make sea silk?"

"Her grandparents brought some byssus back from Italy for her the week before she died. They have family there."

She peered at Harper. "Most people don't know what sea silk even is."

"I make it too. The byssus from around here works well."

Grace shrugged. "She was wild about it. I still have some of the stuff she made. I always wanted to deliver them to Annabelle, but I didn't know how to track her down. Would you take the boxes of her mother's things to her?"

Harper leaned forward. "I'd be honored."

Grace rose and beckoned to Ridge with one finger. "Come with me, young man. I'll let you carry the boxes."

A week ago Ridge wouldn't have expected to be away from his office investigating his father's attack and an old murder. And were they even related? He had a feeling they were following the wrong trail.

15

Her dad's identity seemed so close yet so elusive. The houseboat rolled with the tide as Ridge flipped on some lights in the tiny living quarters. Bear, tail wagging, followed him. The boxes Grace had given them sat on the floor in front of the love seat, and while Harper didn't expect to discover anything about Judy's death, she hoped the contents held a clue to her father's name.

"You don't have to stay tonight. When you leave, I'll take my boat a little farther out. I'm sure I'll be fine."

She'd spent the entire day with Ridge—and she liked it, which was a strange thing to admit to herself. He was an intense kind of guy—far out of her league—but his intensity intrigued her. What would it be like to have his full attention? He lived every minute to the fullest, and she wished she had that ability.

"I don't mind sleeping on the sofa."

"No. Life has to get back to normal sometime. You go home tonight."

Ridge glanced at her. "You seem a little upset. All that talk of blood and death too disturbing?"

"A little. I don't know how this will lead to anything about my dad's identity. It's been a strange day."

Ridge turned back to the small bookshelf and perused the titles there. "You've got all the *Glee* episodes. And the CDs."

Her cheeks went hot at his quizzical look. "I see the contempt on your face. Did you ever actually watch it? It's a great series."

He joined her on the love seat, and Bear jumped up into his lap. "That's not contempt, it's surprise. I didn't take you for the singing type. Were you in choir too?"

"Oh yes. I love music." The reason rushed out like some strange confessional. "Singing always raises my spirits."

No way would she tell him she imagined herself friends with the characters in *Glee* or that she often felt alone in school, even after Oliver found her a home. She'd been shy and hadn't made friends easily. Sara was one who had seen behind her reserved exterior and wanted to be friends anyway.

"An alto, I'll bet?" He grinned and set Bear aside, then got up and slid a CD into the player. Moments later he pulled her to her feet as the chords to "Glory Days" began to play. He snatched two forks off the table and gave her one, then held the other up to his mouth and sang along with Finn and Puck.

Aware her mouth was gaping, she closed it with a snap, then chimed in as he reached the chorus about glory days passing them by.

Was this really happening? She was singing a Springsteen song with Ridge Jackson. Their gazes locked as they "sang" into the forks. A smile curved her lips, and giggles bubbled up until she couldn't sing at all.

She collapsed onto the love seat. "You are a man of surprises."

He waggled his eyebrows at her and went to pop the CD

out of the player. The silence wiped the smile off her face. It felt suddenly intimate and too warm in her little salon. This wasn't how she acted with men. She was usually too tongue-tied to talk to them, let alone sing.

She scooped up Bear as protection. "We could check out the boxes Grace gave us."

He rejoined her on the love seat. "I was trying to help you forget all that for a while. It's been a rough twenty-four hours. And to tell you the truth, I'm not so sure you should stay here alone. The guy from the other night could come back."

"Like I said, I can move the boat farther away from shore. Or back to the marina."

It was hard to trust this camaraderie when they'd been enemies for so long. It left her feeling like she was trying to walk in a carnival fun house and her equilibrium was off-kilter.

"He could swim out or row a boat out to where you are anchored. If you're sleeping, you likely wouldn't hear him with the night sounds and the waves."

She leaned forward and pulled the first box to her. It contained old clothing, lots of browns and oranges like the pictures she'd seen of styles in the sixties. She held out a picture. "Look, Judy is swimming with a manatee."

He examined the photo. "A young one." He peered closer. "It might be that old one we saw at the springs. They can live for decades. We recently lost the oldest manatee in captivity, Snooty. He was seventy."

The next box held old Yardley makeup, hot rollers, a jar of something called Dippity-do, false eyelashes, and hair items. She marveled over the Breck bottles, the Aqua Net hairspray, and Coppertone sun lotion. "No sunscreen for Judy."

"I'm not sure they even had it back then. I think the goal was to get as much sun as possible."

"That's still my goal." Harper pulled the last box to her. "Let's see what's in here."

He sighed but knelt on the floor in front of the box, pulled the flaps loose, then lifted items out and put them beside her. "A kid's stuffed animal, probably Annabelle's when she was little. Lots of marine gastropods."

"I just like saying the name. It's more precise than sea snails." She picked up a shell. "This looks like a Scotch bonnet." She ran her fingers over the polished surface that looked a lot like a Scottish tam-o'-shanter. "Lots of smaller shells, land snails, and sea snails. Some she had drilled holes into."

"Maybe she was making jewelry. Did you used to dabble in it before you started making fiber art?"

How'd he remember that? Maybe Oliver had mentioned it. Then she realized his gaze had dropped to the snail necklace at her neck. She fingered it. "I don't make much anymore. My fiber art is more rewarding."

His fingers scooped the necklace away from her neck. She bit back a gasp at the warm brush of his fingers against her skin.

He turned over the necklace. "That's a nice button-top specimen. Black pearls from the bivalves on either side?"

She barely managed a nod. "It took a while to find ones that matched in size."

"I'd like to see some of your fiber art."

"I have several pieces I'm selling in the auction for Gulf Shore Preservation tomorrow night."

"I'm attending that too. How about I pick you up?"

"Okay," she managed to whisper.

He let go of the necklace, but it still felt warm from his hand when it landed back against her body. "You did a good job."

"Thank you." *Move away, Harper.* She needed to be able to breathe again.

His nearness made her mouth go dry and her pulse speed up. She didn't want him to realize how powerfully he affected her. He wouldn't welcome this growing attraction. She didn't welcome it herself. Where had it come from?

He went back to searching through the box, and she managed to draw in a shaky breath. She needed to get control of herself or she would embarrass them both.

He showed her a sheaf of fabric that looked hand knit. "What's this?"

She fingered it. "This must be the sea silk Grace told us about. I've never seen it made into cloth though. I've only seen a yarn type of material made from it. The quality of this fabric is stunning."

The material glowed golden in the light, and it was so soft and pliable. Harper didn't want to harm it so she placed it beside her. "I wish I knew how she made it. Anything else in there?"

"Nope, we've seen it all."

"I'm supposed to go see Annabelle on Saturday. Want to go with me?" The invitation was past her lips before she could censor it.

"Sure." He hesitated. "But I'm not sure this line of investigation will bring us any closer to who attacked my dad. Once we talk to Annabelle, I want to pay Eric Kennedy a visit."

"Kennedy? You think he could be behind Oliver's attack?"

"He warned you off the shell-bed site. I don't know who cut my dad's air hose, but I have to find out."

She wanted to know too. None of this made any sense.

Where was she? He slammed his palms against the steering wheel and stared out over the empty water. She should have been out there at her mollusk beds. The Taylor woman hadn't docked at the marina, and though he'd driven down every lane near the bay he could find, he hadn't been able to locate her. Had the GPS device been knocked off, or was it malfunctioning?

His employer would not be pleased.

He'd failed all week, and he wasn't sure what to do next. The Rice woman was back home, but he feared her policeman son would be shadowing her constantly.

He plucked his phone from the console and placed the call. "I can't find the Taylor woman. She's not at any of her usual haunts."

"You incompetent fool! If the women get together and talk too much, it will be disastrous. Have you checked on Annabelle Rice again?"

"No, you told me to focus on the Taylor woman."

"I don't care which one you get, just do it. This has gone on way too long, and the situation is urgent!"

"I'll drive past the Rice house and see what I can do."

"What about the old man? Has he started talking yet?"

At least he had good news about that. "No, he doesn't remember anything about what happened."

"I have new information that suggests I need to get him out of the way. He's had an investigator poking into my business, and it appears he may know the truth. I can't allow him to awaken and tell anyone. I want him dead and the report from the investigator destroyed."

He'd have no problem breaking into the house. And hacking into computers was a piece of cake. "It will cost you."

"And I'm prepared to pay! Get the job done, and I'll pay you then. No more upfront money. I can't trust your competence."

He gritted his teeth. "Fine. I'll try to get it done this weekend, and I'll expect payment immediately."

"I'm tired of your 'tries.' Get the job done, or I'll hire someone who can. This has gone on too long."

"Why don't you come down here and do it yourself? This isn't as easy as you think," he snapped.

He heard a click and dead air. He tossed his phone onto the passenger seat, started his car, and turned around to get back to the main road.

Losing this job wasn't an option with his son's life on the line. And fortunately, this new job would be easy.

16

Lights sparkled onto the lawn of Edgewater Park and down to the water in the approaching dusk. Harper felt ill at ease in her slim-fitting black cocktail dress and heels as she strolled through the oceanic wonderland erected on the lawn to showcase the displayed sea art. She was much more at home in shorts or a bathing suit. Ridge looked magnificent in a sports jacket though, and she had to make a conscious attempt not to gawk at him.

Light classical music played in the background—probably Oliver's suggestion to the planning committee. Bach's distinctive Suite no. 1 floated under the flow of conversation and champagne.

He touched her arm. "I'll get us something to drink."

Since Ridge wasn't watching, she let her gaze wander over his gleaming dark hair and wide shoulders. When he was out of sight, she wandered over to the display of her art. Her big mural made from sea silk, pearls, and mollusks depicted Bear in a water setting. The bids on it were already more than she'd hoped to raise for the Gulf Shore Preservation Society.

She spotted Eric Kennedy talking with an older woman who from the resemblance had to be his mother. An elderly man in a wheelchair was with them. Harper didn't want to talk to him, but as she turned to go the other direction, the woman with him beckoned to her with a smile.

Harper's gut tightened, but she pasted on a smile in response and went to join their small group.

The woman took Harper's hand in a warm grip. "You're Harper Taylor, aren't you? I just love your beautiful fiber-art pieces. I've bid on every piece you donated. Fine craftsmanship, my dear." She released her and laughed. "I'm forgetting my manners. I'm Elizabeth Kennedy, Eric's mother. This is my husband, Tom." She touched her husband's shoulder.

Tom looked very ill. His skin color was yellowish and his lips were colorless, but his blue eyes crinkled in a smile, and he took Harper's hand in a surprisingly strong grip. "I've heard so much about you, Ms. Taylor. Your mollusk beds sound promising for the environment. I wish I were strong enough to go out and see them."

"Thank you. It's going incredibly well." She shot a glance at Eric, who was scowling. Should she mention his opposition? Surely his parents knew.

Elizabeth caught the glance and reached over to clasp her son's forearm. "I know Eric has had his reservations, but those beds aren't harming the burial grounds."

"We don't know that, Mother." He shook off her hand and stalked off.

Elizabeth watched him go with a sigh. "That boy always was a bit of a hothead. Don't let him deter you."

Ridge stepped into view, and Harper waved to him. He spotted her and came across the lawn toward her, balancing a plate of appetizers atop two cups of punch.

She rescued the cups and took a sip. "Thanks. This is Ridge

Jackson. Ridge, this is Elizabeth Kennedy and her husband, Tom."

Elizabeth held out her hand, and Ridge took it. "Are you related to the famous Hyannis Port Kennedys?"

"Oh no. People often ask that, but there's no connection at all. My husband is a simple boat builder, and I'm a doctor."

Mr. Kennedy's "simple" company sold more boats in Florida than any other, and its billboards dotted the highway system. Harper hadn't realized the connection. "Good boats."

"We've had a happy life." Elizabeth's brown eyes grew shadowed. "My husband has been ill though."

"Elizabeth." A trace of admonishment creased Tom's features. "They aren't interested in our personal troubles."

Harper touched his arm. "I'm sorry to hear this, Mr. Kennedy. I'll pray you feel better soon."

He patted her hand where it still rested on his forearm. "Thank you, my dear. You're a sweet girl." He looked up at his wife. "Let's go browse the food table. I'm a little peckish."

"Of course." Elizabeth smiled at Harper and Ridge. "Nice talking to you both." She walked away beside her husband as he manipulated the electric controls of his chair.

Ridge frowned as he watched them. "Is their son here too? They seem much nicer than Eric."

"He stalked off when his mother told him my beds weren't causing any harm. I can't imagine anyone voting for the man. I didn't realize his connection to the boat manufacturer."

"We should tell the police to check out his whereabouts when you and my dad were attacked. I'm going to contact the sheriff's office about it. I have the detective's phone number." He set the plate of food down on a nearby table and pulled out his phone, then shot off a text.

"It's hard to believe Eric was the assailant. He's passionate about the health of the Gulf, but most politicians don't get their hands dirty."

Ridge slipped his phone back into his pocket. "Maybe not, but he's got a lot of anger." He picked up his plate again. "You eat anything yet? The shrimp wontons are delicious." He held out the plate.

She took a wonton and bit into it. "Good. Lots of ginger."

Looking around the milling crowd, she saw Ridge's sister. "There's Willow."

He turned to follow the direction of her gaze. "Mom is with her. We'd better go say hello."

She forced herself to nod and walk with him. She'd met Willow and Christina many times over the years, but they'd never made a secret of their disdain for her.

They reached the two women, and Ridge brushed a kiss on his mother's cheek and gave his sister a brief hug. They were both in long, elegant dresses. Willow was in a silvery gray, and Christina wore a black number that made Harper's appear as if it had been pulled off a Goodwill rack. She always felt dowdy in their company.

Christina speared her with a cold stare. "Harper, how nice to see you." Her tone implied it was anything but nice.

Harper's face felt stiff, but she smiled. "I think we're raising quite a bit of money for the foundation."

Christina didn't reply but tilted her head to look up at her son. "How's your father?"

"Pretty chipper. He should be released in another day or two."

"That's good."

Harper felt distinctly excluded as they continued to talk about Oliver's condition. She glanced around. Eric stared at her with malevolence. She shivered and averted her gaze. Maybe Ridge was right about him.

———

Annabelle limped from the kitchen to the sofa. Scott carried her coffee for her while Mark trailed behind with a green smoothie he'd made. He'd arrived yesterday and had been here to greet her when Scott brought her home from the hospital on Thursday.

Scott set the coffee cup on the end table beside her, and Mark handed her the smoothie.

"Thanks, boys." She smiled with fondness at her sons. They were so different. Scott was blond like her while Mark had his father's dark coloring. She couldn't be prouder of them and the lives they'd led. They were both God-fearing men and were active in their churches and communities. It had been hard to raise them alone, but if she had to leave them soon, she could go to the Lord with her heart happy.

Mark's dark-brown eyes examined her. "That bruise on your face looks worse than it did yesterday."

She touched it and flinched. "It will fade."

"Will these injuries keep you from starting your treatment?"

She pondered the question a moment. The chemo might make her more prone to bleeding. Would the doctor decide to delay it? "I guess we'll see. But if it's postponed, it won't be by more than a few days." She reached for her younger son's hand. "It will be all right, Mark."

"But what if it's not?" His Adam's apple wobbled as he

swallowed. "We can't lose you, Mom. I've been talking to Chelsea about moving to Orlando."

"Absolutely not! Your career is in New York. Chelsea loves it there. Don't overreact, honey. I'm going to be fine."

Scott shifted toward the window and peered out. "Someone's here in a black truck."

Annabelle glanced at the clock above the fireplace. Ten o'clock. "Harper is supposed to come by today, but she never said what time."

Scott scowled and marched toward the door. "You're not up to visitors."

"Don't you dare scare her away!" Wincing, she struggled to her feet and shuffled after Scott. "I want to see her."

He paused and looked back at her, then sighed. "Fine. Go sit down. I'll let her in. She's got a guy with her. Big dude with broad shoulders. He come with her the other day?"

"No, she was alone." Annabelle returned to her seat and took a sip of the smoothie, shuddering a little at the faint bitter taste of the kale underlying the sweet taste of the blueberries. Mark was determined to make her well.

Scott's greeting at the door was curt, and she sighed. His cop instincts were on high alert at the moment. She smiled and turned carefully as footsteps came toward her. The tall man with her resembled Chris McNally from *Supernatural* a bit, right down to the thick black hair.

Annabelle held out her hands. "My dear Harper, there you are. I've been looking forward to your visit."

Harper rushed forward, then stopped and surveyed her. "Annabelle, you're all bruised up. Did you fall?" Her narrowed eyes turned to glower at Scott and Mark as though she suspected them of attacking Annabelle.

Scott pulled over two more chairs from the dining table and gestured for them to have a seat. "Someone kidnapped her Tuesday night, and she fell out of the trunk to escape."

Harper gasped and sat beside her. "Are you really okay?"

Annabelle patted her hand. "I'm fine. And who's this with you?"

Harper glanced at the man. "My, um, business partner. Ridge Jackson."

Ridge gave her and her sons a nod, then sat on one of the chairs. "Someone tried to kidnap Harper late Tuesday night too. He used ether, but I arrived at her boat before he could haul her off."

Annabelle gasped and turned to Scott, whose frown had turned thunderous. "This is my son Scott. He's a police detective."

In rapid-fire manner Scott shot several questions at them, and Ridge answered them. Scott and Ridge exchanged a long glance. Scott thrust his hands in the pockets of his khaki shorts. "It might be coincidence that they were both attacked shortly after connecting, but I'm not a big believer in coincidence. Especially not when it involves my mother."

Ridge gave a curt nod. "I'm with you. Not sure how to go about figuring out what this is all about. Harper's attacker didn't say anything."

Annabelle took another swig of the smoothie. "We only met each other a few days ago. There can't be any connection."

Her words rang hollow though. She didn't *want* there to be a connection, because she didn't want Harper to be in danger. She faced Ridge. "Any idea who might want to harm Harper?"

"A sleazy politician warned her off the location of the mollusk farm she's set up. I had thought it might have something to do with that, but with your attack, I'm not so sure."

Harper glanced at Ridge, and Annabelle felt the connection between them. She suppressed a smile. They were more than business partners. If not now, they soon would be.

"We have some things for you," Ridge said. "We found your mother's best friend, the one who discovered her body. She gave us your mom's belongings."

"She kept them all this time?" Annabelle couldn't believe it.

"There are four boxes." Ridge rose and went toward the door.

"We'll help carry them in." Scott motioned for Mark to follow him.

With the men out of the room, Annabelle took Harper's hand. "I'm so glad you came back. You seem troubled. Are you okay?"

Harper stilled, then shook her head. "I'm scared."

"I am too," Annabelle said. "I am too."

17

Ridge opened the tailgate on his truck, then paused in the bright sunlight and turned to Scott and Mark. "One thing I didn't want to mention to your mother . . . my dad had a mishap just before all this started. Someone sliced his air hose and left him for dead. Harper was attacked at the same time."

Scott stopped reaching for one of the boxes. "Tell me what happened."

"He was on a dive to the mollusk beds. He'd gone down at the same time as Harper." Ridge told Scott about how his father was missing until his boat was found miles away with him aboard. "His air hose had been cut. He doesn't remember anything about what took place, but somehow he must have managed to get aboard his boat and motor off."

"Another coincidence?" Scott arched an eyebrow and smirked, then swung his gaze toward the street as a diesel truck spewing noxious fumes lumbered by. "What's this about a politician warning them off?"

Ridge told him about the Native American burial grounds.

"Aren't there some down by Venice too?" Mark said.

"Yes, I'd heard about that." Ridge reached for a box to hand him. "I can't see any connection between Eric Kennedy wanting us to move the mollusk beds and the attack on my dad. Or the attacks on the women. Nothing makes much sense."

Scott hefted the biggest box into his arms. "Our mom has cancer."

"I heard. I'm sorry."

Scott nodded. "The last thing we need is her worrying about her half sister. I can guarantee she won't worry about herself, but she'll be in a tizzy about Harper."

Ridge stiffened. "And Harper will feel the same way about Annabelle. The two of them seem to have bonded quickly. Harper's been searching for her family for a long time."

"So has Mom."

They glared at each other, and then Scott took a step back. "Sorry. I'm a little protective of Mom. You dating Harper?"

"We're just friends." He wasn't so sure he believed his own words. Singing with her night before last had broken down an important barrier he couldn't name. For the first time he felt as if he *knew her.* Really knew her better than anyone else. Which was silly when they'd been at odds for so long. But his desire to discredit her to his father was waning.

He pushed away the crazy thoughts and grabbed the last two boxes. "These things might cheer up your mom."

Mark reached the door first and held it open with his foot for them. "Or it will upset her with thoughts of her mother. She has nagged Scott to death about looking into the murder."

"And there's never time to do it. It's a cold case." Scott stepped into the house and carried the box into the living room to his mother with Ridge and Mark right behind him.

Annabelle's eyes shone with joy as she reached for the box Mark held. Ridge intervened and leaned down toward her. "Take the top box. That's the one you'll want to see first."

Annabelle slid the box onto her lap. "You have a fine young man, Harper."

Harper's gaze locked with his, and a flush spread up her face. She opened her mouth, then closed it again. Ridge knew how she felt—there was no way to counter the romantic assumptions in this room.

Annabelle pulled out the old plushy. In the bright light he realized it was a lamb. The thing had been well loved, and one button eye was missing. The lamb seemed more gray than white, but Annabelle clasped it to her chest.

"This was mine?" She laid the lamb off to the side on the sofa and delved back into the box where she pulled out handfuls of shells. "I still have a little bracelet my mother made me out of shells. It's too small, of course, but I would never part with it."

Harper gently lifted out the sea silk fabric. "Do you have any idea where your mom got this?"

Annabelle studied it. "What is it?"

"It's called sea silk and is made from the fibers that anchor the bivalve pen shell into the sand. People have been making sea silk items for centuries, but this is the first instance I've ever seen of it being made into an actual fabric. It's usually thicker, like yarn. I'd love to learn how to do it."

"I wish I could help you, but I was so small. I don't remember her at all. Is that it?"

Harper nodded. "You wash it in lemon juice and let it dry. There are lots of myths about sea silk. Some have said the Golden Fleece sought by Jason and the Argonauts was made of sea silk. You ever read *Twenty Thousand Leagues Under the Sea*? The crew of the *Nautilus* was said to wear clothing made from byssus, which is what those hairy strands are called."

Annabelle stared at it. "How fascinating."

"Hairy," Scott said in a strained voice. "That rings some kind of bell." He glanced at his mother. "Wasn't there something in the investigation into your mom's death that mentioned fibers in the wound?"

Annabelle nodded. "I think I remember that."

"If she worked with this byssus, could it have been lodged in the wound?" He looked at Ridge as though he might provide the answer.

"Does the evidence room still have everything from the investigation? I could examine it and tell you. The fibers are egg shaped."

"Yep. I'll see about acquiring the evidence boxes."

But what if the evidence did consist of a strand of byssus? What did that tell them?

Harper perched on the closed toilet lid in the head and watched the pregnancy test she'd just activated. Nerves jittered up and down her spine. The next few moments would tell her if she'd have her own family. But if she was pregnant, she would have to tell Ridge what she'd done.

A new awareness simmered between them, and she was beginning to think they might be moving closer to a real relationship. What would Oliver think of that? The way she and Ridge had been at odds all these years had grieved him, but would he welcome a romantic relationship between them? Willow would hit the roof.

Harper held her breath as she thought she saw a second pink line begin to appear on the test. She stared in frozen fascination as the line grew easier to see. It still wasn't as dark as the first line, so what did that mean? Her chest felt tight as she grabbed and read the directions. The lighter color just meant it was positive but early.

She was pregnant? Really?

She leaped off the toilet lid. She nearly floated out to the salon where she scooped up Bear and danced with him around the space. "You're going to be a big brother," she told the wriggling dog.

Her smile vanished as she considered how to tell Ridge. And Oliver who hadn't thought she should do this.

First things first. She had to shower and get ready for church. Sara and Josh had agreed to go to church with her, and they were picking her up since his big truck was more comfortable for three. She dashed into the shower, then threw on a sundress before she put her hair up in a ponytail and headed out.

The perfect Sunday morning full of sunshine, salt air, and the caw of gulls overhead greeted Harper when she stepped out onto the deck of her houseboat.

Josh's blue truck pulled up on shore and he beeped the horn. She gave Bear a final pat, then stepped onto the pier and climbed in the backseat of Josh's truck. She got in behind Josh so she could see Sara.

Sara looked beautiful in a turquoise flowered sundress. Her long blonde hair was up in a French twist. Her welcoming smile held speculation. "I tried to call you several times yesterday and you never called me back."

"I didn't have my cell phone, and I forgot to check it this morning. Listen, there's more that's been happening since that guy tried to grab me underwater." She launched into the events of the last couple of days.

Sara swiveled in her seat to glare at her. "You should have called us."

"I'm sorry. Events came at me so fast I barely had time to breathe." She wanted to tell Sara about her pregnancy, too, but not with Josh there.

His long fingers tapped the steering wheel. "So what's your cop nephew think is going on?"

Harper blinked out of her thoughts about the baby. It hadn't hit her yet that she had more than a sister—she had two nephews as well. Mark was about to get married, and a great-niece or nephew might be in her future. Though her two new nephews hadn't been all that warm, it was early days, and she had faith she could build a relationship with them.

"He doesn't know yet. The sea silk was interesting to him when he saw it though. According to something he read in the police report, Judy had a strand of something unidentified embedded in the wound. She worked with byssus. You should see the cloth she wove out of it. It's magnificent."

"So what's next?" Sara asked.

"Scott will get the box of evidence and see if Ridge can confirm it's byssus. I hope he'll let me take a look too."

They drove through downtown Dunedin with its charming buildings decorated with paintings of oranges on the sides.

Josh slowed to park in front of Dunedin Coffee Shop. "What about the detective who investigated your mom's death?"

"Oh! I forgot to tell you I talked to him." Harper told them about her mother's missing car. "So it's a dead end."

"Could Scott get any notes made at the time of that investigation?" Josh pulled the truck into a space.

"I didn't think to talk to him about it. That's a great idea though."

Sara lowered the sun visor to look in the mirror and slick on rose lipstick. She flipped it back up and smiled at Harper. "How do you feel about being a maid of honor?"

Harper gasped and glanced from her smiling face to Josh who was grinning too. "You're finally getting married? When?"

"In a month. Which means we have to find dresses, order food, rent a venue for the reception—the whole thing. It's about time. We've been engaged for three years and our plans have gotten changed several times."

"No more though." Josh kissed her hand.

"That's wonderful!" She'd heard some of the backstory about Josh's growing-up years and how he was afraid he'd fail Sara. He must have finally come to grips with all of it. "What about a wedding on the beach at Honeymoon Island?"

"I don't think I've ever been there," Sara said.

Harper had grown up here, unlike Sara who had only been stationed here a few months. "It's a barrier island just off Dunedin. It was originally called Hog Island, but honeymooners flocked to it in the thirties and forties. Wait until you see the setting sun turn the white sand pink!"

Josh wrinkled his nose. "Pink? That sounds a little girly."

"It just looks pink," Harper said.

"I think it sounds wonderful! Can we check it out after church?" Sara flashed a pleading smile at him.

"I don't see why not." Josh shrugged. "I guess I can get married on pink sand if that's what you really want."

Harper had to glance away from the expression on Josh's face. It was too raw with love to bear seeing. She didn't know if she'd ever find a man to share her life with, but her heart still longed for family, a child of her own. It was a dream about to come true. She touched her belly again.

She caught sight of a familiar dark shock of hair above solid shoulders as he exited the coffee shop with a cup in his hand. "There's Ridge."

Shoving open her door, she stepped out into the shimmering heat and humidity. He caught sight of her and smiled before heading toward her. He was dressed in khakis and a polo. Josh and Sara exited the truck and Sara lifted a brow her direction as Ridge stopped in front of Harper.

"Sara, Josh, this is Ridge, Oliver's son. Ridge, these are my friends Sara Kavanagh and Josh Holman."

He shook hands with them. "I've heard Harper talk about you two. You're with the Coast Guard."

"How's your dad faring?" Sara asked.

"Okay. I might get to take him home tomorrow. I went to early church so I could stop in and check on him."

"We're grabbing a coffee, then heading to church ourselves," Harper said. "We're going to explore Honeymoon Island afterward. Josh and Sara are looking for a spot to have their wedding."

Ridge lifted a brow. "Nice place. Mind if I join you? I could use a day to clear my head."

Harper's pulse quickened at the thought of him coming along. How soon should she tell him about the baby? She knew enough about pregnancy to know miscarriages weren't uncommon in the early weeks. "Sure. We'll stop by the deli and pick up stuff for a picnic lunch. Want to meet there around twelve thirty?"

"You got it." He lifted his cup toward Josh and Sara. "Nice to meet you two. I'll see you later."

Sara watched him walk away. "You never told me he was such a hunk."

Josh took her hand. "Hey, am I chopped liver?"

"You're the handsomest man on the planet." She displayed a dreamy smile and winked.

"I need a refill and we can go," Josh said.

Once he was out of earshot, Harper told Sara about the results of the pregnancy test.

Her gray eyes went wide. "One baby or two?"

"There was one embryo implanted. I'll have to wait for the ultrasound in a few weeks."

Harper waved at Ridge as he drove off in his truck. She didn't want to notice the breadth of his shoulders or the way his dark eyes crinkled at the corners when he smiled, but she couldn't help it. He was a hunk like Sara had said, and Harper found it hard not to watch him.

18

Ridge couldn't keep his eyes off Harper as she walked the beautiful beach at Caladesi Island State Park with her friends. Her cheeks held a blush of color, and the sea breeze had pulled her hair from its ponytail and tossed red curls that reflected the sunlight.

Had he been wrong about her all these years? Maybe he'd allowed jealousy over his father's attention to her to cloud his judgment. A week ago he would have rejected the notion he could be that wrong about her, but so far he'd seen no deception in her. Just a sweet vulnerability to belong somewhere. He'd never had to worry about belonging or fitting in. His father's money and power had ensured he was accepted no matter where he went.

He'd been blind.

The beautiful turquoise sea merged into the azure sky, and he stood on the sand and listened to the women talk about arches and flowers. He and Josh exchanged commiserating glances.

"I'm just letting her do whatever she wants," Josh said.

"Smart man." Ridge's phone vibrated, and he glanced at the unknown number before he answered it. "Ridge Jackson."

"Ridge, this is Don Ward. I discovered the name of Lisa's best friend."

"Thanks for calling, Don. Hang on, let me grab a pen." He fished a pen and paper from his pocket. "Go ahead."

"Her name is Kelly Gray. She still lives up by Orlando with her husband."

Ridge jotted down the address as the former detective rattled it off. "Got it, thanks."

"Anytime. I'll see if there's anything else I can find. A guy can only fish so much." Don chuckled and ended the call.

Ridge slid his phone into his pocket. He hated to break up the effusive squeals of excitement, but Harper would want to know about this new piece of information.

He walked across the sand to the women and waited for a good spot to break in.

Harper finally took a breath between the food discussion and how many guests would likely attend. She glanced at him. "You have something to add?"

"Weddings are out of my area of expertise." He grinned. "I got a call from Don Ward though. He gave me the name and address of your mother's best friend."

Her eyes went wide. "Does she live in the area?"

"Orlando. We can take a trip up there tomorrow." He waved his hand. "Once you're done planning."

"We're done," Sara said. "We can drive back now, and I'll have Josh take me out to dinner. I started you on this course, and I feel guilty for the danger you've encountered. You have to find out who is behind all these attacks."

Harper hugged her. "Okay, I'll let you know what we hear. But this isn't your fault."

Ridge stared at her. "You think it has something to do with the DNA test?"

"Don't you?" Sara shot back. "It seems clear to Josh and me. None of this happened until Harper met her sister. There has to be some connection."

Ridge had been feeling as if they were wandering in a fog without any clear direction, but Sara's certainty galvanized him. If he could just unravel the threads, he'd be able to figure out this tangled mess.

All her earlier exuberance floated away as Harper let the wind through the open window blow through her hair, and the humidity pressed in on her like a moist blanket. Ridge's truck ate up the miles to Kelly's house as Harper stared blankly out at the egrets eating bugs along the road.

"Earth to Harper. You okay?"

She plastered on a smile and turned his way. "Sorry. I can't believe I'm going to meet someone who actually knew my mother." Her throat tightened and she swallowed. "I mean, I've waited my whole life to learn more about her. This Kelly Gray might even have pictures."

His dark eyes softened as he glanced her way before he focused back at the road. "We're nearly there. Are you going to tell her who you are right off the bat?"

"Yes. Maybe she'll open up more."

He turned the truck onto a narrow street. "I think it's that blue house."

The house was a sixties-style ranch. Its black shutters seemed freshly painted, and the yellow front door added a pop of color.

Harper didn't get out when he first pulled into the driveway and parked. She'd been going over and over in her head what she wanted to say, but every thought had vanished. What if she found out her mother planned to give her up for adoption?

"You want me to go up first? You're as white as the Honeymoon Island sand."

"No, I want to do it." She forced her hand to the door handle and pushed, almost falling out onto the drive. The scent of newly mown grass hit her as she got out, and she heard the distant whine of a power saw from the backyard. Maybe Kelly's husband was building something.

Her limbs didn't want to obey her, and she walked stiffly to the front door with Ridge beside her. Her blood roared in her head, and she wet her lips as she rang the doorbell. Its distant tone chimed inside the house, but no one came to the door.

"Let's go around back. She might not hear us with the noise."

She nodded at Ridge and followed him around the left side of the house, past the one-car garage. The growl of the saw grew louder as they stepped around the corner, and she spotted a woman bent over a chop saw on the back deck. She chopped a long length of treated lumber, then fitted it into place on the deck. The woman's head came up as she spotted them.

She stood and stretched out her back. "Hello, can I help you?"

Harper took a step closer to her, and the color drained out of the woman's face. "Lisa?" she whispered.

Harper's ears roared again as the blood pounded in her head. "I-I'm Lisa's daughter, Harper. Are you Kelly?"

The woman's breath hissed out between her teeth. "You look just like her." Her hand shook a bit as she raked her hair out of her face. "I have a million questions, but I need something to drink after working on the deck. Sweet tea for you both?" Her gaze lingered a moment on Ridge.

"That would be great," Harper said. "This is my friend Ridge Jackson. He's been helping me learn more about my mom."

Kelly nodded at him. "Nice to meet you." She looked like she was in her midfifties, and her light-brown hair curled around her head in a halo. She wore white shorts and a blue tank top that exposed tanned arms.

She led them to a covered porch off the back of the house and pointed to four chairs with blue cushions arranged around a table. "Have a seat. I'll be right back." She went through the back door.

"I have a good feeling about this," Ridge said. "She recognized you immediately."

Kelly came back through the door carrying a tray with a pitcher of iced tea and three glasses. She set it on the table and poured the tea, then passed the glasses around before she dropped into a chair beside Harper. "I can't get over the resemblance. Your mom had those same turquoise eyes. Her hair might have been a touch redder than yours, but you look so much like her it's uncanny." She took a sip of her tea. "How can I help you?"

"I'd love to know about my mother. How long did you know her?"

"Forever. Lisa and I went to school together from the seventh grade on."

"Where was this?" Harper longed to see their high school yearbooks and silly pictures of her mother goofing off.

"Here in Orlando. I never left and neither did she."

"Is anyone in her family still alive?" Harper held her breath as she waited for the answer.

"She was an only child and estranged from her mom when I knew her. I think that's what made her so vulnerable to your father. I heard her mom died of a drug overdose a few years after Lisa's death. I don't know much else about her family."

Harper caught her breath. "You knew my father?"

"Knew him?" Kelly wiped the condensation from her glass. "I don't think anyone really knew him. She called him Huey and was really funny about telling me his real name. I met him once, but the porch light was out when he came to pick her up, and I only saw his white teeth and broad shoulders. He was older than her by probably twenty, twenty-five years. Handsome from what I could see and dressed well, so I thought he probably had money."

"Huey? Unusual name," Ridge said.

"He flew a Huey chopper for the navy. That's about all I know about him."

Harper tucked away that nugget for later examination. "She never married him when she found out she was expecting me?"

"I'm pretty sure he was married, but your mom never admitted it. She was excited she was going to be a mom. We both worked for Disney. We both worked in accounting, and I threw her a baby shower with our coworkers. She had so much stuff it took two trips to take it to her apartment."

Harper's eyes burned and she blinked back tears. "Do you know what happened? How did she die?"

Kelly took a sip of tea. "Truthfully, I never believed she ran that stop sign. She was a careful driver, especially when she knew she was going to be a mom. She came home the night before she died super upset. Shaking and crying. I think his wife came to see her."

Ridge leaned forward. "What makes you say that?"

"She said, 'that witch,' over and over. She wouldn't tell me what happened. The next day she was gone. I tried to get custody of you when your grandma died, but I'd just lost my job and the powers that be didn't think I was the motherly type at the time. It's one of my biggest regrets that I couldn't do anything to save you from her mother. Was living with her rough?"

Harper didn't want to dim the woman's bright hazel eyes with the pain of her childhood. "It wasn't so bad. Better than the foster homes I was in later. And I turned out all right. Do you have any pictures of my mom, yearbooks or anything like that?"

"I have a box of stuff in the garage. Let me get it for you." Kelly rose and went back inside.

Harper didn't know how she felt. How sad to know her mother wanted her yet was never able to hold her. She took a sip of sweet tea. The sugar bolstered her and she drained her glass in one swig.

Ridge reached across the table and squeezed her hand. "How are you holding up?"

"Okay. At least I know my mom loved me, but it makes me more determined to find her killer."

He nodded. "I'm beginning to believe both women might have been murdered. Maybe by the same person."

While she agreed, it was hard to form words or thoughts with his thumb tracing circles in her palm.

19

If Lisa hadn't run the stop sign, what had happened? Ridge listened to the women talk as they went through pictures and yearbooks. The conversation had veered into the things Lisa had liked to do, what courses she'd taken in college, and the type of work she did for Disney. All very interesting to Harper he was sure, but he had more questions about Lisa's death. If Harper's father had killed both women, Kelly might have information she didn't know she possessed.

He set his glass of iced tea on the table. "Harper mentioned we talked to the detective investigating Lisa's death. He also wasn't convinced the crash was an accident. Her car disappeared from the lot before he could complete his investigation. Did you ever hear that?"

Kelly set down her glass of tea. "You mean someone stole it? I never heard that. I saw it before it was hauled to the police lot. It hit the side of a big dump truck. The front end was damaged but not so much that it couldn't be driven. Lisa only lived about two hours."

Ridge had assumed she'd hit her head or suffered some other kind of traumatic injury and had died at the scene. He'd even wondered if paramedics delivered Harper at the scene.

He shot a glance at Harper to make sure she wasn't overly upset by talking about her mother's death, and she gave him a slight nod.

"The detective said no one seemed to know what had happened to it. He also told us her last words were, 'The mermaid was right.' Do you have any idea what she might have meant by that?" When Kelly's eyes widened, he knew the words meant something to her. "What is it?"

Kelly wet her lips and glanced at Harper. "I'd been trying to decide if I should mention this or let it go. Lisa had been with her boyfriend at Cocoa Beach, and he left to go get them some food while she bathed in the sun. A woman approached her out of the blue and told her she was dating a dangerous man. This woman told her to check into the murder of a Weeki Wachee mermaid in 1971."

Harper caught her breath. "Judy Russo."

"That was the name the woman gave her. She told Lisa she needed to back away from the guy she was dating or she'd end up dead too."

"Did Lisa say what the woman looked like?" Ridge asked.

Kelly shook her head. "The whole thing gave her the creeps, but she decided she'd see what she could find out. She went to Weeki Wachee and asked around. Some friends of Judy's still worked there, but no one could tell her the identity of the man Judy had been seeing."

"Do you know who she talked to?" Ridge suspected it might have been Grace or Silvia, who would have been around twenty at that time. If so, why hadn't either one mentioned it when they saw her?

"She probably told me the woman's name, but I don't remember after all these years."

"We'll see if we can find out anything."

Kelly nodded, and her gaze went to Harper. "I know I've said it before, but it's downright crazy how much you look like Lisa. You even had red hair when you were born."

"You saw me after I was born?"

"Of course. I was in the waiting room when you were born, and I was there when your mom died. I wanted to bring you home with me, but DCF took you straight to your grandmother. You had several visitors the day you were born."

"Visitors?" Ridge asked. "Friends of yours and Lisa's?"

"No, it was a couple I didn't know. I thought they might have been prospective foster parents."

"Do you remember what they looked like?"

Kelly pressed her fingers to her forehead. "It was so long ago. All I can remember is that they were older. Maybe in their forties. I can't even remember their hair color. Sorry."

And the hospital would have no record of visitors. Maybe it was nothing, but what if it had been Harper's father and his wife? Maybe he had to make sure Lisa never awoke.

Ridge drank the last of his iced tea. "We've taken up enough of your time. Thanks so much for all the information."

Harper rose too. "And I really appreciate these pictures of my mother. I didn't know anything about her except that she died in an accident."

"I'm glad." Kelly stood and embraced her. "Come back any time. I've got your phone number, and I'll call if I think of anything else. I'm so glad to have finally met you. Your mother would have been so proud of you."

Tears glinted in Harper's eyes as she hugged Kelly back. He was becoming more and more ashamed of the assumptions he'd made about Harper all these years. Was it any wonder she'd absorbed the love Oliver had given her like a dry sponge? She'd received very little of it in her life.

She released Kelly, and Ridge picked up the box of pictures and yearbooks. They walked back to his truck, but before he put the box into the backseat, Harper grabbed Lisa's senior yearbook.

"I'm glad we came. I feel I know my mother now."

He nodded and pulled out the drive and headed into the glare of the setting sun. "Let's stop and get some dinner."

"Okay, I'm starving. How about The Melting Pot? Fondue sounds different and fun."

Cozy too. Maybe he'd get a chance to apologize for being so mean to her. He was discovering maybe the reason he'd been that way was because it was the only method he had for resisting her.

Feeling comfortably full, Harper sat across from Ridge at a booth. The aromas of cheese, steak, and garlic hung in the room in a tempting mixture.

The dessert of cake pieces to be dipped in the chocolate fondue appeared appetizing, but Harper sat back anyway. "I don't think I can eat any more. This was so good."

Ridge dipped chocolate cake in the fondue, then held it up to her lips. "You have to at least try a bite."

How could she refuse with that challenging expression on his face? She opened her lips, and he deposited the nugget of chocolaty goodness in her mouth. The explosion of flavors hit her tongue. Chocolate, hazelnut, maybe a touch of cinnamon.

It was so good she reached for her fondue fork. "Okay, maybe a couple of bites."

He grinned. "I thought I could persuade you."

He was so handsome in his red and black Tampa Bay Buccaneers shirt. So many times lately she'd been tempted to plunge her hands into his thick black hair. She'd spent way too much time imagining how it would feel. This pull she felt toward him was something she'd never experienced before.

She realized she was staring when his smile faded and his brows rose. "Something wrong?"

Heat scorched her cheeks and she busied herself with getting another bite of dessert. "Just lost in thought."

She put down her fondue fork and didn't look at him until he reached across the table and took her hand. She slid her gaze up to meet his, and her pulse stuttered at his expression. She should say something—anything—but all thought left her head at his touch.

"I've been wrong about you, Harper, and I want to apologize."

Before he could continue, she blurted out, "I know I was a pain when I was a teenager. We got off on the wrong foot, and it was as much my fault as yours. I wasn't very trustworthy."

"You're being way too gracious. It was all my fault. I told myself I didn't like the way Dad catered to you, but now after spending so much time with you, I realize I was fighting my attraction to you."

Her fingers convulsed around his. Did he just say what she thought he said? She shook her head slightly to clear it. That couldn't be right. She was projecting her own feelings into this conversation. "I-I don't understand," she managed to say.

"I want us to start fresh if you're willing. You may hate me for the way I've treated you all these years, but I hope you can forgive me."

Her pulse was doing crazy things in her chest, but she managed to move her head in an up-and-down motion. "Of course."

Did this mean they'd spend more evenings like this as well as evenings under the stars on her boat while they talked? And maybe it meant more nights like when they'd sung together and clowned around.

His grip on her hand started to slide off. "You don't have any feelings for me?"

Her paralysis had sent the wrong message. She grabbed hold of his hand and didn't let him pull away. "I-I do have those feelings, Ridge, but I didn't think you could possibly feel the same way."

His dark eyes lit up and he smiled. "Well, that's a relief. I thought you were about to crush all my hopes."

"Y-Your sister won't be happy."

"Willow doesn't run my life. When I'm with you, I feel— happy. Complete. It's not just been our search into what's going on—it's you. It's not easy to admit I was wrong and misjudged you. I thought you were pregnant and trying to use Dad to support you. He told me I'd misunderstood a phone conversation I overheard, and I'm realizing he was right. I'm sorry for misjudging you."

Cold prickled her neck and shoulders. "P-Pregnant?"

He'd overheard them talking? How did she even begin to explain?

"Silly, I know, but he'd said something about always being there for the baby. I'm not sure now what he was talking about. Or even who he was talking to."

She needed to tell him the truth, but she didn't want to spoil this magical moment. She couldn't bear to tell him he wasn't wrong—that she was hiding something monumental from him. They'd had so much fun together. There would be time to tell him later.

20

The hospital halls were like a morgue at three in the morning. His sneakers made no sound as he slipped like a wraith down the hall toward Oliver Jackson's room. With any luck the guard would be gone and the room would be empty of staff. He'd attempted to do this yesterday, but there had been an accident involving several people and the hospital had been packed. He hadn't been able to get into Oliver's room without being seen.

He paused where the halls intersected and peered down the final turn to Oliver's room. The door was closed and unattended. Perfect. He darted a glance back toward the nurses' station, but the two women on duty were talking together, and he caught snatches of conversation that indicated one was pouring out her marital problems.

Good. That would distract them from any soft noises.

He made the turn down the hall, quickly pushed open the door, and stepped into a shaft of moonlight, then closed the door behind him. He could hardly hear above the pounding of his blood in his ears, but he stayed by the door until he calmed down and could hear there was no pursuit on the other side of the door.

He slipped over to the bed and looked down into the old

man's face. His mouth was slightly open, and his black hair contrasted against the white pillow. Oliver's breath whispered in and out in a gentle rhythm.

He pulled out the needle and vial, then drew the liquid into the syringe as he'd been taught. This was the part he dreaded. Murder. His love for his son spurred him on, and he steeled himself to do what was required. Fast and silent.

The needle slipped easily into the IV tube and he pressed down on the plunger. Oliver flailed out an arm and knocked the empty vial from his hand, and it rolled away into the darkness. Oliver whipped out his hand and knocked the needle out of the IV.

He bit back a curse when he heard a nurse in the hall, then whirled and slipped into the bathroom until she passed by.

He needed to get out of here. Hopefully he'd injected enough poison to do the job. He rushed for the door and made his escape.

Dad has to be all right.

The litany repeated over and over in Ridge's mind as he parked in the hospital lot and rushed inside. He'd called Harper on his way in, but she hadn't answered so he left a message that the hospital had called and Dad had taken a turn for the worse. He was in a coma again.

When he stepped out of the elevator onto the cardiac floor, he found it quieter than expected at four in the morning. It was too early for surgical patients to be arriving, and he didn't pause at the information desk.

Several nurses sat at their computers, and a young and pretty one saw him. "Mr. Jackson. I'm so sorry about your father."

Though he wanted to rush to his dad's room, he stopped to talk to her. "Do you know what happened? He was improving enough that I thought I would get to take him home soon."

Compassion filled her hazel eyes. "I have no idea. His alarm was beeping for a new IV bag, and I went to change it. I found him unresponsive and called for help. We got his heart started again, but he's in rough shape. We're waiting for the results of his blood work. His condition is fragile."

Ridge's gut clenched. He had a sinking feeling his dad was going to die. "Can I see him?"

"For just a moment."

He hurried down to his dad's room. The door stood open, and as he neared, he heard the sound of machines beeping and breathing for him. Ridge drew in a deep breath before he stepped to Dad's bedside. His color was pasty and he was as still as death.

He wasn't ready to lose his dad. What could he do? He'd been praying constantly since the call came, but this was so much worse than he'd been expecting.

His father's forehead was cool when he touched it. "Dad?"

No flicker of eyelids, nothing to indicate his father heard his voice. Ridge dropped his hand back to his side. Willow needed to know, too, but he didn't think he could get through the phone call without breaking down. He pulled a chair closer to his father's bed, then dropped into it.

"Ridge?"

He blinked and looked up into Harper's worried face. He reached up and touched a wisp of red hair that had fallen out of her ponytail. "Harper?"

He was tired clear to the bone and struggled to rise. All the stress was catching up with him.

She took his arm. "I came as soon as I got your message. How is he?"

"Totally unresponsive. I think I fell asleep for a while. What time is it?"

"About six."

"He's in a bad way, Harper." He choked out the sentence. "I need to call Willow, but I don't want to tell her."

"You want me to call her?"

He shook his head. "It's my responsibility."

And he'd do it once he could think clearly. He fixed his gaze on his father. Dad was all that mattered to him. "It would probably be best for Dad if you're not here when Willow arrives. I don't want him to overhear any kind of raised voices, and I don't know how she'll react if you're here."

A flicker of hurt passed over her face, but she nodded. "Call me if you need me. I'll be at the coffee shop with Josh and Sara."

He touched her arm. "I will. Thanks for coming. I'll keep you posted." He watched her leave. This was for her own good. Willow and his mother could be cruel.

He clasped his dad's hand. "Dad, can you hear me?" There was still no response, so he went back to his chair.

A doctor entered the room, but Ridge couldn't recall his name right now. He wobbled to his feet. "Doctor."

The doctor didn't smile and went directly to check Dad's monitors. "We're not sure what happened overnight, Mr. Jackson. Your father seems to have had a massive heart attack."

"I-Is he going to pull through?" Ridge managed to ask.

"I wish I could say yes, but it's too soon to know." The doctor patted Ridge on the shoulder. "I'll do the best I can."

Which was doctor-speak for all that could save his dad was prayer. Ridge wheeled on his heels to go to the chapel.

21

Ridge heard his mother's commanding tones in the hospital before he saw her. She had one of those loud voices that carried throughout an auditorium—and in this case down the hallway. Why had she come? He'd only called Willow. He stopped short and contemplated turning tail, but his sister was standing outside their father's door and saw him before he could skedaddle.

Willow didn't match her name. She was barely five feet tall and softly rounded. Men wanted to take care of her, but the instant some guy thought he could treat her like a fragile doll, they found themselves thrust out of her apartment with the door slammed and locked before they knew what was happening. She'd been engaged three times as far as Ridge knew. He didn't think she would ever find a guy who measured up to her exacting standards.

She shot him an annoyed look from her green eyes and slipped her phone back into her purse. "Ridge, there you are. I was just texting you to ask where you were."

She wore a lace top over designer jeans and red heels. The red Coach purse—the only brand she ever carried—slung over her shoulder was nearly as wide as she was. Her blonde hair was a neat cap with the fringes grazing her jawline. She was a walking advertisement for high class and money—an image she worked hard to project.

Her gaze skimmed over him, and her expression registered approval. He'd evidently dressed up enough to please her. "You saw Dad? Any change?"

She shook her head. "He's the same. The doctor said there's no brain activity. I'm not sure he's going to wake up. Mom wants to talk to you about turning off the machines."

He stiffened. "When was the doctor here? I don't believe there's no brain activity. And even if there isn't, I'm not turning off the machines. I won't kill my own father."

She wrinkled her nose. "I told Mom you'd be difficult."

"It's none of her business. She divorced us and walked away." He stalked to the door of his father's room and peered in at his mother, who was continuing to harangue the nurse.

"All these machines are ridiculous. Oliver would never want to live like this."

"That's not my call, ma'am." The nurse adjusted the drip on his IV line, then darted for the door.

As she passed, Ridge caught a glimpse of fear in her eyes. He pressed his lips together. "Mom, Willow said you wanted to talk to me. There's an empty waiting room down the hall. Let's go there. I don't want to disturb Dad."

"He's beyond any disturbance, Ridge." She brushed past him, the scent of Dior wafting in her wake.

Her red high heels clattered on the tile as she stalked down the hall to the waiting room, Willow right behind her. Even though Mom was fifty-five, she was as slim as a girl. Not a glimmer of gray was allowed to remain in her hair, and her blonde hair was short and spiky like a punk rocker's. It suited her though, and she had a constant stream of men asking her out.

He sighed and followed Willow into the room. His mother whirled around by the window looking out into the parking lot. Willow went to join her, and they stared at him with identical defiant expressions.

So it was going to be war—two against one. He folded his arms across his chest. "I'm not turning off Dad's life support. I have power of attorney over his medical decisions, and there's no way I'll do that, so save your breath."

His mother lifted a perfectly shaped brow. "Have you spoken with the doctor?"

"Earlier this morning. I haven't heard anything about no brain activity."

"He was in fifteen minutes ago." Mom flicked her fingers as though shooing away a pesky fly. "Oliver always said he didn't want to be kept alive by machines. He wanted to donate his organs."

"He changed his mind and signed a living will. He had heard some horror stories about organ donation and didn't want to do that any longer."

Surprise hit her eyes. How was she going to deal with that? And why did she care what happened to Dad? She'd get nothing from his estate. His gaze landed on Willow. But she probably expected to receive half. She'd be surprised when the will was read someday.

His mother wet her lips. "I find that hard to believe."

He shrugged. "I have a copy if you want to see it. We discussed this at length." Should he tell Willow she wouldn't be receiving what she thought? No, now wasn't the time. This felt like they were vultures hunched around his father's bed, waiting for their prey to die. It was odd, distressful, and repugnant.

An alarm blared down the hall, and two nurses and a female doctor rushed past the open door. He whirled. "That sounds like Dad's room." He raced after the medical personnel as they disappeared into his father's room. He knew the drill and stayed outside the room. His mother tried to duck past his arm blocking the doorway, but he stopped her. His gut clenched and all he could do was pray.

They worked on Dad for what seemed like hours before the doctor said, "I'm going to call it. Time?"

"Ten-ten," one of the nurses said.

The other nurse caught a glimpse of them in the doorway and touched the doctor's arm. They whispered together for a few moments, and then she drew the privacy curtain around the bed.

The doctor came toward them. "I'm sorry, Ridge. I'm not sure what happened. Your dad's heart stopped suddenly. I got some odd readings too." She frowned. "I'd like to perform an autopsy since we aren't sure what happened."

Gone. His dad was gone. A hole opened up inside him, but he fought falling into that dark chasm. His eyes burned, and he knuckled away the moisture. Not now.

"An autopsy?"

"Yes."

"Okay. Let me sign whatever you need." He shook off his mother's hand and brushed past Willow.

Neither of them had ever loved Dad. They were no comfort, but he knew who would understand his pain.

He parked by the water, then ran his window down and cut the engine before he reached for his phone. At least he'd been able to eliminate one threat. He had more good news for his employer as well.

He watched a dolphin play out in the water. "The old guy is dead."

"And the women?"

He knew that question was coming, but he'd thought there would be at least one attaboy before the grilling began. "I've been driving by the Rice woman's house. Her son pops in and out, so if I'm watching, I should be able to slip in while he's gone and grab her. I might get the Taylor woman instead."

"I don't care which one, just get the job done!"

"I'd like my money for the old man." He put as much grit in his voice as he could.

"I'll wire it today, but I'm keeping out the advance for taking care of the women. This should have been done a week ago. When it's over, you'll receive the full payment."

He couldn't just sit in the car and take that, so he thrust open his door, got out, and paced through the weeds in front of his car. "That's not fair."

"And it's not fair that I've paid you for something you've failed to accomplish. I shouldn't have trusted an amateur."

"You knew I'd deliver. And besides, I'm not an amateur any longer. I've done what you required, and I don't expect to be treated like some kind of kid."

"You're what—all of twenty-seven? You are still a kid. But maybe you're right. You did dispose of the old man. Just bring me one of the women. Time is running out. And make sure that box of newspaper clippings disappears. It would be helpful if you get that investigator's report as well. Besides, a robbery might throw off the police and make them think the attack on him had something to do with business or a personal matter."

"Not a problem." He ended the call, got into his car, and started the engine.

While the Rice woman would be the easiest mark, it might be problematic to abduct her by himself. He could get his brother to help. Allen loved Alex, too, and this was the only way to save his life.

Calm down. Ridge parked on the street and took a deep breath, then another, until the pressure eased in his chest. He blinked the moisture from his eyes and swallowed hard. His mother and sister had tried to talk to him, but knowing they wanted his dad dead made it impossible to be in the same room with them.

Maybe he'd see things differently in a few days, but it was hard to feel his sister or mother cared about losing Dad. They only wanted his money.

He scanned the tables out front of the coffee shop and didn't see Harper at first. Then someone moved, and he spotted her bright hair. He shoved open his door and got out. His legs trembled a little. Shock evidently. He tried to smile as he strode her way but couldn't. Her friends were with her, but he only had eyes for Harper.

Her smile faltered, and her gaze searched his face. "What's happened?"

"I-It's D-Dad." He gritted his teeth and got hold of himself. "He's dead, Harper."

Her eyes went wide, and the color drained from her face. "No," she whispered. She rose and took a step toward him.

He gave a jerky nod. "They're performing an autopsy because it occurred so out of the blue. They got some odd readings too."

He didn't know what to do with his hands so he started to stick them in his pockets, but she moved toward him and embraced him. Ridge wasn't sure what happened, but he found himself nestled in her arms with his head tucked into the crook of her neck. She smelled of vanilla and sunshine, fresh air and sea salt. Emotion welled in his chest, but he stuffed it down.

A man didn't cry, not even when he lost his father.

A few tears slipped out in spite of his resolve, but he managed to hold back the sob building in his throat.

"I loved him too." Her voice wobbled, thick with tears.

He allowed himself to absorb the comfort she offered. This was why he'd wanted to come to her. She understood because she loved Dad too. Maybe the two of them were the only ones who did.

He pulled away, and she let him go, then swiped at the tears streaming down her cheeks. Her beautiful turquoise eyes locked on to his face. "Did you call your sister?"

He nodded. "She and Mom were there when he died. Neither of them shed a single tear." He told her about the chat in the waiting room. "I heard the alarm going off."

"And the doctor has no idea what happened?"

He shook his head. "His heart just stopped for no reason they could tell."

She touched his hand. "I'm sorry, Ridge, truly. He was so proud of you and loved you very much."

"He thought I should have done something more with my life."

"He might have said that, but he often showed me articles

about research papers you'd written. He said he didn't know where you got your brain, because he wasn't that smart and neither was your mother."

He straightened. "He said that?"

"Many times." She gestured to the outside table. "Want to have a seat? We can grab coffee. We don't have to work today."

Tears ran down her face again. Proof positive that he'd pegged her wrong all these years. Even after their truce, he'd wondered a little. No longer. Her expression was tragic when she pulled away from Sara and hugged Josh, then moved to stand by Ridge.

"I need to go to Dad's house." He wanted to be around his father's things, find a copy of his will, and dive in to the myriad details that went along with managing a death in the family.

"I'll go with you," Harper said. "Are you hungry?"

"I wouldn't be able to eat anything right now."

"Me neither."

Ridge took Harper's arm and steered her toward his truck. "Mom's been texting me. She wants me to let Willow come by the house and take whatever she wants. I haven't answered her."

Harper stopped and looked up at him with a troubled gaze. "Now would be a good time to make up with your mom and sister. I'm sure they cared more about Oliver than they're showing."

"I don't trust either of them. I don't want them in the house until I've had a chance to go through things." He drew in a deep breath. "I need to notify his attorney. He's got the notarized copy of Dad's will."

He helped her into the truck and shut the door behind her, then pulled out his phone as he went around to the driver's side. He stood outside and called Mr. Booth, then left a message when he didn't answer.

Later would be soon enough for a return call. Ridge had plenty to do.

22

The ten-foot-high double doors closed behind Harper, and Oliver's mausoleum of a house seemed to swallow her up. She'd never felt this way before, but today all she felt was death. She'd stopped by her houseboat to retrieve Bear, and she set him on the floor to let him explore familiar territory.

Ridge headed for the hallway off the entry that led to the office. "I think I'd better find Dad's copy of his will first. There might be a list of small gifts attached. Then if Willow asks for anything, I'll know if it's okay. I don't expect her to hold off her arrival long. You can come with me."

Harper followed him into the enormous office. The ceilings were tall in here, too, and floor-to-ceiling bookcases loomed from opposite walls. Books filled the dark oak shelves. A massive dark wood desk took up the space near the bay window that looked out onto a garden area filled with flowers. Fresh tears flooded her eyes when she saw the azalea garden. She'd given him most of the azaleas over the years she'd known him, and Oliver had loved them.

She glanced at Ridge to see how he was doing. His set face was pale and his lips pressed into a firm line. He was powering through this like many guys, refusing to allow himself to feel and experience the grief. He'd probably hold it in until he was alone in his bed tonight.

Ridge stepped to the bookshelf near the window on the right and fiddled with something she couldn't see. A few moments later, he swung the hinged shelf open, revealing a recessed hidden space containing a massive safe.

She peered past his shoulder. "I had no idea this was here."

"Not many people do. Maybe only I did, actually." Ridge went inside and pressed several numbers on the keypad of the metal safe, then swung open the drawer. "It's fireproof."

When he stooped to reach inside, she saw stacks of money, some files, and several envelopes. "You need help?"

"I'm not going to touch the money. I just want to skim the papers and the envelopes." He scooped them all up, then shut the safe door. It locked with a click behind him, and he walked to the desk and dumped the contents on top of the polished surface. "The will is probably in an envelope and labeled. Help me look if you don't mind."

She nodded and picked up a thick envelope. The outside was blank and the inside held a list of guns. "I'll bet his gun safe is in here somewhere too."

"It's behind the bookshelf on the other wall." Ridge held up an envelope. "This has to be his will. It's got his attorney's name in the return address. He pulled out the papers and unfolded them. "This is it. Have a seat while I read it."

She settled into the large armchair opposite the desk while he dropped into his dad's chair. He flipped through the papers. "Here's what I was looking for—the bequest. There's quite a list of items for Willow. She gets all of her bedroom furniture, any books or electronics she wants, the grandfather clock in the hall that belonged to our grandparents, and all our grand-mother's jewelry. The jewelry is probably what she's itching to get her hands on. She's asked Dad for it several times over the years. Still, she's not going to be happy that this is all."

It seemed like a lot to Harper—especially the jewelry. "Do you want me to help you gather the jewelry for her now?"

"No thanks. It can wait until the lawyer reads the will." His brows winged up, and he caught her gaze. "He left you some things too."

"Me? I've never asked him for anything."

He shrugged. "Dad always noticed when people commented about liking something. My guess is you had admired the blue-and-white bowl in the display case."

The one in the dining room. "Who wouldn't? It's beautiful."

"It's yours now."

"I can't take it! He told me it's very valuable."

"It's a Chinese palace bowl from the Chenghua period. You could easily get seven million for it."

Her stomach plummeted and she felt faint. "I can't possibly take it," she whispered. "You say everything is worth so much money, but most of the things he left Willow don't amount to much. She can have the bowl."

"He wanted you to have it. Most everything in that display case is worth millions. And you let me worry about Willow."

She shivered. "Oliver must have been much wealthier than I dreamed. No wonder you always suspected me of using him for his money."

"He was a great collector of antiquities and valuable art-work. After growing up poor, he believed it was important to own beautiful things. Insurance estimated the contents of this house at two hundred million."

"I'm sure the bowl belongs with a family member who would want it."

He bent his head over the document again and didn't reply. Was that speculation in Ridge's dark eyes? Were all his doubts about her surging back?

———

Ridge wasn't yet sure how he felt about the huge bequest his father had left Harper. She was in the kitchen making coffee while he wandered through his father's bedroom. Dad always wore Clive Christian Original cologne, and the room reeked of it. He opened the closet door, then blinked in disbelief before he entered the cavernous walk-in space.

The closet had been trashed. Suits and shirts lay crumpled on the floor, and every box on the shelves had the lid torn off and the contents dumped out. The armoire was upended, and Ridge righted it, then pulled open the drawers. Dad's many Rolexes were missing, and so were his rings and gold chains. All his clothing from the drawers lay out on the floor too.

A thief had been in here, but how? The alarm hadn't gone off. Ridge exited the closet and called the alarm company only to find out the alarm had been off since this morning. He distinctly remembered setting it when he left the house.

"What time was it taken offline?"

"About ten, Mr. Jackson. It appears it was turned off by an online command."

He thanked her and hung up. No one knew the code, not even his sister or mother. Some kind of IT expert? Dad had thought his security system couldn't be hacked, but maybe someone had managed it.

What could the intruder have been seeking? Only jewelry? He doubted it. This seemed to have been a systematic search. He went back to the cavernous closet and pressed the opening for the hidden safe containing his grandmother's jewelry. It was all there. He went back into the bedroom and pulled out the dresser drawers. His dad was a neatnik, but the stacks of underwear and socks were rumpled, so someone had been in here. They'd clearly tried to search without worrying about detection.

He looked around the room. The understated gray quilt on the four-poster bed held a faint handprint embedded in the soft fabric, so he dropped to his knees on the gray carpet and glanced under the bed. Nothing. He rose and shook his head. Was it possible someone was looking for something else but took Dad's jewelry to throw off their true motive? The house contained many objects worth far more. Any thief worth his salt would have raided the locked display cabinets.

The doorbell rang. He glanced out the window and sighed. Willow's red Porsche was parked in the driveway. He'd known she wouldn't stay away for long. He hurried to the front door to answer before Harper felt the need to open it. Willow would pierce her with an icy stare and order her out.

The aroma of coffee permeated the downstairs, and he heard the distant sound of Bach's Cantata no. 4. Harper must have turned on Dad's MP3 player in the kitchen. Ridge was well versed in every piece of classical music in his dad's library. It had constantly played all his life.

The doorbell pealed again, and he unlocked the door and opened it. "Willow." He stepped aside to let her in.

She'd changed since this morning and wore a gray power suit over a pale-blue blouse. The blue heels were even higher than the ones she wore this morning. "You aren't answering your phone." She swept past him.

He shut the door and locked it again. "I turned the ringer off. I didn't want to be disturbed."

"I got ahold of Dad's attorney. He's coming here with the will in a few minutes."

"Willow, Dad's body hasn't even made it to the funeral home. There's no need to bother Mr. Booth today. There's plenty of time to read the will."

"He's already on his way." Diamonds twinkled in her ears as she tossed her head and went past him into the living room.

He rolled his eyes and followed her. She was like a hurricane, a fierce wind that demolished everything in her path. "There's fresh coffee."

"No thanks."

The locked display cabinets caught her eye, and she smiled as she ogled Dad's collection of Chinese vases. Even one of them would be worth several million dollars. She probably expected that some of them would be hers. His gut clenched as he contemplated the coming battle. He wanted to follow his father's wishes, but he didn't like drama, and it would abound once Willow and Mom found out the will's contents.

The doorbell rang a third time, and he went to let in Bernardo Booth. "Sorry to bother you on a moment's notice," he told the attorney. "It wasn't my idea to call you."

Dressed in his ubiquitous navy suit with not a hair out of place, Bernardo gave him a sober nod as he entered. He and Dad had gone to school together. Though nearly seventy, not a gray strand peeked through Bernardo's thick black hair. He was whip thin with an erect bearing he still carried from his years in the military.

"Willow is in the living room."

"And Ms. Taylor? I called her and asked her to be present as well."

That was news to Ridge. "She's here. I'll get her. Would you like coffee?"

"A stiff drink might be better." Bernardo's impudent grin lit up his gray eyes. "But since your father was a teetotaler, that's out of the question. At least your mother isn't here." He walked through the huge foyer into the living room.

Ridge went to the back of the house and found Harper unloading the dishwasher. "You don't need to do that."

She stood and pushed her thick red hair out of her face. "It's not a problem. Hey, the lawyer called."

At least she was admitting it. "He's here now and asking for you."

She winced. "Do I have to go?"

"He says you do." Ridge found a tray and poured four mugs of coffee. "I need something to get through these next minutes."

"I've been praying ever since he called." She squared her shoulders. "Let's get it over with."

23

Harper couldn't let anyone see her knees shaking. Holding Bear in her arms was her one steadying influence. She pasted on a gentle smile and nodded to Willow.

Willow turned from the display case, and her green eyes widened. "What are you doing here? We're having a private family meeting."

Bernardo cleared his throat. "I called her, Willow. She's named in the will and has to be here for me to proceed."

Willow waved a hand encrusted with rings. "Fine." She shot Harper a glare before she seated herself as far away as possible near the fireplace.

Harper wasn't sure where to sit or what to do until Ridge handed coffee mugs to everyone, then sank onto the sofa and beckoned to her. She put the mug on the coffee table, then settled on the sofa with room between them. Bear lay down on her lap and put his head on his paws. She took a few deep breaths and prayed to stay calm no matter how upset Willow became.

Bernardo took a sip of his coffee, then set it on the table beside his chair. "First off, let me say I'm personally grieved to lose my longtime friend. Oliver was a good man, an honorable man. I stopped to see him at the hospital and he seemed to be improving. I really thought he'd make a full recovery. I'm very sorry for your grievous loss."

"Thank you, Bernardo," Ridge said. "I know you loved him too."

The lawyer pinched the bridge of his nose. "Indeed." Bernardo opened his briefcase and extracted a sheaf of papers. "Ridge, you of course know you are the executor."

"Yes."

"As executor it will be your responsibility to ensure your father's wishes are followed."

"I intend to do whatever he wanted."

Bernardo riffled through the papers. "Excellent. I'll read the body of the will now. At the end I'll give you each a copy of the list of personal belongings he's assigned to you."

Harper tensed and Bear lifted his head. She listened to the lawyer drone on about minor gifts to charities Oliver supported. Nothing there for Willow to object to as the gifts were a few thousand each. Willow sat slightly forward in the chair with her hands clasped in front of her. Her intent gaze never left Bernardo's face.

The attorney took another sip of his coffee. "To my daughter I leave two hundred thousand dollars. To Harper Taylor, daughter of my heart, I leave five hundred thousand dollars. The rest of my estate including all bonds, securities, property, and cash I leave to my son, Ridge."

Willow's face surged with red, and she leaped to her feet. "You're lying! That can't be right. It should be evenly split!" She turned to her brother and jabbed her finger his direction. "You won't get away with stealing my share, Ridge. I'll contest it!" Her eyes narrowed as she faced Harper. "And you! I hope you're happy."

The attorney cleared his throat again. "If you contest the will, Willow, you'll lose whatever your father left you. He's very specific in his will. All of us know Oliver was a man who knew his own mind. He was not impaired in any way, and by law he can dispense his possessions and money however he pleases. Please sit down so I can continue."

"What's to continue? Ridge gets it all, just like he did when Dad was alive. All the support, all the attention, all the love." Angry tears hung on her lashes, but she sank back into the chair. She clasped herself with her arms and shook her head.

"That's not true," Ridge said. "When was the last time you came to see him? Texted him? I glanced through his phone's history. He rang you twice last week and must have left a message because the connections were only about thirty seconds long. You never called him back."

"It was a busy week." She stared at the ground, her expression sullen.

"And the week before that? Same pattern. You've always kept him at arm's length. It's a wonder to me that he kept trying to spend time with you. The last three Christmases you never even stopped by."

"You keeping track or something, Ridge? Is that how you got him to give you everything? You reminded him of my neglect?"

"I never said a word. I didn't have to remind him—the truth was constantly in his face. When you left with Mom, you never looked back. She molded you into her own image—cold, calculating, and remote."

"Mom's not like that!"

"No? You could have fooled me. I call her and she never calls me back, just like you did with Dad. When was the last time you were here in this house? Years?"

A shaft of pity darted into Harper's heart. Willow was probably grieving her father, so this news must seem like even more of a rejection.

Willow glared at her brother. "Fine, so you get the property. What about the items in the house?" Her green eyes took on an avid shine. "The vases are worth millions."

The sympathy balloon popped in Harper's chest. Willow really did seem to care only about the money and property.

"Ah, yes," Bernardo said. "I have the bequest list here. He did leave you a few items."

"Yes!" Willow took the paper Bernardo handed her, but her smile faded as she read it over. "Grandma's jewelry, the grandfather clock? Those are pittances!" She balled up the paper and tossed it into the fireplace as she stood and loomed over Harper. "What service did *she* perform for Dad to get that bowl?"

Heat ran up Harper's neck. Before she could reply, Ridge leaped to his feet and inserted himself between his sister and Harper. "She was a daughter to him, Willow. That's more than you can say."

She sneered back into his face. "You'll be hearing from my lawyer." Her heels clattered on the marble floors as she rushed to the door and slammed it behind her.

Ridge ran his hand through his thick black hair, leaving it standing on end. "Well that went well."

⌒

Ridge's jaw ached from clenching it so tightly during the confrontation. He carried the empty cups back to the kitchen, then returned to find Harper still on the sofa with Bear on her lap. He studied her for a moment and wished the two of them could curl up on the sofa and watch a mindless movie. He didn't want to remember his father's face in the hospital bed. He didn't want to close his eyes and see his sister's angry face.

He sat beside her and patted his leg. Bear scampered over to lick his fingers. "Did you think I was too harsh with Willow?"

Harper looked tired. Circles shadowed her eyes and her skin was pale. She hesitated, and he shook his head. "I was, wasn't I? You don't know her well though. Give her room to negotiate and the next thing you know, she owns everything you have. I promised to follow Dad's wishes."

"What if his wishes were wrong?" Harper's voice was soft. "I loved Oliver like a father, but I have to wonder if this marked difference in the will was one last way to punish Willow for leaving him. He was a good man, but he didn't find it easy to forgive."

Ridge forced himself not to answer immediately. To think about her words. "You're right, he didn't forgive easily. He hasn't spoken to his brother in several years after what seemed to be a minor spat. I can't even remember what the squabble was about anymore."

She reached over and touched his hand. "If you pray about it, God will tell you the right thing to do. One thing I do know is family is important. I'd give anything to have had a real family all these years. Mend fences with your sister, and you'll never regret it."

Ridge wasn't so sure. "Dad had strong feelings about making us both stand on our own two feet. He never gave us money. We had to earn our own. All that money he's left me leaves me a little appalled. I'm not sure what to do with it. It's way more than I'll need in ten lifetimes, but I know Willow. She's likely to spend it on fancy houses, luxury cars, and who knows what else. She has very expensive tastes. And Mom would also get her hands on some of it. After all his hard work, Dad would roll over in his grave if he thought Mom and her boyfriends would blow through it."

Harper nodded and removed her hand. "I understand. I'm not sure there is a perfect answer. Maybe give some of it to his charities. I'm sure you'll figure it out with God's help."

He started to answer but his phone rang. "Hello, Dr. Newman." He'd known Dad's doctor a long time. Dad and the doctor had often golfed together.

"Ridge, I'm afraid I have some upsetting news to tell you."

"The autopsy is done?"

"Not yet. When your father's hospital room was cleared, our cleaner discovered an ampoule of potassium chloride under his bed."

"What does that mean?"

"When injected into an IV line, it causes an instant heart attack."

"You mean his death was accidental? It wasn't an actual heart attack?" Ridge didn't quite understand the doctor's uneasy tone.

"At first I feared the nurse made a mistake and instead of flushing his IV with sodium chloride, she used potassium chloride, but that's not the case. I've checked the supply cabinets myself. There's no missing potassium chloride in this hospital, and his IV wasn't due to be flushed until tomorrow."

Ridge rose and walked to the window to stare out at the greenery. "Then what are you saying?"

"I believe someone came into his room and injected him with the potassium chloride with the express purpose of killing him. Unfortunately, I've had to notify the police, and you and the rest of the family will probably be interrogated. I was told not to warn you, but I've known you a long time, Ridge, and I know you loved your dad. I didn't want you blindsided when the cops show up."

Ridge's lips were numb, and he licked them until he could speak. "My mom and sister were with him before I got there. I never even went into his room. How long would this take to cause the attack?"

"If he got a full vial of the stuff, seconds, maybe a minute or two tops. As soon as it hit his heart. The only reason he survived it initially is because it wasn't a full dose, and a nurse found him immediately. We'll know more from the autopsy."

"Mom, Willow, and I had been talking for about fifteen minutes when I heard the alarms go off."

He became aware of Harper's presence close beside him. Her turquoise eyes were wide and scared. He pulled her into a one-armed embrace.

"Make sure you tell the police," Dr. Newman said. "I'm sorry about this, Ridge. This will delay getting your dad's body back for burial. The police will probably order a much more complete autopsy than we might have done in a routine way."

"I understand." Ridge thanked him and ended the call. "You got the gist of that?" He didn't let Harper go. Holding her was a comfort to his hurting heart.

Someone had murdered his father.

She nodded. "I could hear that booming voice of his. We have to find out who attacked me in the water. I'll bet it was the same person who hurt your dad and then killed him. Maybe he heard Oliver had woken up and had to make sure he didn't remember."

"Maybe. I can't help but think about how Willow and Mom

wanted me to turn off the machines. Even though they were with me, they could have hired someone to go in there and administer the drug."

"They wouldn't."

"Maybe not Willow, but I can see Mom making those arrangements."

How did he go about figuring out the truth? One thing for sure—he wasn't giving his mother a heads-up that the police were coming.

24

Harper glanced at Ridge from under her lashes. When he'd driven her home, he seemed reluctant to leave. Realizing he didn't want to be alone, she invited him aboard her houseboat. She'd fixed them turkey sandwiches and a fruit salad, but neither of them had eaten much. Bear had enjoyed the leftover meat.

They sat in companionable silence on the old furniture in her tiny salon. Harper reached for the box of clippings Annabelle had given her and put it on the love seat between them. "I still haven't gone through this box."

Ridge capped his water bottle and set it down. "It will occupy us until the police show up."

"You think they'll come here?"

"You're an heir and were close to Dad. They are going to question everyone."

The thought of being interrogated wasn't pleasant even though she had nothing to hide. If the police talked to Willow, she'd point them Harper's direction. She pressed her lips together and opened the box. Empty? She glanced up at Ridge. "Did you put the clippings somewhere else?"

He peered into the empty box. "I didn't touch them. When did you look in here last?"

"It's been several days. Someone's been here while I was gone." Chills snaked up her back at the thought of someone prowling around. "But why? What could be in here that some-one would want? Judy's murder was decades ago."

Ridge rose and lifted magazines and shifted items on the shelf before he ducked into her bedroom, looked around, then exited. "They're clearly not here. Is anything else missing?"

She stood and drifted around the small space. Possessions weren't something she noticed or cared about. Her six-year-old MacBook Air was still on the floor beside her bed as was her phone. The only necklace she owned was the one she'd made that hung around her neck. The small boom box was still tucked in a cabinet.

"To tell you the truth, I don't have much, but I didn't notice anything else missing."

Ridge dropped onto the love seat. "There has to be some-thing we're missing in all this. My dad's murder has to be connected somehow to everything that's going on—Annabelle's abduction, the attacks on you, and now these missing clippings."

"I know neither of us like the thought of coincidences, but maybe that's what we have this time."

"I don't buy it. We aren't seeing the connecting threads, but we will."

Headlights swept the room through the bank of windows facing the shore. Harper went out to the deck, and Ridge fol-lowed. The muffled sound of doors slamming was followed by the shadowy forms of two people heading toward the pier.

"Who's there?" Ridge called.

"Police." A woman stepped out of the shadows into a swatch

of moonlight. "Detective Daly. This is my partner, Detective Sanchez. We need to speak with both of you."

"You want us to come down to the station?" Harper glanced at Ridge for confirmation of what to do.

Daly shook her head. "That won't be necessary. Yet. We can speak aboard your boat if that's comfortable."

"Of course." Harper led the way into her salon.

There wasn't much seating, just the love seat and one other chair, so she settled on the floor and pulled Bear onto her lap. "Have a seat."

Ridge took the chair near her, and the detectives sat on the love seat. In the light Harper got a better look at the two detectives. The woman, Daly, was in her forties with fine lines fanning the outer edges of her eyes. Her blonde hair was in a short, easy care cut that just covered her ears. Sanchez was older with a thick neck and strands of white in his black hair.

Harper's blood pumped in her neck, and she swallowed. There was no reason to be nervous. She hadn't done anything wrong, but her assurances failed to settle her agitation.

Daly took out a notepad. "When was the last time you saw your father, Mr. Jackson?"

"Minutes before he died, though I didn't go into his room. I was standing in the doorway talking to my sister. My mom was in his room when I got there."

"Staff at the hospital told me you and your sister had words?"

"We did. She said she and my mother thought I should turn off Dad's life support. I refused because Dad had a living will specifying how he wanted his care."

"She got angry?"

"She thought I was being unreasonable." Ridge's voice was even.

Harper listened as he went through the rest of the day's events, all the way through his sister's appearance and her anger at being shortchanged by Oliver's will. The two detectives exchanged glances when he got to the part about her threatening to get an attorney to break the will.

Sanchez turned his attention to Harper. "When did you last see Oliver, Ms. Taylor?"

"After the hospital called Ridge to let him know Oliver had lapsed into a coma. If you mean when did I last seem him alive and well, it was the day of the accident." Harper told them how Oliver had come to help out with the pen shell beds but had vanished. "Ridge found him aboard his boat later that night."

"Someone had cut his air hose." Ridge crossed his arms over his chest.

"There's bad blood between you and Oliver's daughter and ex-wife?" Daly asked.

"Well, not exactly bad blood." Harper glanced at Ridge for support. "They didn't like the fact Oliver was a mentor to me. They thought he spent too much time and money on me."

Daly nodded and put away her notebook. "That's all the questions for now. We'd better see the rest of the family."

Harper escorted them to the pier and turned to find Ridge right behind her. His arms enveloped her, and she pressed her face against his chest. How did he make her feel so safe? And when he knew the truth, would this tenuous relationship explode?

November 1969

Judy dried her hair with a towel and stripped off her one-piece suit. Her muscles ached and she felt off. She hadn't felt right in weeks, not since he'd left port. No matter how much joy she took in swimming in front of thousands of people a month, she missed him. The Vietnam War raged on, and she worried about his safety every moment, though she didn't talk about it much. There was too much antiwar sentiment around, and she would suffer no one to disparage Huey for serving his country.

Her stomach gripped her in a sudden spasm, and she rushed for the toilet where she vomited up her lunch of a ham sandwich and chips. She rinsed her mouth and stared at herself in the mirror. Her red hair clung damply to her forehead, and her green eyes were huge in her pale face. How many times had she thrown up this week? She thought back. Four. Was it the flu?

"You okay?"

She turned to look into Grace's worried face. The two of them had become good friends in the past three months even though Grace was married. Judy adored baby Silvia who would be three soon, and she babysat her whenever she wasn't swimming. It helped the time slip by.

"Don't make a fuss. It's just an upset stomach."

Grace stared at her. "You're pregnant, aren't you?"

Judy gasped. "Hush now! How could you say such a thing?"

"Are you sure? You have to take a nap every day after our afternoon performance, and you've been throwing up. When did you have your last period?"

Three months. The terrible realization drained the blood from Judy's head, and she grasped the edge of the sink to keep from falling. "I can't be pregnant." She forced the whisper out of a tight throat.

"Oh, honey." Grace stepped to her side and embraced her. "You need to see a doctor and find out. How long has it been?"

"I think it's been three months."

Her dad and stepmother would make a fearful ruckus. She pressed her palms to her cold cheeks. "It can't be true." But she felt the truth of it in her heart. "I'll go see the doctor and find out before I tell him."

"Is it someone from back home? Will he do the right thing?"

Judy shook her head. "It's someone I met my first day here. He's in the navy."

Grace's hazel eyes darkened. "You know what they say about navy guys—a girl in every port."

"He's not like that. It's not like he's forgotten about me—he still writes."

"When did you hear from him last?"

"Two weeks." She lived for his letters. "Mail takes so long from Southeast Asia though. I reckon I'll get a letter soon."

Would Huey do the right thing though? She didn't really know him all that well, though her heart felt as if they'd been together all their lives. Did he feel the same way? He said he missed her, but what did that mean?

Her stomach clenched again, and she ran for the stall. Squatting in front of the cold porcelain, she wiped her mouth and considered her options. There weren't many. Who would want to watch a mermaid who was as big as one of the manatees? If Huey didn't stand by her, she'd have no choice but to go back to Abilene. Her kin would whup her and send her out with her tail between her legs.

She exited the stall and found Grace, deep in thought, standing in the bathroom doorway. "I don't know what I'm going to do if he disappears and doesn't help."

Grace's full lips flattened into an expression of determination. "I do. You can swim until you start to show, then you can work for me in the office. If you want to go back to swimming after the baby is born, you can do that."

"You're the best, Gracie! I'll still help with Silvia all I can."

"You think he's going to come back?"

"I-I think so. I hope so." What would Huey think when he got her letter? Fatherhood would look good on him, but he might not think he was ready.

She washed her hands and went to lie down on her cot. Several other girls lived here, too, but the rest of them went out with friends or beaus while she fell into bed with exhaustion. That should have been her first clue. She was the only one who had to nap after a performance.

"Get some rest. We'll talk about this later when we know what he's going to do." Grace shut the door behind her, and the room plunged into silence.

Judy groaned and sat up. Her agitation had driven away her fatigue. She picked up the newspaper one of the other girls had left and leafed through it to the society page. Her gaze landed on a familiar face smiling into the camera with his arm around a beautiful young woman with long hair.

She skimmed the article and gasped. This was an engagement picture. The woman was the daughter of a US senator. Marrying her would open many doors for him, and she didn't think any man would give up that kind of future for a penniless girl with so little sense who found herself pregnant. Tears burned her eyes, and she threw the paper to the floor. How could he? Sobs wracked her as she realized her life wasn't going to turn out the way she'd hoped.

She gave into the storm of grief for several long minutes, then wiped her eyes and blew her nose before she reached for the newspaper again. It didn't say when they'd gotten engaged, but it had to have been before he left two months ago. Maybe he didn't really love this girl and would be willing to break the engagement.

Once Judy knew for sure she was pregnant, she would write him. If that didn't work, she'd go see this girl and lay out her case. At least there was hope.

25

What was so urgent that Grace had called first thing at six in the morning? When she had gotten up, Harper found a voice mail from Grace who asked her to come see her again. She'd called Ridge, and he said he'd be there soon to go with her.

She unfastened her seat belt as Ridge parked at Weeki Wachee, and they stepped out into an overcast sky. With the news of Oliver's murder, Harper was ready to occupy her mind with something other than the danger that felt like it was closing in on her.

Inside, Ridge asked for Grace and was directed to an employee door into the auditorium. She was swimming in the springs, and Harper watched her graceful movements as she trained a new mermaid. Her dyed red hair floated in the water as she spun in the water in a mesmerizing movement. The young woman she was training gave Grace a thumbs-up, then swam off to exit the water. Grace saw them through the glass and held up one forefinger before she quickly kicked away to the exit as well.

While Harper waited for Grace, she watched two manatees swim around in the springs. Ridge joined her, and his warm presence calmed her. He'd been quiet since learning of his father's murder. If only there was a way to comfort him.

He pointed out the bigger of the two sea mammals. "That's an old manatee. He's got quite a few boat scars, and his skin is leathery. I've seen him before, too, out in the coastal waters."

"How old?" She loved hearing him talk about his passion for the gentle creatures.

"I'd guess at least fifty years old, maybe sixty or seventy. He's probably been coming here year after year to shelter from the cold water in the ocean. The last few years Three Sisters Springs has been home to hundreds of manatees through the winter months. Marine biologists have been trying to balance access to seeing them against protecting their well-being. It's quite a tightrope to walk."

She watched the manatees lazily swim around and nose along the bottom. "He might have been around when Judy worked here."

"Maybe. He's quite a handsome fellow."

In the old days mariners were said to mistake manatees for mermaids, but she didn't understand how that was possible. A manatee looked more like the sea cow it was called than a beautiful part-woman, part-fish creature. They were protected, but visitors to the area took guided excursions to be able to swim with them. They were as smart as dolphins in spite of their ponderous movements and small eyes.

The door opened and Grace, her wet hair corralled in a braid, stepped inside. She still wore her modest one-piece bathing suit, and her limbs were as lithe and smooth as a twenty-year-old's. "Thanks so much for coming."

Harper stepped closer to her. "You said you forgot to tell us something?"

Grace nodded. "Maybe it's nothing, but it came to me in the night. Judy said her boyfriend was engaged to someone else, but she was sure once the woman knew about Annabelle, she'd let him go. She was planning to take Annabelle to see her the day before she died. I'm not sure if she went or not. We didn't get a chance to talk."

"Do you have a name for the fiancée?" Ridge asked.

"No, but her family had money. I told Judy her beau wouldn't likely be willing to give up that family connection, but she was sure he really loved her."

"Money." Harper hid her disappointment. "That could be anyone."

"This was much more of a backwater in the early sixties," Grace said. "You might research wealthy families near Clearwater in that decade. It was quite the scene. The Rolling Stones wrote 'Satisfaction' in a Clearwater hotel after a performance on *The Ed Sullivan Show*. They had to cut the concert short to escape the rabid fans. Judy and I were there." She gave a sigh. "I'll never forget those days." Her hazel eyes cleared of memories. "There was record-setting growth in the Tampa Bay area in the fifties and sixties. Land developers made a killing. You might find some leads in history."

Harper had her doubts, but she nodded. "Thanks so much for your help, Grace. If you think of anything else, let us know."

Grace smiled and walked to the glass where she tapped on it. The old male manatee swam closer and pressed his snout against the glass on the other side. "This is Roger. He's been here forever. People come back year after year to see him. He was born here in 1960."

Ridge peered intently through the glass. "It's great you know his age. We seldom do. He's in good shape."

"He's a fixture around here."

Harper turned toward the door. "Thanks again, Grace."

"You'll let me know if you find out anything? Not knowing what happened to Judy has been one of the biggest regrets of my life."

"We'll let you know if we discover anything," Harper promised.

Ridge held the door open for her, and she stepped out as thunder rumbled. A hint of ozone in the air warned that a storm was about to let loose, so they ran for the truck. She jumped into the passenger seat as the clouds opened up. Rain battered the windshield and hood as Ridge climbed behind the wheel.

She handed him a napkin from the glove box. "You think her clue is of any use?"

He mopped the rain dripping down his forehead and cheeks. "I know she meant well, but it's like looking for a specific fish at the reef. I don't know when we'll know if we are on the right track."

That had been her impression too. "At least we have something to dig for."

"The bigger question is whether Judy talked to the fiancé. If she did, either this woman or someone in her family might be implicated in Judy's death."

"Or my dad," Harper said. It always circled back to her father.

⌒

Annabelle's boys had run to the grocery store together to get food for the rest of the week before the sun was up. Mark planned to make her his vegetable soup for when the nausea hit, and Scott thought they needed to stock up on things like ginger ale and smoothie ingredients. She couldn't imagine having a green smoothie when the sickness hit, but she'd shooed them out to give her a little peace before the ordeal began.

Her dear boys. She couldn't leave them—she had to fight this with every ounce of her being. Her boys would have children someday, and she intended to be the best grandmother on the face of the earth. Tears filled her eyes, and she brushed them away. She *wouldn't* feel sorry for herself. She would do her best and leave the results in God's hands.

While she didn't fear the chemo, she knew she needed to gird herself for the battle with some praise music and her favorite Bible promises. She looked at herself in the full-length mirror in her bedroom. Her calm expression concealed the way her pulse skittered.

She'd forgotten her supplements this morning so she went to the bathroom counter to grab them. As she exited her bathroom into the dim bedroom, she felt rather than heard a movement to her right. She glimpsed a figure in a ski mask before a suffocating cloth covered her head. *Not again!*

She fought the dark with the sickeningly sweet odor, but her strength was no match for the drug, and the edges of consciousness slipped away.

This time when she came to, she was in a small room with a bit of light slicing through the slats of the blinds. She blinked and sat up. Her head throbbed and nausea roiled. Panic hovered at the edges of her mind, but she fought it back. If she had any hope of escaping, she had to keep a clear head. She didn't understand why anyone would want her. This was far beyond a normal sort of attack. Whoever had taken her last time hadn't harmed her.

She forced herself to detail her surroundings to calm herself. She grabbed a fistful of white bedding, which felt like something from a luxurious hotel. High-quality carpet covered the floor, and Annabelle knew carpet and furnishings well. Even the plantation shutters were expensive.

Her head still spun when she slid her bare feet onto the thick carpet and padded to an open door. It was an attached bathroom with lavish fixtures. She retraced her steps and went to the closed door, but it refused to open. She eyed the windows, then opened one of the blinds and looked down into a yard fringed with forest. She couldn't see any other houses.

The window was plate glass without a sash to raise. She could break the glass, but she was on the second floor, and there was only a steep drop to the ground below. No escape that way. Unless she could tie the sheets together so she could manage to get within a few feet of the ground.

Her stomach rebelled, and she ran for the bathroom where she threw up in the toilet. It knocked the pain of her headache back some, and she rinsed out her mouth, then went back to the bedroom. Once she got the drug out of her system, she'd feel better.

She looked around for something to throw through the window. There didn't seem to be a single loose item in the room though—no lamp, no dresser drawer, no soap dispenser, nothing. She swallowed her panic, then sat on the bed to consider her options. Maybe she could wrap her hand in some of the bedding and use her fist to punch through the glass. It was worth a try.

The sound of metal scraped in the lock, and she stood to face the door. A man entered the room. This guy wasn't hiding his face with a ski mask, and a cold shaft of fear scraped down her spine.

Maybe he didn't need to hide his identity since she wouldn't live to tell anyone.

Her breath quickening, she backed away until she reached the wall with the windows. "What do you want with me?" Her thin, reedy voice sounded odd.

He was in his late twenties with a shaved head and a scar on his left cheek that he fingered silently as he stood watching her. About six-one, he had a rugged face with a crooked nose that appeared as if it had been broken at least once. He wore pressed khaki slacks and a striped shirt with a red tie. His dark-brown eyes raked over her without expression.

"What do you want with me?" she asked again in a stronger voice.

His lips twisted into a terrifying smile. "You look frightened."

"Wouldn't you be scared? You drug me and take me from my home. I wake up here with no idea what you want from me or why I'm here. I want to go home. I want my boys." Her voice dropped on the last part as her panic increased, and she forced herself to take several deep breaths.

"I'm not going to hurt you."

She didn't believe him, not for a moment. If only she could figure out what was going on. It made no sense.

Without another word he exited the room.

She ran to the door in time to hear the lock *snick* into place. She sank to her knees and let the tears flow.

26

arper stood at the counter of Kookie Krums, her favorite bakery in Dunedin. The mouthwatering aromas of red velvet cupcakes, peanut butter cookies, and chocolate chip cookies mingled with the smells of coffee drinks being prepared. Though she wasn't sure what kind of cookies Ridge liked best, she picked out peanut butter and chocolate chip. He had to like one of them. She ordered four cupcakes and two coffees as well.

He was meeting her here, and they were going to see Annabelle. Since the clippings were stolen, Harper was even more eager to read them. Someone had wanted them kept secret, and hadn't Annabelle said she'd locked them up because she felt uneasy? What was that all about?

Harper emerged into the bright sunshine and saw Ridge exiting his truck. The lights flashed as he punched the lock button on his key fob.

He didn't look like he'd gotten any more sleep last night than she did. He looked pale and drawn, though he lifted a smile her way and took the coffee she offered. "Just what I need. And cookies?"

"Cupcakes too." She indicated a cafe table under the awning. "We can eat here before we head to Orlando."

Tires squealed on the road as a blue sedan threw on its brakes and swerved into a parking space. Scott Rice, his blond hair askew, leaped from the car. Mark jumped out on the passenger side.

Scott reached her first. "I was on my way to see you and saw you sitting here."

Harper rose. "What's happened? Is it your mom?"

He nodded. "She's missing. Mark and I went to the store, and when we got back, she was nowhere to be found. I smelled ether in her bedroom, too, and she'd lost one of her slippers."

"How long ago was this?" Ridge asked.

Mark looked subdued. "About six this morning. We left at five. She was supposed to start chemo this morning at seven. I know she didn't go by herself, because her car is still in the garage. The back door was unlocked too. I've got a BOLO out for her, but no one has reported seeing her."

"What can I do?" Harper asked.

"I thought maybe we could go over everything that's happened since you met her. The chain of events are just weird, but they have to connect somehow."

"Something else has happened I'm sure you haven't heard," Ridge said. "My father was murdered yesterday."

Scott's gaze sharpened. "How do you know it was murder?"

"The cleaner at the hospital found a vial of potassium chloride under his bed." Ridge told him everything including the visit from the police.

"I have the physical evidence from my grandmother's murder in the car," Scott said. "None of this happened until you showed up, Harper." His tone sliced with the dagger of accusation.

Ridge frowned. "This has nothing to do with Harper."

"Maybe not, but you have to admit it's strange. The first attack on Harper occurred before she came to see Mom, so it's like she brought the danger to our doorstep."

Harper clasped her hands together. "I didn't think about that—you're right. But I don't see how any attack on me is related to your mother. She and I are virtual strangers still." She rubbed her head. "I'm beginning to think these have to be individual incidents with no ties."

"I don't believe that," Scott said flatly. "The connection is there—we just have to find it. Let's go over this again, step by step, as events unfolded." He looked at Harper. "When did you discover the genetic link to Mom?"

"A week ago Saturday. On the following Monday I went to see your mother for the first time."

"You didn't waste any time, did you?"

Ridge leaned forward in his chair. "And I don't like your tone. Quit accusing Harper with that sneering expression."

Scott clenched his fists. "Look, my mother is missing. I'm a homicide detective. This is the only interrogation manner I possess. I don't mean to appear accusatory, but the first twenty-four hours are critical."

Harper reached over and put her hand on Ridge's arm. "It's okay. I want to do whatever I can to find Annabelle."

He fixed Scott with a stern glare. "Fine. Just remember we're on the same team here."

Scott nodded. "So the two of you spent hours together and really hit it off. She told you about her mother's murder, and you told her about your mom's death in an accident. She was taken the next night but managed to escape."

"So that was Tuesday night. Later that same night someone

put ether over my face and tried to take me from my boat. Ridge happened to come by in time to save me."

"You were both attacked the same night," Scott muttered. He paced the sidewalk for a few moments, then came back to stand by their table.

Harper looked up at Scott. "There's something I forgot though, and I don't know when it happened. Your mother gave me copies of the newspaper clippings from her mom's murder. I hadn't had a chance to really go over them, but last night we opened the box and everything inside was missing. Someone had broken into my boat and taken everything from the box."

Scott glanced at his brother who had been standing quietly listening to the rundown of events. "That does seem to indicate this is tied to my grandmother's murder. I put Mom off a dozen times about looking into the evidence. I should have listened. I have that fiber evidence I told you about. That's why I came instead of calling. Time is running out."

"We'll take it to the lab right now and test it," Ridge said.

Harper wished her first visit to the new lab Oliver had put together were under better circumstances. If only she'd been able to come here with him and hear all of his plans.

The sharp sting of alcohol or some other kind of antiseptic assailed her as she stood beside Ridge at the microscope. She took stock of the room as he focused his lens on the bit of fiber found in Judy's wound. Various types of equipment filled the lab. There was a full wall of metal cabinets containing drawers filled with mollusks, snails, and other invertebrates.

He was in his element here surrounded by the sea life he studied. "How soon before you're ready for experiments?"

He looked up briefly. "I still need to hire a few people, but the lab equipment is all in place."

"And what about your new job at the museum?"

"I'm going to turn it down. Dad's gone, and I'll have to focus on figuring out what to do with this lab and his pharmaceutical business long-term. It's Dad's legacy. I can't just walk away and ignore it."

"You could sell it. Oliver wouldn't expect you to give up your dream for his."

"He knew me better than I know myself. The minute he mentioned this lab, I was hooked."

She wished she had the words to comfort him. She settled for squeezing his arm. "I'm praying for you, Ridge. I'm not really sure what the right answer is either. You'll take over as head of Jackson Pharmaceuticals?"

"And all the other businesses. That was always Dad's wish. I would be happier staying here in the lab and puttering around with new directions to explore. But if I just hired a CEO for the company, it would slowly fail. No one cares about a business as much as the owner."

He was right, but she couldn't see him behind Oliver's big desk dealing with a mountain of paperwork.

His arm brushed hers as he fiddled with the microscope, and she caught the scent of his shampoo, something clean and enticing. She should step away, but she stayed where she was and inhaled. Ridge would be mortified if he knew how attractive she found him.

"Ah, I've got it. It's definitely byssus. It has that characteristic egg shape. It's possible the murder weapon was a bivalve shell. When the killer removed the shell, it could have left a strand of byssus behind." He straightened and removed the strand from the microscope.

He turned and picked up a pen shell and held it with the point toward her. "If the killer hit her in the temple or the eye with just the right angle, it would penetrate and kill her instantly. Or he could have hit her with something else that had been contaminated with some byssus strands."

"This was someone who was harvesting sea silk maybe?"

"Maybe not. We know Judy was a sea silk artisan. She likely would have had her work conveniently sitting around that the killer used."

"I've never seen anything like the work she did." Harper leaned against the counter. "Have you heard from your mom or sister?"

"They've left several messages, but I haven't listened to them yet. I can't stand to hear their only interest in Dad was his money." He swept his hand around the lab. "All this was bought with his hard work. His pharmaceutical company will thrive because of his knowledge and dedication. They don't see any of that. All they see is what he left."

Ridge put his hand over hers. "You've been so great, Harper. When Dad died, all I could think about was getting to you—you were the only one I knew who loved him. I needed to grieve with someone who understood. It's sad it couldn't be with my own family."

His words initially warmed her, then sent her elation spiraling to the ground. Was that connection she felt because he thought of her more like a sister? If so, she needed to guard her heart. She was feeling so much more than sisterly affection. Her thoughts turned to him way more frequently than she wanted to admit.

She pulled her hand back. "What now?"

"I'll text Scott the results." He pulled out his phone and sent a text. "I'd like to talk to Josh about the guy who grabbed you that morning. I want to find my dad's killer."

"And you've decided it's not your mom or sister?"

"Yes. They wanted his money, but I can't quite believe they'd do something that drastic. Maybe I'm being naive."

"You know them better than anyone." She followed him out of the lab and into the parking lot. The setting sun was putting on a show out over the ocean, and her stomach rumbled to remind her it was dinnertime.

"I heard that. My stomach is serenading me too. We could stop at Cafe Alfresco. I love their chicken curry with mango chutney. I'll buy."

She wished she could consider this a date. She got into the truck. "That's my favorite too. If I eat all my dinner, can I have the carrot cake? Though the thing is huge. Maybe I should just eat the carrot cake and skip the dinner."

"I'll split it with you after dinner."

The thought of sharing a plate with him seemed surreal and way too intimate if she was going to work on guarding her heart, but she couldn't say no. She sat in silence as he drove them to the restaurant. They were quickly seated outside at a table with lots of privacy near the iron railing. The restaurant, along the Pinellas Trail in downtown Dunedin, was a favorite in the Tampa Bay area. Aromas of Italian, Asian, and seafood dishes permeated the air in a tantalizing bouquet.

Ridge's dark eyes were pensive as his gaze wandered. "What would you do about my mom and sister if you were me?"

Treacherous waters ahead. The wrong advice could backfire. The server brought water to the table and gave her a reprieve while they gave their orders. She laced her fingers together when he looked back at her expectantly.

"There's really no place for your sister in the pharmaceutical business, is there? What about his other businesses?"

He barked out a derisive laugh. "She wouldn't be caught dead working in one of Dad's businesses. She likes telling her patients what to do."

"She probably makes good money. Do you know why she's so wrapped up in having more?"

His troubled gaze locked with hers for a long moment. "You're right. I should find out. Maybe there's some valid reason she needs the money. If that's the case, I should help her, shouldn't I?"

Harper didn't want to say her true feelings, so she just nodded.

Ridge took a sip of his water. "You think I should give her the money even if she doesn't need it, don't you?"

"Someone with that much anger and rage is usually covering over something painful. The divorce may have taken a bigger toll on her than you know. She doesn't seem to be the type to tell you what she's feeling."

"And she's been so influenced by Mom. Mom doesn't deserve a cent though. She took half of everything when she left Dad. If she's blown her half while Dad built his up, that's her own fault."

"I would agree with that. I know God expects us to be generous and forgive. Maybe you and your sister need to have a long talk."

She felt the blood drain from her face when she spotted a figure over Ridge's shoulder. "Um, here comes Willow now. She's spotted you and she looks angry."

27

Ridge rose to greet his sister, but when he moved to give her a perfunctory hug, she held out her hand to stop him. Her eyes were red as though she'd been crying.

He folded his arms across his chest. "You okay, Willow?"

"What do you care?" she shot back. Her voice trembled and she bit her lip.

He pointed to the seat. "Want to sit down and talk about it?"

She shook her head, then dropped into the chair anyway. "I haven't been able to sleep or work since Dad died."

Since Dad died, or since she knew he hadn't split his estate? Ridge didn't voice the question twisting his insides. He didn't like being so cynical about his sister, and he wished they could be close. He couldn't remember the last time he'd felt warmth from her. Wasn't family supposed to mean something—to be a safe harbor from the storms of life? It often felt like his mother and sister *were* the storms, blowing in and wrecking any harmony he'd found.

"I'm sorry," he said.

She looked at him with watery eyes. "Are you going to do the right thing?"

"What is the right thing, Willow? To follow our father's wishes he spelled out very clearly, or to throw it all aside? What would you do if Mom did the same thing? What if her will leaves everything to you? Will you follow her wishes or ignore them?"

Her face darkened to a dull maroon, and Ridge suspected Willow already knew their mother had named only her in the will. Mom had told him she'd made a will in Willow's favor because she was a woman and alone. He had shrugged and let it go. He'd rather have had Mom's love, but since he never felt anything approaching motherly affection from her, part of her estate was no substitute.

He could make his own way. If he could have his dad back right now, he'd take that in a heartbeat over the wealth. It meant nothing.

"I'd share it with you," she muttered.

"I don't believe you. Are wills meant to be ignored? Everything belonged to Dad, and it was his right to leave it however he wanted." He could feel Harper's gaze boring into him, and he softened his tone. "Why does it mean so much to you? You're a doctor, so you don't really need the money, do you?"

She laced her fingers together, then released them and plucked at a napkin without making eye contact. "I'd rather talk about this in private."

Harper rose. "I'm going to the restroom."

She stepped away before Ridge could grab her wrist. Maybe it was best this way. Willow probably wouldn't talk in front of Harper, and something was clearly wrong. "Well? Why is the money such a big deal?"

She sighed and fingered a lock of her blonde hair. "I was stupid, okay? I was dating this stockbroker, and he claimed he could double my investments. I had about three million, and I turned it over to him."

"Oh, Willow."

Her lips flattened. "I know. I know. Oldest scam in the book. But he looked the part—he drove a Porsche, had a huge house in Miami and another one in New York. I believed him. The worst thing is that I thought I was in love with him."

"Your money is gone?"

"Every cent." Her voice wobbled. "And he's gone too. He isn't answering his phone, and I put a private investigator on his tail. He flew to Belize, and I don't think he's coming back."

He absorbed the story. This was very unlike Willow, which probably added to her distress at her naïveté. She prided herself on her brain and good sense. She'd abandoned all of it for this guy. "Did you tell Mom?"

She caught his gaze in a steady stare. "What do you think?"

"You were ashamed to tell her."

She looked down at her hands that were still pleating the napkin. "She'd think I had no sense. And in truth I didn't show much. And even if I told her, she wouldn't bail me out. You know how she always says we have to learn from our mistakes."

He'd heard that adage many times over the years. "What do you think happened to Dad?"

Her head jerked up. "What do you mean?"

"Did the police come to talk to you and Mom?"

"Yes. They suspected we might have had something to do with it, but that's ridiculous. You don't believe we'd do anything like that, do you?"

He shook his head. "I wondered for about a minute after you were both so adamant about turning off life support, but I don't think you'd actually murder anyone."

"Thank you. That means a lot." She shifted and rose to her feet. "I'd better go. I saw your truck and decided to stop. It was stupid. You don't owe me anything. Mom's right—we do need to learn from our mistakes. This is one I won't make again."

He stood and faced her. "Lucky for us there's such a thing as grace."

She stopped and blinked up at him. "Wh-What?"

"I'll transfer the money tomorrow. It's the right thing to do."

She threw her arms around him, and he hugged her back. Maybe grace really did beget grace.

Annabelle pushed her wet hair out of her face, then looked down at the hospital gown. A stone-faced woman with gray hair had taken her into a bathroom with a lock on the outside. She'd been told to bathe. At first she'd thought to refuse, but the thought of a shower enticed her into obeying. What could it hurt to be clean to face what was coming?

She'd planned to put her old clothes back on, but the moment she'd stepped naked into the shower, the door had opened and the woman had taken her clothing and left this gown behind. Slippers, too, the kind hospitals used.

She tried the door and found it unlocked. Pausing outside the door, she listened and absorbed the atmosphere. Somewhere in the distance music played. It sounded like a radio station. Was that the smell of pizza or some other Italian dish?

In her slippers she moved to the top of the staircase and stared down into a large room that held only folding tables and chairs. The carpeting seemed new, and she could see the front of a fireplace.

This was a house, not a commercial building. From her bedroom window she could tell it was the middle of nowhere, so screaming wouldn't get her anywhere. She hung poised over the first step. Should she try to slip out the front door? She eased down a step, then another until she stood on the last step before she put a toe into the downstairs. Her heart pounded in her ears, and she exhaled in a series of short gasps. Someone was bound to come out and find her any moment.

She looked to her left. The door enticed her to step that way. It had a dead bolt, which would be sure to make some kind of sound, but maybe the radio would drown out the slight click. What was she—some kind of coward? She had to try to escape.

She stepped off the final tread and rushed for the door. The dead bolt felt stiff and unwieldy under her fingers, but it finally clicked open. She tried the knob, but it still wouldn't open. She released the lock and the knob twisted easily under her hand. The door let in the fresh breeze of freedom, and she slipped through the opening and onto a front porch.

Someone grabbed her by the wrist as she started to pull the door shut behind her. The door jerked out of her hand, and the same woman who had escorted her to the bathroom stood in the opening. Her hazel eyes blazed with anger, and she pressed her lips in a tight line.

Annabelle tried to pull free, but the woman was muscular and determined. She jerked Annabelle back into the house and slammed the door shut without letting go of her.

Annabelle twisted and yanked, but the woman was like an immovable rock. "Let go of me!"

"I thought I locked that door." The woman's gaze swept over her and down to her feet. "No harm done, I guess. You didn't make it far. Back upstairs." She shoved Annabelle toward the steps.

Annabelle dug her feet into the carpet. "Look, just let me go. I won't tell anyone about this."

The woman planted her other hand between Annabelle's shoulder blades and shoved her toward the staircase. "Shut up and move."

Annabelle stumbled when the woman shoved her again, and she fell onto her already sore knees. The woman jerked her up, but as she stepped to one side, Annabelle wrenched her arm free, then darted around her and ran in the direction of the music. She reached the kitchen and ran on through to a hallway where she found another door. She flung it open and stepped into a garage. Maybe she could find a weapon here.

She shut the door as the woman rushed toward her, then grabbed a shovel off a rack by the door and wedged it under the handle. The garage was dark so she flipped on the light switch and looked around for a weapon. More tools hung on another wall: another shovel, an ax, hammers, a crowbar, and a shop broom.

The door rattled behind her, and she ran to the rack of tools and removed the other shovel. She swung around to face the door, but the woman wasn't shaking it anymore. The silence felt ominous, and Annabelle swallowed down her fear. Where was she?

She held the shovel on her shoulder, ready to swing it into the woman's head, but the silence stretched on. Where was she? A sound brought her around to face the garage door. It was rising. Annabelle darted toward the opener by the door into the house and hit the button. The movement stopped. She hit it again and it started back down as a face peered under it.

The woman was outside, so Annabelle removed the shovel from the door to the house. She tried to turn the knob, but it was locked. She looked around for another way out. There was another door into the backyard. She ran to it, unlocked it, then stepped outside into the morning sunshine.

"Stop right there." The woman came through a gate into the yard.

Annabelle registered the black gun pointing her way and stopped. "Look, I haven't done anything to you. Let me go. I'm supposed to start chemo today."

The woman's flat hazel eyes widened, and the gun wavered a bit. "Chemo?"

"Yes, I have lymphoma. I need treatment." Maybe the woman had a bit of pity in her heart.

The woman narrowed her eyes. "Inside."

Or maybe she was heartless.

28

April 1970

The squeak of the nurse's shoes in the maternity ward faded as Judy stared at her baby's perfect bow-shaped mouth. She cuddled the baby closer and caught the sweet scent of Annabelle's skin. This was true love of the best kind. Little Annabelle had her father's blue eyes below a fluff of blonde hair. A wave of inexpressible love constricted Judy's heart. Until she'd seen her daughter's face, she hadn't realized how much she would love her little one.

Wrapped in pink flowered flannel, the baby's little face was perfect in every way. He'd have to love his daughter too—he wouldn't be able to help it. Huey had promised in his letters to hurry home as soon as he could. He'd said he would break his engagement and marry her. Judy was so lost in a pleasant daydream of the three of them in a beautiful waterfront home that she didn't hear her door swing shut.

She blinked and looked up at the woman standing in the dim light at the foot of her bed. It wasn't a nurse, but someone dressed in a slim-fitting knee-length dress and pumps. Judy squinted, then pulled the string to turn on the light. The baby mewled at the brightness and closed her eyes. Judy shifted Annabelle to shade her face, then stared at the woman. She struggled to sit up as recognition flooded her.

The woman stepped closer into the light. "So you're the trollop who thinks she can steal my fiancé. He'll never marry you, you know. My father would ruin him."

Judy lifted her chin. "He loves me."

But maybe the woman's family was powerful enough to make good on the threat. Her hands shook a little as she adjusted the blanket around little Annabelle. Judy didn't want any harm to come to him because of loving her.

The woman gave an elegant sniff. "You're deluded. I'll admit he's infatuated with you, but he wouldn't dare cross my family. Or his either, for that matter. His father would disown him, and he wouldn't be able to support you and your brat anyway."

Judy sat up and swung her legs over the side of the bed. She wasn't about to put down Annabelle while this she-wolf was in the room, and Judy wanted to be in a position to defend them if this woman made a move in their direction.

Her rival was even more beautiful in person, and her elegance reminded Judy of Jackie Kennedy. Her thick dark hair was lustrous, and she had a thin patrician nose. The handbag she carried looked like an Oscar de la Renta. She was used to the best of everything, and she probably got everything she asked for.

Though the woman's social standing was far above Judy's, they were just two women who loved the same man. Judy almost felt sorry for her as she saw through the woman's stiff carriage to the fear that had driven her.

She stared at the woman. "If you're so sure of that, why are you here?"

The woman pressed her lips together. "I'm here to offer you a deal. Take your child and go far away from here. I'll give you a check for a hundred thousand dollars, which is enough for you to live nicely for a very long time."

Judy bit back the gasp gathering in her lungs. "You must really fear he'll leave you."

"Let's call this a little insurance. I'm sure you're only after him because of who he is. Men are so easily lured by a pretty face."

"I love him."

"You don't even know him. You met him for what—two minutes? This was really all my fault. If I hadn't blown him off to shop for wedding dresses with my friends, he never would have met you. He showed up unexpectedly and thought I should change my plans. That picnic you ate was planned for me, you know. He'd bought all my favorite foods and wanted to show me his new boat." She wrinkled her nose. "I couldn't disappoint my friends after we had an appointment to look at dresses. It would have been rude."

Judy heard the way she was trying to convince herself she'd made the right call, but it still stung that he'd lied to her that day over a year ago on the boat. Even so, this woman had made a mistake to choose her friends over her fiancé. "I don't want your money."

The woman scowled and stepped closer. "I'll ruin you. I'll make sure the newspaper carries this story. People will point and sneer when they see you."

"And you'll be pitied. I'm sure you won't like that." Judy saw her flinch as the barb hit home. She was feeling more and more confident. "He told you he wanted to break the engagement, didn't he?"

"He's a man after all—he doesn't know what he wants. But I know what you want, and it's more money. Okay, fine. I'll up the offer to one hundred and fifty thousand." She fumbled through the leather purse in her hand and withdrew a checkbook. "I'll write it out right now."

"I don't want your money. Not even a million dollars would make me agree to leave him."

The woman gaped as she stared at Judy, then dropped her checkbook back into her purse. "You'll be sorry." She wheeled on her heels and stalked out the door. It creaked closed behind her on its spring.

The baby made a squeak and sucked on her tiny fist. Judy pulled her close and fed her while she mulled over what had just happened. Wait until Huey heard what his fiancée had offered. He'd surely realize she loved him for himself and not for his money. And who could resist this beautiful baby?

The future looked bright now that she knew she'd won.

⌒

Annabelle was still missing though there'd been a massive police search for her all day. Harper sat on the upper deck of her houseboat under the stars and prayed for her sister. Where was she? What had happened to her, and was it her fault like Scott implied? She stared out over the water and inhaled the salty tang of the sea. A fish splashed somewhere nearby.

Ridge came up the ladder with two bottles of water in his hands and a bag of potato chips under his arm. He dropped into a chair beside her and gave her one of the bottles. "You look pensive. You worrying about Annabelle?"

"What if Scott is right and this is my fault? Maybe I brought the danger to her door when I showed up. I was attacked first, though I still can't see what Annabelle has to do with my mollusk farm."

He uncapped his bottle and took a swig. "I can't see any connection either."

"All my life I've longed for connection, for family. What if my obsession to find my roots has brought this trouble to Annabelle?" Her hand settled on her belly. And it was also risking the life of her unborn child.

He leaned forward. "One thing you have to remember is that even if there is some connection, you didn't cause it. The kidnapper chose whatever path he's taken. Don't get all guilt-ridden on me, or we'll never figure this out."

"I know you're right." She pulled her laptop over and launched her email program, then scanned the dozen or so messages. "Looks like the pen shell meat was a hit for the restaurant. They've increased their order for the next harvest."

She shut the computer lid and set it back on the floor. "Um, how did your talk go with your sister?" They'd both been quiet on the way back to the boat, and she hadn't wanted to break the silence.

His dark eyes warmed as he held her gaze. "Good, thanks to you. She'd gotten taken in by a shyster who stole all her money. I'm going to give her what she needs."

A rush of heat ran up her neck. "Really? I'm so glad you sorted it out."

"We seem to have called a truce."

"And your mother?"

He shrugged. "Nothing different there, and I don't expect our relationship to change. She is who she is. But maybe Willow and I can start over. She let her mask down for the first time in years. Maybe ever. That guy really did a number on her. Sometimes our biggest heartaches bring the most blessings."

She nodded. There had been plenty of heartache in her life over the years. Losing her mother at such an early age had scarred her. No matter how hard she looked, she'd never been able to replace what she'd never had. Here she was nearly thirty, and she was still alone. Where was the blessing in that?

Ridge ripped open the bag of potato chips. "What's going through your head?"

"Just thinking about what you said. I don't see any blessing in being without a family all my life. It's been hard."

"I'm sorry. Here I am complaining about my mom and sister and you haven't had either of those things. After all you've gone through, it's probably hard to trust anyone."

Trust. She sat back in her chair as the word hammered into her brain. It was true. She had trouble trusting anyone. She'd gone to every one of her foster homes full of hope that this time might be different, but every time, she'd soon learned her place in the family. That place had been slaving away in the kitchen or doing the laundry for a household of ten. In one home she was expected to care for the babies while the foster parents partied every night. Everyone always wanted something from her.

Was this lack of trust the real reason she was still alone? It was impossible to have a relationship with anyone without some level of trust. Even Oliver was someone she'd circled around, waiting for him to betray her. Maybe it was the real reason she left her phone at home more often than not. She wouldn't expect some call to come through only to find out it never happened.

It was better to expect nothing than to face disappointment.

"You're right." Her words came out a hoarse croak. "I guess I really don't trust much of anyone. You were able to start over with your sister today. How did you get enough trust to do that when she's disappointed you so many times?"

A frown settled between his brows. "What's the alternative, Harper? To live in a constant state of trepidation and fear? She might revert to the old Willow, but I'll never know if she can change if we don't both try. And if she disappoints me, so what? A little disappointment never killed anyone."

"Sometimes it's felt a little like death," she murmured.

"I know you're a Christian, so you must trust God, right?"

She considered the question. "Maybe I don't, not really. I keep waiting for the other shoe to drop. Just like Annabelle's disappearance. I've been praying for him to save her and rescue her, but what if he doesn't?"

He bobbed his head in a slow nod. "I get it. I prayed for my dad, too, and God still took him. That's when trust comes the hardest, but it's also when it brings the most blessing. I trust that God has my dad's best interests at heart even when I can't see it. We often don't understand why things happen, but we trust anyway."

She reached for the chips bag and took out a handful. "I'll try to do better, but I'm making no promises."

The tang of vinegar and sea salt hit her tongue. Could she lay down her guard enough with this man who seemed so steady? The truth would be revealed when she told him about her pregnancy.

29

Annabelle was back in the locked room, but she hoped she was going to be turned loose soon. The woman had seemed surprised to hear she needed chemo treatments. Surely she would be released.

She paced the floor and looked out the window for a while. A white SUV pulled up and a man got out. He moved so quickly, Annabelle didn't get a good look at him, just a vague impression of size. It might be the guy who had grabbed her. A door slammed from somewhere, and faint voices traveled up through the register, so she flung herself onto the floor and pressed her ear to it.

"Where is she?" a man demanded.

"Locked in the room." The woman answering sounded like Annabelle's captor.

"What's this nonsense about chemo?"

"She says she has lymphoma and was supposed to start treatment today."

The air-conditioning kicked on, and Annabelle couldn't make out the man's answer. She pressed her ear so tightly to the register that it would leave marks.

"I think she's telling the truth."

The man exhaled an exasperated sigh. "This changes everything."

"Yes, sir."

"We'll have to get the other one."

Annabelle's breathing quickened. Other one? One of her boys? Panic clawed at her, but she forced herself to stay calm and keep listening. Maybe she would hear something useful.

"We don't have much time," the man said. "I can take care of it tonight."

"What about the Rice woman?"

"She's of no value to the boss. Get rid of her."

Annabelle held her breath as she waited for the woman's answer. Her fingers curled into her palms. *Please God.* She wanted to see her boys again. Her sister too. If she'd been waffling about fighting this cancer, she realized in this moment that she'd do everything she could to stay with her family. To have a future with them.

She hadn't allowed herself to think of the future much. Every time she did, the reminder that she might be dying flashed through her mind. But not anymore. She would take it one day at a time and live every day to its fullest.

"You're sure?"

"If her body is found, the cops will be swarming, especially Annabelle's son who's a cop. We might find it harder to nab the sister."

Sister?

Annabelle bit back a gasp as she remembered Harper telling her about someone trying to snatch her using ether. Why would either of them be a target?

The conversation grew too muted again to hear, then grew louder again.

"I'll get the Taylor woman and let you know when I have her at the location."

"Of course."

Annabelle heard footsteps, and then the door shut. She leaped to her feet and ran to the window where she saw the SUV pull out. Squinting, she tried to make out the license plate number but couldn't. The vehicle drove out of sight around a turn in the long drive. She had no idea how far away this place was from Orlando. She'd been unconscious on the drive here.

There had to be some kind of clues she could tell Scott. What if Harper was taken before she could warn her?

She whirled away from the window at the lock clicking behind her. Her captor stepped into the room with a paper plate.

"I brought you some food. I'm going to take you home in a little while." The woman's voice was gruff, and she didn't meet Annabelle's gaze. She set the sandwich and chips on the end of the bed and backed out of the room.

Annabelle eyed the thick slice of turkey with avocado slivers between two pieces of toasted bread. The chips looked homemade, like something from a gourmet restaurant where she'd eaten, but she couldn't quite name which one. She needed to remember. Everything was a clue.

"Thank you," she called as the door locked behind the woman.

She hadn't eaten since she'd been brought here, so she sat on the edge of the bed and put the plate in her lap. She devoured the sandwich and chips, then washed it down with the bottle of water the woman had brought her earlier.

She took the plate over by the door and placed it on the floor. When she stood, the room began to spin and her mouth felt dry. Had she been drugged again?

She staggered to the bathroom and fell to her knees in front of the toilet where she jammed her fingers down her throat, trying to make herself throw up. She couldn't expel the food though, and darkness began to close in on her vision.

After crawling to the sink, she pulled herself up and splashed cold water on her face. She had to stay awake so she could figure out how to find this place again.

She put her wrists under the stream of cold water, but she could barely stay upright by clinging to the sink. Her knees buckled as darkness claimed her.

30

The heavy rain had begun to flood the parking lot outside the school gym as they waited for Jamal to exit the locker room. Harper buckled her seat belt and waited for Ridge to get off the phone. Her stomach rumbled, and she glanced at the time. Three o'clock. She hadn't had a chance to have lunch.

Not that she was hungry when worry about Annabelle gnawed at her.

Ridge put his phone away. "Annabelle's been found! Scott says she's in the hospital being checked, but she's fine. She was found unconscious."

"Has she said what happened? Do we know if she escaped or someone turned her free?"

"Scott said she was drugged and dumped out after the kidnapper found out she had cancer."

"That's so odd."

Jamal loped to the Jeep and got into the backseat. "Sorry it took so long. Lots of congratulations. I can't wait to tell Mom I made the most points!"

"Let's get you over there so you can tell her."

Ridge struck the right lighthearted note with the boy. He was good with kids. Harper put the Jeep in Drive and pulled out of the parking lot toward Jamal's house. His mother was caring for his grandmother and hadn't been able to attend the basketball game.

They dropped Jamal off at home before she asked more about Annabelle. "It's beyond strange that they just let her go. Does she have any idea why she was taken?" She pulled away from the curb.

"She doesn't know, and she wasn't harmed in any way." His gaze captured hers, and he chewed his lip. "She overheard them say they'd have to take you instead of her."

Harper's foot went to the brake, and the Jeep jerked to a stop. Her pulse fluttered in her chest. "Why?"

"They plan to grab you tonight. I think we should swing by and get Bear and some clothes so you can stay at Dad's until we get this sorted out. I still can't believe someone could break into his place with his expensive security."

She started shaking her head before he finished. "My life has been disrupted enough. I can take my boat over to the marina and stay under the lights and near lots of people. There's no reason to bother you."

"I miss Dad, and I could use the company." His words were low, and he stared down at his hands.

Her chest squeezed. It took a lot for a strong man like Ridge to admit he needed a little help. "Well, when you put it like that . . . I guess I can stay at least tonight. Scott should have more news by tomorrow. I'm sure he's trying to turn over every stone."

This was an opportunity to test her resolve to work on her trust issues. And maybe she could get up the courage to tell Ridge about the baby.

She put her foot back on the accelerator and pulled out into the traffic. As they drove back to Dunedin, she kept stealing glances at his strong profile and found him staring out the window. Losing his dad had knocked him hard.

When they got to the cover, her boat bobbed in the waves at the small dock. She parked and got out. "You want to wait here while I grab a few things?"

"I'll come with you. I can take charge of Bear while you gather your stuff." He shoved open the passenger door and headed for the houseboat.

Bear barked at their approach, and she could see the top of his head as he kept jumping in excitement. "I'm here, Bear." She stepped aboard and scooped him up. He licked her chin and wiggled all over before she set him down.

"Harper, wait!" Ridge leaped aboard the boat and grabbed her arm. "Get to shore. I think there's a bomb."

She let him propel her and Bear off the boat to a safe distance before she asked questions. "Where's a bomb?"

He shone the flashlight on his phone onto the bow of the boat. "See those pipes taped to the bow?"

Black duct tape attached several pipes to her boat. It hardly looked big enough to do much damage, but she grasped the gravity in Ridge's tone. "A pipe bomb?"

"Looks like it. I'll call 911 and get it checked out, but I don't want to take any chances."

"What could be the reason to bomb my boat though? I don't have anything of value."

"Maybe to force you to land? You've been moving the boat all over, and if you're forced to stay on land, you might be easier for them to find. It's just a guess. We still don't know what they want."

She hurried toward the Jeep and slung herself under the

wheel. She started the engine with a shaking hand. How did life get totally upended in just a few days? And why would anyone want to hurt her? Or Annabelle, for that matter?

Ridge approached with Bear in his arms. He opened the back door of the Wrangler and settled the dog and his food onto the seat before he got into the passenger seat. "Let's get out of here. I'll call the police while you drive."

Ridge pulled out his phone and made the call. He informed the police that they weren't staying at the location and gave the dispatcher his number. "They'll let us know what they find out."

He tapped on an app. "Let's list the things we know. You and Annabelle both ran a DNA search and found each other and discovered similarities between your mothers' deaths. The current situation seems to indicate the killer is still alive."

"Our dad."

"Or someone else. Let's not limit our possible perpetrators." He tapped in several lines of text. "I'm texting Scott what we heard about Joe Mitchell. Maybe he can find him and interview him."

"Their deaths were twenty years apart. Who else would do it besides my dad? I doubt this Joe Mitchell knew my mother."

"Maybe not, but someone knew them both somehow. A mentor."

"Another mermaid? Though my mother was never a mermaid as far as I know."

"We know she went to talk to a mermaid before she died. We need to ask questions about that."

Harper pulled into Oliver's drive. "We're going in circles and nothing is really clicking."

"Not yet, but we'll figure it out."

Harper got out and retrieved her satchel. Time was running out on finding the truth, and they weren't any closer than they were last week.

———————

The gentle flame in the fireplace added a homey feeling to the room. Ridge had made sure the alarms were activated before he settled in a big armchair by the fire. Harper was on the white leather sofa across from him with Bear on her lap. Bear had sniffed around the house before he decided it was acceptable. He seemed at home now curled nose to tail on her legs.

She looked beautiful tonight. Her red hair was loose on the shoulders of her orange T-shirt, and her long tanned legs were in denim shorts. He liked being able to sit and admire her. Things had changed so much between them over the past week. He'd considered her an enemy for so long, but this complete turnaround felt right.

"How could my dad's death be related to the attacks on you and Annabelle?"

Her hand paused midstroke along Bear's back. "You dismissed that idea when I brought it up. I thought you suspected it had something to do with his estate."

"I assumed so at first, but I've been thinking about what you said. The charities in his will wouldn't have arranged for his death. At least I can't imagine it. And I don't believe Willow had anything to do with it. So that leaves the original attacker. If the killer is the same person who attacked him underwater, what might Dad have seen that he wanted to keep quiet?"

"The person's identity."

He'd already considered that. "I'm not sure Dad would have been able to describe him. He might never have gotten his memory back. And water distorts everything. The mask and the mouthpiece would make the guy hard to recognize too."

Ridge passed her a bowl of peanut M&Ms, and she took a small handful. He took a couple himself and popped them in his mouth. "What else?"

"It could be whoever is trying to sabotage the pen shell beds."

"Eric Kennedy," he said.

She ate a piece of candy. "What would be his motive for it though? All he wants is for us to move the beds. That's not worth committing murder to accomplish."

"True. So we've got several players and not just one? Someone is after you and Annabelle for an unknown reason. Someone killed my father, and someone wants to disrupt the pen shell beds. That seems a stretch to have all of those interested parties lash out at once. My priority right now is keeping you safe. Which means we need to figure out who's behind the attack on you and Annabelle."

What was the key piece of information they were missing?

Harper drew her legs up under her. "Your father could have been an innocent bystander to the attack on me. I still think whoever attacked me tried to get him out of the way first. Then he was killed so he couldn't identify the attacker."

She put Bear down and rose. "I think I'll make some coffee. Want some?"

"I can do it."

"You might not make it strong enough for me." She left the trailing scent of plumeria behind her as she headed for the kitchen.

He stood and stretched, then followed her into the cavernous kitchen with its bank of gray cabinets and marble counters. She stood in front of the coffeepot looking around. "Where'd this thing come from? Last I knew, Oliver had a Cuisinart."

Ridge grinned. "I knew you'd need help. He brought this monstrosity back from his last trip."

Dad's copper contraption took up its own special bar. It almost looked like a copper and brass R2-D2 with arms coming out on the sides.

She held her palms up. "What is this thing?"

"It's an Elektra Belle Epoque. Made in Italy. Dad saw one when he was there a few weeks ago. Let me show you." He demonstrated how to grind the coffee and direct the hot water. In minutes he had two cappuccinos.

She took a sip and sighed. "Heaven."

"That's what Dad said. He thought it was worth the twenty grand."

Her beautiful eyes widened. "He paid that much for a coffee machine? I think his old Cuisinart would do."

"You know how Dad was. He had to have the best of everything."

"I didn't see that side of him quite so clearly as I do now."

He put his coffee mug down on the marble counter. Ideas flooded in so fast he could hardly articulate them. "It appeared the attacker wasn't out to kill you but to take you with him. And Annabelle wasn't harmed either. She was abducted, then released when they found out she had cancer. That's pretty odd."

She nodded. "Why not kill her? Whoever he is, he has already killed two women in the past. Why try to take us alive?"

"I don't know. I think we have to start back at the beginning again. And let's examine the DNA company that matched up the two of you. Annabelle believes you're still a target, so we have to look at any connection between the two of you. Something is there—we just can't see it yet."

"It feels like a wild-goose chase."

"We don't have any other places to try so it's worth a shot. We'll talk to Annabelle tomorrow."

She looked so pretty standing there in the kitchen with her amazing turquoise eyes burrowing into his soul. It took all his willpower not to step close enough to take her in his arms. Now wasn't the time though. They had to find who was targeting her before it was too late.

31

Oliver's home was the first place she'd ever felt safe, so it seemed appropriate she'd come here for refuge. Harper sipped her decaf in his enormous armchair in his office and watched the flames flicker in the fireplace. The office always smelled of the clove gum Oliver was fond of, and she caught the scent of his cologne as well. If she closed her eyes, she could almost see him standing by the bookcase with a leather-bound edition of one of his precious Zane Grey novels in his hand.

Tears pricked her eyes, and she looked down at her dog. Bear's head was on her lap, and she trailed her fingers through his fur. She had to tell Ridge tonight about the baby. It might ruin everything, but he wouldn't throw her out when he feared for her life.

At least she didn't think he would.

"What are you hoping to find in here?"

Ridge glanced up from behind the desk. "Anything that might tell us who killed Dad. You know he would have done anything for you. What if he was looking into your lineage again? I know he poked around early on, but there would be a lot more resources now. He might have decided to have another go at it."

225

Her chest squeezed, and she remembered a conversation she'd had with him when she first told him she wanted to have her own baby.

Ridge's gaze sharpened. "What? You just went white."

How did she say it—just blurt out the truth? He would be apt to think she'd tricked him all this time.

And maybe she had. She'd allowed them to get closer when the truth was a barrier to a future together.

Should she stand or stay where she was? The thought of approaching him and having him turn away when he heard the truth would be more than she could bear.

Her grip tightened on Bear, and she pulled him to her chest for comfort. "There's something I have to tell you."

His gaze locked on her face and he leaned back in the desk chair. "Okay." His tone went as wary as hers.

She tightened her fingers in Bear's fur, and he lifted his head and whined. She loosened her grip and stared back at Ridge. "I won't blame you if you hate me."

His brows drew together. "It's that bad?"

"I-I think it's good, but you might share your dad's opinion." She drew in a deep breath. The only way to get through this was to just say it. "I'm pregnant." She rushed on when his mouth slackened and his eyes narrowed. "It's not what you think, Ridge. I-I had an adopted embryo implanted a couple of weeks ago. Your dad tried to talk me out of it, but I wanted a family of my own."

When he said nothing, she swallowed hard. "You don't know what it's like to feel lost and alone. To have no one. You always had Oliver, but I bounced around from foster home to foster home. I'm nearly thirty, and I was afraid if I didn't have a baby soon, I never would."

"Wow, you really don't have much trust, do you?" His words were strangled. "So you're pregnant with some stranger's baby."

She tried a watery smile but didn't manage it. "I've met both parents. The father has dark-brown hair and blue eyes. He's six-one and a doctor. He doesn't drink or do drugs. He passed a health screening with flying colors before he filed for divorce. The mom is lovely and passed all the tests too. She has blonde hair, gray eyes, and is a teacher. After her husband left her, she wanted the unborn baby to have a chance at life."

"I see." He rose and paced from bookcase to bookcase. "How long have you known?"

"I found out I was pregnant on Sunday. Just a few days."

He still said nothing, but she could see the thoughts churning. "You've known since before I told you how I felt."

"I-I was falling for you, Ridge, and I didn't want to ruin everything." Her words were a bare whisper, and she was finding it hard to hold his betrayed gaze.

"It would have been the best time to tell me the truth instead of me having to drag it out of you."

His harsh tone made her flinch, but she deserved it. She'd ruined everything. Truth was important to him and always had been. She'd known that but she risked her heart—and his—by playing with the truth.

"I'd always intended to tell you, but I was waiting for the right time."

"The right time for truth is every minute of every day." He raked his hand through his thick dark hair making it stand on end. "I don't know what to do with this, Harper. To say I'm disappointed and hurt is an understatement. I apologized to you, for Pete's sake. And you let me act like I'd had it all wrong and hadn't heard what I'd heard. Sap that I am, I wanted you to be as true and honest as you appeared to be. I was wrong."

"I deserve every bit of your condemnation. I-I'll go now." Her vision blurred, and she got up with Bear in her arms.

"You're not going anywhere. A killer's still out there."

"I can take care of myself." She had to get out of here before she disgraced herself by crying.

He moved to block the door. "Your death will not be on my hands. You're not leaving until we know what's going on." He scowled down at her. "And you realize Dad might have died because he found your father."

She felt faint and swayed where she stood until he reached out and took her arm. "That's what I'm afraid of."

———

There was no way she would be able to sleep. Harper slipped out the French doors in the bedroom to the balcony and texted Annabelle. You up?

The answer pinged back almost immediately. I wanted to call you but was afraid you were asleep.

The buzz of a call came on the heels of the text, and Annabelle's name flashed on the screen. Harper answered the call with a laugh. "You're fast. Are you really all right?" She settled on a chaise lounge and stared out at the moon glimmering on the bay's dark water. The white beams of Oliver's boat gleamed in the dim light.

"It was so strange, Harper. They fed me, let me shower, and gave me a hospital gown to wear. They seemed to care about my well-being."

"Then let you go."

"They didn't seem to want me once they knew I had lymphoma. Have you seen anyone hanging around? And you're not by yourself, are you?"

"I'm at Oliver's with Ridge. It's been quiet." Tears tracked down her cheeks.

"Honey, what's wrong? You can tell me."

Harper choked back a sob. "I'm not sure anything can help. I really messed up. I knew honesty was important to Ridge, and I kept something from him. I was afraid."

She launched into the story of her pregnancy. She could tell by the way Annabelle fell silent that the situation was every bit as bad as she had believed.

"I'm not even sure now I did the right thing. What if I'm a terrible mother? I never had a role model to know how a good mother acts."

Annabelle's wistful sigh came over the phone. "You're about to embark on the greatest journey in the world, Harper. You'll make a great mother."

"I just wanted a family. Even with Oliver, he wasn't always there for me, you know? He would promise to show up to school events or to take me out for coffee and often had to cancel for business. I always floated around the little bubble of his real family and knew I didn't fit in—that I wasn't part of that family. Oh, I'm grateful for all he did. He took a rebellious, smart-mouthed kid and found me a foster home where I was safe. They were good to me, but safe isn't loved. Safe didn't mean I belonged."

"I'm so sorry you went through something that hard so young. One thing I want to warn you about though is not to put unrealistic expectations on yourself. You're going to make mistakes—and often. We all do. But that doesn't mean you don't love your child. And he or she will love you."

"I don't want to make mistakes."

"You'll want to do everything possible for your baby—and you should—but within reason. Don't make your child the sole reason for your existence. It's too much pressure on you and your child. Just relax and let them be a kid. Let yourself be human. We all do the best we can, but we all fail too. And it's okay."

Harper didn't like the sound of that. She'd thought Annabelle would tell her how perfect life would be as a parent. "You were a single mom when your boys were young. How did you manage to be both mom and dad?"

"I wasn't. I was mom. I made friends at church and at work and found people who would pinch-hit for the spots I couldn't fill."

More facts Harper didn't like. "I don't really know people like that, especially now that Oliver is gone. Sara has always been a good friend, but most of the time we haven't been in close proximity. She won't be at this duty station long either. I don't know if I'll have much of a support system."

"Then you'll find them. Friends are the family we can choose. Reaching out and receiving both have a place in a rich life. Don't get so fixated on doing that you forget to let others reach out and help too. I'll do all I can—you know that. But the main thing to remember is you have to forgive yourself and try to do better next time with the Lord's help. Give yourself grace."

The pressure in Harper's chest began to ease. Failure wasn't permanent. There was always grace. "I'll try. What should I do about Ridge?"

"I've seen the way he looks at you. He's just lost his dad. Give him time to come to grips with this. I think he'll realize you're too important to him to just let go of what you've got."

"I hope you're right."

"I'll be praying for you."

"Thank you. What about your chemo?"

"I'm starting day after tomorrow."

A boat with its lights on moved through the bay close to shore, and Harper rose and went to the railing where she could hear the faint sound of music coming from the craft. People out enjoying each other's company. She needed to remember to take one day at a time and enjoy each moment for what it was.

"I can come and sit with you if you want the company."

"My boys will be here. You've got enough going on. Find out who is behind all this. I couldn't bear it if something happened to you now that I've found you."

"I love you, Annabelle."

"I love you, Harper. And it has nothing to do with the blood running through our veins. I would have loved you if we weren't sisters. When I'm through with chemo, I want to come see your boat and help you refit it. I have so many plans for our future."

"I'd love that too. Sleep well, and I'll come see you tomorrow."

"Good night."

Harper ended the call and leaned on the railing. Annabelle would be a good teacher to show her how to live in the moment every day. Grace. It was a word she hadn't thought about much except in how she'd been undeserving of God's grace. She hadn't thought about giving it to other people and to herself.

She intended to learn how to do that—starting with Ridge. She only hoped he could give her grace for keeping something so important from him.

32

P regnant.

Ridge should have been in bed because it was nearly eleven, but he sat on his dad's back deck under the stars. The sound of the ocean should have soothed his agitation, but his knee still jiggled. The salty sea air cleared his head, but nothing could calm his thoughts.

He'd persuaded Harper to go to bed, but he had no idea what to do with this new information. She could have told him the truth multiple times and hadn't.

He stood and walked across the expansive cedar deck to stare out at the moon glimmering on the waves of the bay. His heart was already involved, and she'd deliberately waited until that had happened. It felt sneaky and manipulative, traits he'd suspected she possessed before he put down his guard.

What did he do with this?

Everything in him wanted to forgive her and move on, but though he'd pointed out her trust issues, he had his own. His mother would say it was because he felt abandoned by his father, but that felt too clichéd. Everyone wanted to blame someone else for their bad behavior, and he'd sworn never to do that. If he had trust issues, it was up to him to resolve them.

"Couldn't sleep either?"

He looked over to see Scott striding across the grass toward the deck. "When did you get here? Did you ring the bell?"

The detective nodded his head. "Just got here. I rang the bell and when you didn't answer, I decided to check the back deck. How's Harper? Mom is still worried about her."

"She's inside in bed. How's your mom?"

"Okay. Nothing much slows her down." Scott moved over to sit on an upholstered chair. "I thought losing my dad was hard, but knowing what Mom'll have to go through is agonizing. I'd take it from her if I could."

Ridge joined him in another chair. "My mom moved out when I was a kid, so I know something about losing a parent. I didn't see her much after she left, and my sister went with her."

"Nearly losing Mom has made me treasure every moment with her. And I have to get to the bottom of this so I can sleep at night. It's been days since I was actually in bed. I've been napping in the car when I can."

The bags under Scott's eyes underscored his words. Ridge liked the man's dedication to his mother. He remembered how defensive Scott had been the first time they'd met. "You married?" He hadn't seen a wedding ring, so he guessed the answer was no.

"Nah. Engaged once in college, but I found out she'd cheated on me with my best friend. I haven't dated much since I became a detective. My schedule is unpredictable, which isn't conducive to a relationship." Scott's face lit up in a mischievous grin. "You dating Harper yet?"

"I thought we were heading that direction, but now I'm

not so sure. She told me tonight she's pregnant." He held up his hand. "I'm not the father, obviously. She wanted a baby so she went to a fertility specialist to get one."

Scott's eyes widened. "Wow, that's a hard pill to swallow. Basically, you don't get her without taking on a ready-made family. She might be worth it though, depending on what you think of kids." He gave a wry grin. "I don't know why I'm offering advice when I have no experience with something like this."

"I like kids, but she had the opportunity to tell me before tonight and hid it from me. That's the biggest problem I have with it."

"Mom told me Harper grew up in foster homes. Fear usually drives dishonesty. She was probably afraid of your reaction. I would guess she's painfully familiar with rejection."

"Probably, but I'm not sure that gives her a pass for dishonesty with something so important. It feels manipulative."

"Mom thinks the world of her. Just make sure you're not throwing the baby out with the bathwater as my mom always says." He stopped. "I guess that's a bit of a pun in this situation."

Was he willing to throw the dream of a future with Harper away over this? It was going to take time for him to figure this out. "Any word on the whereabouts of Joe Mitchell?"

"Actually yes. He was shot and killed when he broke into a woman's house in 1975."

"So he's not the one after Harper and your mother."

"Nope. He might have known something about what happened to Judy, but we'll never know. And he's clearly not the one who took my mom and tried to abduct Harper. I did some digging, and he seems to be implicated in a series of rapes that occurred from 1966 to 1975. They stopped when he was shot, so that's a pretty good indication he was involved."

"So we're at a standstill."

"That's just a dead end. There's still plenty of investigation into the earlier deaths. I'm not discouraged, at least not yet. You have to keep Harper safe until I figure it out though."

"What about your mother?"

"I don't think she's in danger anymore. They wouldn't have released her if they intended to harm her. I have those police notes into Judy's death you were asking about. If I'd thought my insomnia would drive me this far from Orlando, I would have brought them. Come by tomorrow and I'll have them for you."

"Will do."

Scott stood and yawned. "I might take a nap in my car."

"Plenty of beds here in Dad's house. You're welcome to crash inside."

Scott's phone rang, and he glanced at the screen. "Duty calls, so sleep will have to wait." He answered the phone and walked off toward the front of the house.

Ridge yawned, too, and headed for the back door. Maybe once he slept on this problem, he'd know what to do.

Sunlight streamed through the windows and danced on the marble counters in Oliver's kitchen. Harper turned the bacon over in the skillet. "What would you like in your omelet?" She kept her voice light and neutral.

She resisted the urge to ask how he was feeling this morning. She felt as fatigued as he looked. It had been hard to sleep in the unfamiliar space with all her thoughts crowding her out of the bed. The thought of some unknown assailant lurking outside the window had startled her awake every time sleep tried to sweep her to dreamland, and Ridge's stunned expression when she revealed her pregnancy had kept her tossing and turning.

He stepped around the big island and poured a mug of coffee from the fancy machine. "Everything you've got. The more jalapeños, the better."

He sounded normal, without the edge his voice had last night. The faint scent of soap from his shower mingled with the aroma of coffee and bacon. She had a strong sense of déjà vu from somewhere, though she couldn't remember ever cooking a man breakfast like this. Maybe it was because it felt natural to be in such an intimate setting with Ridge.

But it might not ever happen again.

She finished the omelets and slid one across the island to him where he sat on a stool sipping coffee. "I'd like to see Annabelle today and make sure she's okay. What are your plans?"

"I'll go with you. Scott's supposed to get me copies of Judy's homicide investigation notes since yours came up missing. We can start looking there."

They ate in a strained silence, and Harper barely tasted her omelet and bacon. As soon as the clock hit eight, she planned to call and check on Annabelle.

The doorbell rang, and Ridge slid off the bar stool. "Wonder who's here this early? It's only seven."

Dread curled in her belly. Maybe it was more bad news. She followed him through the house to the front door. He disarmed the security system, threw back the dead bolt, and opened the door.

Scott stood on the other side with two boxes in his arms. "I know it's early, but I thought you might be up."

Ridge stepped out of the way. "I was going to track you down today to get the files. Looks like a lot."

"It's more than investigation files." Scott entered and shut the door behind him. "Grace Beck called and said she'd found a box she'd missed of Judy's. I don't want Mom delving into this herself so I brought it for us to check out. Where do you want them?"

"This way," Ridge said. "We'll use the kitchen island."

Harper's pulse quickened as she followed the men into the kitchen. Maybe there would be answers in the boxes. "How is your mom today?"

Scott set the boxes on the end of the island. "She started off the morning hounding me to bring you the investigation files." He lifted one shoulder in a half shrug. "Nothing much keeps her down for long."

Harper eyed the boxes. "Want some breakfast?"

"No thanks, I've already eaten. But I wouldn't say no to coffee."

Ridge got him a full mug, then grabbed the first box. "What's in this one?"

"The box Grace still had. I haven't looked through it yet."

Ridge opened the flaps, lifted out the contents, and made a pile of tiny pots of cream eye shadow, a pair of white ankle-high boots, fishnet stockings, and an orange plaid beret. He frowned and removed a handful of small metal canisters. "Anyone know what these are?"

"They look like home movie films." Scott opened one of the canisters. "Super 8mm films. We run into them during investigations sometimes. They won't have sound."

"How do you watch them?" Harper asked.

"You need a special projector, but we have a digitizer at the station. I'll take them in and get them converted. It might take a day or two, but I'll ask them to expedite 'em."

Harper doubted the old movies would tell them much about the current situation, but one of them might provide a clue on where to look. "Is it possible to buy a projector locally?"

"I don't know where you'd find one other than online, which would take longer to get than for me to digitize them."

Ridge loaded them back into the box, then reached for the other box. "At least we can review the files on Judy's murder. These are the originals, right?"

"Right. I checked these out of the evidence room."

He'd gotten them the byssus strand for Ridge to examine, but they hadn't read the original reports and witness statements. Harper held out hope there would be something new here.

She reached for a stained manila folder, opened it, and scanned the first page. "These look like investigation notes."

Ridge was perusing another folder. "These are witness statements. This will take a while. Let's take our coffee into the living room while we read them."

Scott took a last gulp of his coffee. "I'm investigating the homicide of a working girl, so you guys have at 'em. Call me if you find anything interesting."

Ridge rose. "Will do. I'll walk you out and set the security system behind you."

Harper listened with half an ear to their footsteps heading to the door as she leafed through the detective's notes. Most of them she recognized, but she ran into a small notebook that wasn't familiar. It was shirt-pocket size, and she flipped open the red worn cover. The crabbed writing was hard to read, and she turned on the light to see it better. It was the detective's impressions of the murder scene.

A silver bracelet with gemstones found clutched in victim's hand. Evidence tagged.

This was the first mention of a bracelet found at the scene. Harper rose and went back to dig in the box. She found the bracelet in a crumpled paper envelope. It was unique with fine silvery filament around a large opal stone and inset diamonds. The rest of the band was made up of simple silvery links. The metal looked like platinum to her.

Had it been Judy's or was it a real clue?

33

The murder scene pictures were hard to take. Ridge swigged down water, but it didn't help the dryness in his mouth. He set down his glass on the end table and studied the bracelet Harper had given him. He'd found his gaze straying to her more and more often. Her red hair was on top of her head in a cute ponytail that made her look about eighteen, and the green top she wore deepened the green in her eyes.

She looked so innocent, but she'd shown him she wasn't completely honest.

He turned the bracelet over in his fingers. "I feel like I might have seen something similar to this once, but I can't remember where."

"I recognize most metals, and this appears to be platinum. How could Judy afford something that expensive? She didn't come from a moneyed family."

"I'm just sure I've seen something similar, but I can't think where. There's a jewelry store my mom has used all my life, and the jeweler is a friend of hers. Let's take it there and see if he can tell us anything about it. I'll stick the plates in the dishwasher and we can go."

"I can do it."

He shook his head. "You cooked so it's only fair that I clean up."

Her brows rose and she smiled. "Your mom taught you well."

Maybe she had. He hadn't stopped to think about how she'd at least taught him manners. His phone rang and he reached for it. His mom must have known she was being talked about. His gut clenched as he answered the call. He hadn't talked to her since their last explosive meeting.

"Hi, Mom."

"I'm outside in the driveway and thought I'd warn you so you could turn off the security." Her clipped voice held no emotion.

"Come on in." He ended the call and went to turn off the alarm and unlock the door.

His mother's stylish heels clattered on the walk, and she looked professional and all business in her navy skirt and white shirt. He stepped out of the doorway to allow her to enter. She lifted her cheek to him, and he kissed it dutifully.

He shut the door behind her and reengaged the security. "Would you like coffee?"

"No, my first patient will be at the office in an hour, so I don't have long." She walked down the hall to the living room and stopped abruptly when she spotted Harper sitting on the sofa with her legs curled under her and Bear snuggled up beside her. "I didn't know you had company." Her blue eyes were ice chips as she glared at him. "Like father, like son."

Harper's chin came up, but she said nothing and got up to step into the kitchen. He wanted to throttle his mother for insulting her, but he took a few deep breaths until his anger went from boiling to a slow simmer. His mother would have even more to say when she discovered Harper's pregnancy.

When he had control of his emotions, he stepped away from the overpowering scent of her perfume. "You don't have any idea what you're talking about. What do you want?"

His mother ignored him for a long moment as she looked around the living room. Ridge saw it through her eyes—the expensive rug and furniture, the elaborate crown molding and beautiful fireplace, the priceless objet d'art. Was she evaluating the worth of everything here? It would do her no good. These things were his father's, and Dad wouldn't want her nosing around like a bloodhound trying to tree its prey.

"Your sister told me about the check you gave her. That's kind of you, Ridge, but don't you think you should split your father's estate with her? She's his child too."

He'd transferred ten million dollars to Willow, but even that wasn't enough to pacify his mother. He crossed his arms over his chest. "Dad wouldn't be happy I gave her what I did. She ignored him for most of her adult life. What's your will look like, Mom?"

Her cheeks colored as his barb hit home. "That's different."

"Of course it is."

The silence between them stretched into something uncomfortable, but he wasn't going to speak first. Pleading Willow's case wasn't why she'd come. His mother was the master of subtext. Her first attack was always subterfuge to cover her real agenda.

She glanced up at him. "I don't know how our relationship devolved to this degree." The twist of her lips should have spoken of sadness, but her eyes were expressionless.

He could have pointed out a thousand reasons for their estrangement, but he pressed his lips together and resisted. She'd tell him what this was all about eventually.

When he didn't answer, she put her hand on his crossed forearm. "I'd been talking to your father about letting me have the Monet painting. He never hung it, and it's in the attic. It would be perfect for my office. I'll be honest and tell you he hadn't said yes, but he hadn't said no either. He was thinking about it. Could I have it?"

He wanted to reject her request, but he found himself held by the sincerity in her blue eyes. She was his mother, after all. While he knew she was playing him, shouldn't he be kind? Shouldn't he forgive her even if she never asked for it?

And forgiving her meant he should turn his attention to the other elephant in the room—Harper's subterfuge.

He gathered his thoughts. "I don't know what painting you're referring to."

Her smile emerged, and this time it reached her eyes. "I can show you. I deal with a lot of depressed patients, and the moment I beheld that painting, it lifted my spirits. We were in Paris to celebrate our tenth anniversary, and your father bought it because I loved it."

"Why didn't he hang it?"

The light in her eyes died. "It was silly. A painter saw me in a sidewalk café and sat down. Your dad thought I'd made a date with him, and he never believed it was a chance meeting. That incident started the collapse of our marriage. No matter how hard I tried, he never forgave me even though it wasn't my fault. Your father could be hard and unforgiving."

The story took him aback. What else had he been wrong about? His mother, his father? He didn't know anymore.

"You can have it. I'll get it for you."

Harper could barely look at Ridge as she drove her Jeep to the jewelry store in Tampa. Even though she'd splashed cold water on her face since hearing Christina Jackson's snide comment, her cheeks still burned. She shouldn't be staying in the house with Ridge by herself.

When her condition became apparent, people would think he was the father.

She'd thought no one would know she was there, and to know his mother assumed the worst was a wake-up call to make other arrangements. She couldn't deny the fierce attraction she had for him, and it was dangerous being around him this much. She already had too many feelings for him welling up in her heart, and his reaction last night had made it clear he no longer trusted her.

If he ever had.

She pulled the Jeep into an empty spot in the lot right in front of the store and switched off the engine. "I hope we learn something today."

Ridge turned toward her. "You've been quiet. I hope my mom didn't upset you."

What did she say to that? She didn't want to cause more trouble between him and his family. She cleared her throat and shook her head. "I've been thinking about where to stay. I texted Sara to see if I could stay with her."

"She has to work, and you'll be alone during the day." His tone stayed measured, but his fingers tightened into fists.

Her phone dinged, and she received a message from Sara. "Looks like that won't work anyway. She's on special assignment down in Miami for a few days."

"Good. I want to make sure you're safe."

She dared a peek at him, and the warmth in his dark

eyes made her face flush. "Did you tell your mom why I was there?"

"No. I thought if she assumed the worst, she wouldn't tell anyone. If I told her you were in danger, I was afraid she might blab it around to people and the attacker would hear about it. I didn't like it, but I didn't see a good alternative."

He was always thinking about the best course of action. Not every man thought through things the way he did.

"We'd better go inside."

Brown and Sons Jewelers was in a strip mall that looked like it dated from the sixties. The parking lot was mostly empty as she stepped into the shimmering heat. It was only ten so it was going to be a scorcher of a day. The blast of the air-conditioning was a welcome relief after the humidity frizzing her hair.

An older man with fine white hair and long thin limbs placed a velvet tray of rings in the display case and smiled their way. "Good morning. How can I help you?"

He might be old enough to have worked here in the late sixties. Harper reached into her purse and pulled out the bag containing the bracelet. She shook it out into her palm and held it out to him. "Have you ever seen this?"

He gently picked it up from her palm and examined it. "I think this is my father's work. We do custom jewelry here and have been in business since 1955. I'm the son part of Brown and Sons."

She glanced at Ridge as he stepped forward. "Is your father here?"

Mr. Brown pursed his lips. "He lives at Blue Heaven Assisted Living. He had a stroke, but his mind is still sharp."

"Could we take this to him and see if he remembers who he made it for?"

Mr. Brown stared at Ridge. "You make it sound very urgent."

Ridge nodded. "We think it might be related to a murder, and we need to know who owns this bracelet. Would he remember?"

Mr. Brown put the bracelet on a velvet display pad and snapped a picture with his phone. "He might, but I don't think it would do you much good to talk to him. His speech is garbled, and he's very hard to understand. Let me show him a picture of it. I might be able to find it in some old books too. We've always taken pictures of our custom work. It might take me a few days to find it though. I'll see my father tonight, and maybe he will remember."

"We appreciate it." Ridge passed over a business card. "Here's my number. You can call or text me when you find out any information."

Mr. Brown fingered the card and slid it into his shirt pocket. "A murder, you say? Might I ask the victim's name?"

"It was Judy Russo," Ridge said. "Maybe your father will have heard the name. The murder happened a long time ago— 1971. Though it's a cold case, we think it might be related to a current attack on Ms. Taylor here."

"Past sins have a way of affecting the present. I'll let you know what I find."

A man with ropy arms covered in tattoos came in, and Ridge took Harper's hand to steer her to the other side of his body. That automatic and highly protective gesture took her breath away.

Once they were outside, she slid into the driver's seat and started the engine. "Now what?"

He clicked on his seat belt. "Now we go to Weeki Wachee and see if Grace ever met your mother."

34

The Wrangler smelled of hot peppers and cheese. Harper had stopped at Chipotle, and they scarfed down burritos on the way to Weeki Wachee. The silence between them had been awkward, and several times she wanted to ask him again if he could forgive her deception.

The problem was she wasn't sure she was ready for his answer.

Rain drizzled as she stepped from the parked Jeep and hurried to the auditorium with Ridge. They had an hour before the three o'clock show, and they found Grace in the office with her reading glasses perched on her nose. She turned away from a filing cabinet. She had on bright-blue yoga pants and a blue patterned top.

Her hazel eyes widened when she saw them. "I wasn't expecting you today. Did you find Joe?"

"He's dead," Ridge said. "Shot when he broke into a home in 1975."

Harper locked down her surprise. When had he heard that?

"It's no wonder. That guy was a weird one." Grace motioned

for them to follow her to a small room containing only a battered card table and chairs. It smelled of stale coffee. "How can I help you?"

"I never mentioned my mother's name was Lisa Taylor," Harper said. "Her best friend told me she came here to find out about Judy's death. She had been in Cocoa Beach with my father, and a woman approached her and told her to look into the death of a Weeki Wachee mermaid, so she came here. Did you speak to her?"

Grace scrunched her nose and tucked a wisp of dyed red hair behind her ear. "I think I did, though I don't remember the name. A woman came to see me and asked me if I knew Judy's boyfriend. She showed me a picture of herself with a man and asked if it was him. I couldn't tell her since I'd never met Judy's boyfriend. I told her about Judy's murder though."

Ridge took a step closer to her. "You saw Lisa's boyfriend?"

"Well, a picture anyway." She frowned. "Let me try to remember. That was a long time ago."

The pause while she thought about it seemed to last forever. Maybe this was the break they'd been waiting for.

Grace finally nodded. "Nice looking man, though older than her. He had wings of white in his blond hair. Snappy dresser, too, all slick. This would have been maybe 1989? I can't remember for sure, but it seemed strange she'd be asking questions about Judy's boyfriend after all that time."

"Any hint to who he might have been?" Ridge asked.

Grace's brow puckered. "They were standing in front of a Datsun Bluebird. Lisa, if that was her name, said her boyfriend had just bought it for her."

"Was that the car she wrecked?" Harper asked.

"I'll text Don Ward and find out." Ridge typed away on his

phone. "He was going to try to get the notes from the investigation. It should include photos at the scene."

Ridge's phone dinged, and he glanced at it. "It was a Datsun Bluebird. He's got the records for us and says we can stop by and look at them."

Another lead to follow. Harper thanked Grace and followed Ridge to the door. The skies had darkened, and the drizzle had turned to a downpour.

"Great. My hair is going to look like I stuck my finger in an electric socket."

"I'll go get the Jeep. Wait here." He took the keys from her, pulled open the door, and ran through the rain and puddles to the Wrangler.

A pretty brunette came to stand beside her. "That man's a keeper. Guys seem to have lost a sense of chivalry lately."

Harper's heart squeezed at what she'd done to him. "He is a good man."

Ridge stopped the Jeep by the door and got out, leaving the driver's door open. She dashed out into the rain to leap through the open door. The brief contact with the rain had plastered her hair to her scalp.

She yanked the door shut and grabbed the napkin he handed her. After mopping her face, she noticed his stare. "What?"

"You look beautiful with frizzy hair." His gaze left her face. "Let's go see what we can find out from Don. I feel like we're on to something. I'm not sure what that something is, but it feels like progress."

His tone was softer than it had been all day. Was he going to forgive her?

The pounding rain left streams of water on the pavement by the time Harper pulled her Jeep onto the highway. She gripped the steering wheel with both hands. "The Wrangler keeps wanting to hydroplane."

"Want me to drive?"

She shook her head. "I'll put it in four-wheel drive. I know this old Jeep pretty well." She pulled off and messed with the transmission lever, then drove back onto the road.

The inclement weather had evidently deterred other drivers, and he spotted only a few other vehicles heading their direction.

He glanced at Harper, whose focus was intent on the road. She hadn't had much to say since they left Weeki Wachee, and he knew she was still mulling over his reaction to her news. He pushed away the stab of guilt. What had she expected? Joy and congratulations?

The Jeep hit a patch of water, and the rear tires swung to the left as the vehicle began to hydroplane. She fought with the wheel and managed to get it under control again. Glancing behind them, he spotted a gray car bearing down on them. The guy would run into trouble if he didn't slow down on these treacherous roads, but maybe the driver couldn't see them. The rain was so heavy the windshield wipers were having trouble keeping up.

The big car behind them continued to gain ground. "There's a car coming up fast behind us. You might want to slow down and let him pass," Ridge said.

Harper braked to decelerate and let the other vehicle pass, but instead of swerving into the passing lane, the gray car crept closer until its bumper was inches from her Jeep.

Ridge sat twisted in the seat to watch what the guy was doing. "What the heck?"

Harper glanced in the rearview mirror. "What's wrong?"

"That guy behind us is still tailgating. It's not safe in this weather."

The words had barely left his lips when the big vehicle smashed into the Jeep's bumper. The steering wheel spun in Harper's hands, and the vehicle veered to the right. The right front tire hit the gravel, which pulled it farther off the road and toward the field.

The Wrangler's wheels sank into the muddy ground, and the resistance slowed the vehicle enough so Harper could steer them back toward the pavement. The Jeep came to a stop with the front left wheel on gravel and the other tires in mud and water.

"Are you all right?" The racket from the rain on the hood nearly drowned out Harper's frantic question.

"We're okay." He twisted in the seat to try to see out the back window at the vehicle that had struck them. It had felt deliberate, and he was reaching for his phone to dial 911 when the glass in his window shattered. Before he could react, a stun gun came down on his bare right arm.

The jolt was like nothing he'd ever experienced. The voltage shot up his arm and neck, then spread through the rest of his body in a painful contraction that seemed never ending. He was conscious of Harper's door being opened and of her screaming his name as she was yanked out from under the steering wheel. Try as he might, he couldn't break the grip of the electrical shock until the attacker pulled his arm back out of the broken window.

Ridge slumped against the seat for what seemed like an eternity but was only a few minutes until mobility coursed back into his muscles. He fumbled for the door and managed to thrust it open and stagger out into the pounding rain as the big car roared off into the downpour.

His mind was still foggy as he stumbled back to the Jeep and grabbed his phone. It took several tries to punch in 911 and reach the dispatcher. He told her what had happened. When he came to himself, he was lying beside the Wrangler with his face turned up into the rain. He blinked and sat up, then looked for his phone. Sirens blared in the distance, and he staggered to his feet to wave down the police car.

He should have been in the Jeep chasing after Harper's abductors, but instead he'd passed out and been lying out there in the rain for who knew how long. If anything happened to her, it would be his fault.

The police car stopped behind the Jeep, and he stumbled back toward the two officers who got out into the rain. They had to find her.

Harper's arms ached where the man had grabbed her. She'd fought with all her might, desperate to get back to Ridge, who had been rigid in the grip of that stun gun thing. The man who'd grabbed her had dragged her to a gray Cadillac, then thrown her into the trunk.

The claustrophobic darkness pressed in on every side, and her scraped cheek lay pressed against the rough fabric of the trunk's carpeting. Rain drummed against the top of the car, and the tires threw up more water that struck the bottom. The sound in both directions drowned out any other noise and added to her disorientation. She patted her pocket for her phone, but of course she'd left it at Oliver's.

She touched her belly. Was the baby all right? There was no pain or blood to indicate that the accident had harmed the baby.

She reached out and tried to find some kind of weapon in the dark, but the space was totally empty except for her. There didn't seem to be a void beneath the floor for a spare tire and tire tool either. She was trapped here until her captor chose to release her.

Her lungs ached, and she forced herself to slow down her breaths until her hands quit shaking. She prayed over and over again for Ridge. Could that stun gun kill him? His agonized expression played over in her mind in a terrifying sequence.

Where were her attackers taking her? Annabelle had warned them, but there'd been no way to anticipate an attack like this out on the highway. The rain had played right into their enemies' hands. As far as she could recall, there'd been no other vehicles on the road at the time of the attack. No one would have had a chance to get the license plate number or make and model of the Cadillac.

It felt as though the car had hurtled through darkness forever by the time it slowed, and she thought they were on city streets. She had no idea of direction or location. The car stopped and started, turned and drove more until the tires rolled over a slight hump as though up a drive. The vehicle stopped, and she rolled to her back and sat up as far as she could in anticipation of the trunk lid opening.

If only she had a weapon.

She clenched her fists and waited. The lock clicked and the trunk lid opened, letting the rain strike her in the face. She sat up the rest of the way and tried to scramble out, but a man in a ski mask grabbed her arm. He hauled her out the rest of the way and propelled her through the puddles toward a small building nestled in pines and southern oaks. There were no other houses around as far as she could see, and her mouth went dry.

She was out here facing this alone and without help.

But no, that wasn't right. No matter what happened, God was with her in this. He might choose to save her or he might not, but either way, he had her by the hand.

Where was the driver? She hadn't seen him get out. She heard splashing behind her and saw the gray car glide out of the drive. Its lights moved down the road and disappeared as the tree line blocked them out.

The hitch in her chest smoothed, and she lifted her head. If she quit fighting him, his grip might loosen. She eyed the surroundings through the rain again. The trees and vegetation to her right were thick. If she could get away from her captors, she might escape detection in the foliage.

She yelled so it would carry over the pounding rain. "You're hurting me. You can let go. I know I can't escape."

His grip only loosened a fraction, not enough to wrest free. "I don't trust you."

"Where are you taking me, and what do you want?"

He didn't answer as they reached the building. The door was unlocked and he opened it, then pushed her inside to a brightly lit space. It looked like an operating room, all clean tile and stainless-steel counters. An operating table and lights occupied the center of the room.

He released her arm to lock the door before he pocketed the key. "This way."

He pushed her through the room to an open door on the far side. It had no window, so she got only the vague impression of a bed.

She glanced back at the operating space. "What is this place?"

"Just a spot to keep you for now." He reached past her and flipped on the light, which illuminated the bed with its stark white sheets. Another room opened to a bathroom with a small sink and shower.

She turned to him and splayed her hands in a pleading gesture. "Look, I don't understand what this is all about."

She guessed his height at about six feet. His muscles were thick and ropy, even the ones on his neck. Likely a bodybuilder. His eyes behind the ski mask were dark brown and stony. No sympathy there, and she didn't really expect any.

"You'll know soon enough. It's not for me to tell you."

So he was a hired gun. She'd suspected as much, but she hoped to find out something about the motive behind all these events.

"Did you kill Oliver Jackson?" She blurted out the question, then took a step back.

His gaze never faltered, but he turned around and went out the door, slamming it behind him. That was enough of an answer since he hadn't seemed surprised. She didn't understand why she would be a target, but she had to find a way out of here before the person who hired him showed up.

Maybe there was a window in the bathroom. She peeked into the room, but no window. Could she find some way to pick the lock on the door? She went over to the lock and peered at it. It was a dead bolt, locked from the outside.

She was stuck in here and at the mercy of her captors.

35

The rain had finally stopped, and the oppressive humidity steamed the air like fog. Harper had been gone nearly four hours, and the encroaching darkness made him feel even more helpless. How did they go about finding her? Gray Cadillacs were hardly scarce in this part of Florida. The only hope was if the car's bumper or grill had been damaged in the blow to the back of her Jeep.

The police car reached Dunedin and stopped at the Coffee Shop. Ridge pulled the Jeep in behind the cop car. Scott was supposed to meet him here, and he recognized Scott's car parked along the street.

He got out and approached the police car. "Detective Rice is here. Thanks for the escort."

Scott exited the Coffee Shop with two cups in his hand. "You don't look so good. Getting stunned can do that to you."

"It wasn't much fun."

Scott gestured to an outside table and sat in the chair closest to the door. "No news about Harper's whereabouts? My mom is beside herself. She's texted me every few minutes telling me I have to find her. Can you go over the events for me step by step?"

Ridge dropped into the other chair and went through every-thing that had happened, including the sudden attack with the stun gun. "She was screaming my name as the guy dragged her away." His voice trembled, and he took a quick sip of hot coffee. "I failed her."

"It wasn't your fault. A stun gun is impossible to fight. Those guys knew what they were doing. There were two, right?"

"As far as I know. I didn't see who grabbed Harper, because I couldn't turn my head while I was being paralyzed by the gun. There were at least two though because someone grabbed her while someone else attacked me. I heard two doors slam before the Caddy drove off."

One of the worst moments of his life had been hearing that car drive off with Harper in it while he could do nothing. He'd never felt so helpless, and it was an agonizing sensation.

"I've been in touch with the detectives handling the case, and they have no leads. They can't stop every gray Caddy out there, but her picture has been disseminated and cops are looking for her. That won't help much if they stashed her in the trunk. And it's been long enough they probably have reached their destination."

Scott sipped his coffee and stared at Ridge over the rim of his cup. "There has to be some tie between Harper and my mom. They didn't even know each other existed before the DNA test and had no contact."

Ridge set his coffee down. "Harper and I talked about this last night. I've racked my brain on how their relationship could play into this. Revenge against their dad maybe? Perhaps someone is trying to use them as a hostage to flush him out, though as far as I know, he doesn't know they exist. No father has popped up on their reports. And how did my dad play into this? Harper thinks the killer believed Dad could identify him as the person who attacked her underwater."

A thought hit him. Just before Harper had told him about her pregnancy, he'd wondered if Dad had gone back to trying to discover her father's identity. Could there be something about that in his desk? Maybe her father had figured out he was being investigated.

He told Scott what Harper had said. "Let's take a look at Dad's desk."

"We can check that out." Scott frowned. "I'm going to review Mom's DNA report. I want to see who all had access to their blood connection. A revenge motive sounds possible, that is, if this is all about their being related."

"You have any other theories? It's the only thing connecting them."

"Not the only thing. When you and Harper showed up, my grandmother's homicide case was reopened. Maybe the murderer heard about that and wants to stop us from solving it. And the detective investigating Lisa Taylor's death believed it wasn't accidental. I think it's more likely related to my grandmother's murder than to the accident that killed Harper's mom. There would be no connection to my mom if that was the underlying cause."

"True enough. Let's focus on looking at who had access to those DNA results and who might have heard about you reopening Judy's murder case. We don't have much time though. Harper is in their hands, and I doubt they will let her live long."

Scott whipped out his phone. "I'll call Mom and get her log-in information." He placed the call and jotted down something in his notebook. "Got it. I'll grab my laptop in the car."

He sprinted to his car and pulled a bag out of the passenger seat, then returned and handed it to Ridge. "See what you can find while I call in and find out what I can about the company who tested their DNA."

Ridge took the computer and the notebook and logged into Annabelle's profile. It didn't take long to discover the only close match was to Harper, but there were four other matches who appeared to be distant cousins. Any one of them could be the culprit.

He jotted down the information and slid it across the table to Scott, who had ended his call. "Could you see if your mom would contact these distant cousins? If we can get their names, it would be a good place to start."

"I'm sure she would." Scott tapped out a text message and got back an almost immediate response. "She's doing it now, but it could be days before they answer. We have no way of knowing how quick they'll be."

"Can we get a court order to reveal their identity?"

"We don't have any real evidence yet, so no, we can't get that. I should have a phone number for the company owner soon though."

"Maybe you can sweet-talk the owner into helping me."

Scott raised his brows. "Doubtful. Companies aren't usually willing to disclose confidential information without a court order."

Ridge took another gulp of his coffee. He couldn't sit here and do nothing when Harper was in mortal danger, but he didn't know where to look. "Let's check Dad's files."

Ridge flipped on the lights in his dad's office. The scent of his father—cloves and cologne—made him wince. He'd never inhale the smell of his father during an embrace again.

The overhead light was dimmer than he'd like, so he flipped on the bookshelf lights as well. This might take a while, but he wasn't sure where else to search.

He moved to the desk and began pulling out drawers. "I'll take this set of files, and you can look in the ones on the other side," he told Scott.

The detective nodded and reached into a desk drawer to extract an armful of files he dumped on his side of the big desk. He picked up the first folder and began to peruse it.

Ridge sorted through his first file full of utility bills. Astronomical ones but then this place was huge. He found his dad's telephone bill and glanced over it. There were several calls to a private investigator.

"I think I found something." He showed the number to Scott. "If we don't discover the report here, we could try calling the guy to see what he found out."

He laid the bill aside and continued to scan through the files. Scott worked in silence, too, and half an hour later, they'd turned over every piece of paper in the desk. Their only clue was the investigator's number.

Scott picked up the telephone bill again. "The first call was a month ago and the last one was a week before Oliver's death. It's possible the investigator couldn't discover anything."

"Or he was still working on it and was reporting progress."

"That too. I'll try giving him a call." Scott whipped out his phone and placed the call.

Ridge heard him leave a message asking for a call back. Scott identified himself as a police detective and referenced

Dad's murder. That would either make the investigator call right away or run for the hills if he knew something he didn't want to divulge.

Ridge's phone rang. He didn't recognize the number, but he answered it anyway.

"Ridge? This is Sara Kavanagh. I just heard about Harper being kidnapped." Her voice held an edge of panic. "What can you tell me?"

"It's true." He ran through the events on the highway. "We're looking for her and trying to follow any trail that might lead us to her."

"She's pregnant!"

"I know," he said evenly. "She told me."

Sara swallowed hard on the other end of the line. "I've been trying to think of anything that might help us figure out who is behind this, and I keep coming up empty. Please let me know right away when you find her."

"I will." He ended the call as Scott's phone rang.

While Scott talked to the caller, Ridge went back to the desk. Had they missed anything? He glanced at the bookshelves and remembered all the papers in his dad's safe. He'd been on a mission looking for the will when he'd opened it last time. Something might be there.

He opened the bookcase and revealed the safe, then punched in the code. He wrinkled his nose at the stale air inside, then sorted through the stuff, pushing the stacks of money to one side. He removed the rest of the contents and took them to the desk as Scott ended his call and joined him.

"The videos I took in to be digitized are ready, and one of my buddies will drop them off here. We can take a look at them and see if we can find any clue as to who killed Judy. More papers?"

Ridge nodded. "From Dad's safe. He might have locked up the report until he was ready to talk to Harper about it." He pushed part of the pile to the other side of the desk for Scott to go through and continued to examine the documents he'd kept.

Scott held up a thick envelope. "This is from the investigator." He opened the flap and pulled out the sheaf of papers inside, then unfolded them and laid them on the desk between them so they could review them together.

Ridge's pulse quickened and he scanned them. "This just looks like a contract with the payment spelled out."

He wanted to slam his fist into a wall or something. Every moment that passed brought more fear and uncertainty. Annabelle hadn't been harmed. He could only hope and pray they wouldn't hurt Harper either.

36

Harper had paced the ten-by-ten room and prayed for what seemed like hours though her watch indicated it had only been ninety minutes. She stepped to the door, then retraced her steps to the opposite wall. She'd stripped the bed, and the mattress lay on the floor, but she'd still found nothing to help her get out of this place.

Was Ridge alive? The question had spun around and around in her brain through these long hours. She couldn't bear it if he was dead. She'd been kidding herself for years that she didn't find him appealing. Now she might have lost any future she might have had with him.

If he'd have her and the baby. She touched her belly. There'd been no sign of an imminent miscarriage.

Her mouth felt dry and cottony, so she went to the bathroom and cupped her hands under the stream of cold water. She slurped it down and wiped her wet face with the back of her hand since there were no paper towels or a hand towel. There was no soap either. Nothing to indicate her captor intended for her to shower or stay here long.

Her heart kicked in her chest. Did that mean her death was already planned?

She retraced her steps to the door and pounded on it. "Let me out!"

Every previous time she'd shouted for release there had been no answer. But this time she heard a sliding sound. Someone was throwing open the dead bolt. If only she had some kind of weapon—a lamp, a drawer, anything. Unarmed, she crouched toward the door with her hands clenched. When the door swung open, she leaped toward the woman in a white uniform entering her room.

She body-slammed the woman, and they both went down in a tangle of limbs with Harper on top. The kit of supplies the nurse had in her hand went sliding across the floor. Harper leaped to her feet and charged through the door toward the exit past the operating table.

She didn't see her kidnapper until her hand was on the doorknob. He came at her from the left, and desperate to escape before he grabbed her again, she yanked open the door and took a step through the threshold.

His hand came down on the bruises he'd left on her forearm, and she winced but continued to rush for the outside. He was too strong though, and he hauled her back inside, then shut and locked the door.

The ski mask was gone and seeing his face shot tremors through her. He had a lurid scar on his left cheek, and his dark-brown eyes held deadly intent as he spun her around to face him. He gripped her shoulders with both hands, and his fingers bit into her flesh. She smelled sweat under the overpowering scent of his cologne.

She'd seen him somewhere before. The pizza place maybe?

"Nice try." He pulled a length of rope from his pocket and

tied her hands in front of her, then turned her toward the bedroom door and goose-stepped her back.

The nurse was just getting herself up off the floor. She was young and looked like she was barely out of college. Her blue eyes were wary, and she patted her mousy hair back into place.

The nurse gestured toward the bed. "I need the mattress put back."

Harper's captor shoved her to the corner. "Don't move." He locked the door, then heaved the mattress back onto the bed before returning to Harper. "Sit." He jabbed his forefinger at the bed.

He didn't wait for her to comply but marched her to the bed and forced her to sit down. His grip was hard and unyielding, and though she tried to get back up, he kept her seated.

He nodded to the nurse. "Get it done. Once this is over, the doctor will take care of my little boy."

She had retrieved her supplies and approached with the caddy in hand. Harper spied syringes, alcohol swabs, and other medical items. She tried to jerk away again, but the man held her left arm in a tight grip. He moved out of the way while still keeping hold of her.

The nurse took out a blood pressure cuff and slipped it onto Harper's arm. She pumped it up and put the cold stethoscope on the bend of Harper's elbow, then began to let out the air. Once she noted the blood pressure in her notebook, she listened to Harper's lungs and chest, then took out an elastic band.

Harper shook her head. "No, I'm not sitting here for this." She bit the man's arm as hard as she could and tasted blood, but he didn't even flinch.

"It's your funeral, girlie." He sat on the bed beside her and dragged her onto his lap, then wrapped both of his arms around hers from behind and held her firmly in place. "Do it," he said to the nurse.

She approached with a wary expression. "If you flail around, this will hurt. A lot. I have a sedative if I need to use it, but I guess you would prefer not to be knocked out."

The fight drained out of Harper. She couldn't struggle if they sedated her, and the sedative wouldn't be good for the baby. She let the nurse take vials of blood, and then her captor finally released her. She sprang off his lap and shuddered when he gave a coarse laugh at her distaste.

"I wouldn't mind feeling you up again." He leered at her and went toward the door. "Milly, get her some food. Even a condemned person should have a last meal."

Condemned? Did that mean they were going to kill her? Why not just do it instead of bringing her here?

Harper didn't understand any of this. Her arms ached from being manhandled, and her head throbbed. Food might give her strength—and a tray might bring a weapon with it.

Ridge put his coffee cup on the counter in Dad's kitchen. "I can't sit here and do nothing. Maybe we should drive around searching for gray Cadillacs."

Scott nodded toward the front of the house. "While I was waiting for you at the Coffee Shop, I watched for gray Caddies. I saw three. One had two kids in the backseat. Another one drove past with two elderly women in it. And that was just in the span of fifteen minutes. They are common."

Ridge clenched his right hand into a fist. What could he

do? His phone rang, and he saw his sister's face on the screen. "Willow?"

"Ridge, I'm on the porch. Could you let me in?"

"Be right there." He walked through the house to the front door and let his sister in.

She wore heels and a suit very much like the one he'd seen their mother in earlier in the day. Her white shirt was a bit creased and tendrils strayed from the French roll on her head.

"Are you okay?" He didn't know when he'd seen her even a little bit disheveled.

She waved her hand. "I'm fine. It was a rough day. One of my patients had a meltdown and attacked me." Her voice wobbled.

He took her in his arms. "You're shaking."

"My receptionist had to call the police. It got a little intense." She pulled away and fumbled for a tissue from her purse, then mopped her wet cheeks. "I'm not usually so emotional. I think it's Dad's death. Have you heard when we can have his funeral?"

"I had a message from the coroner's office that they've released his body. I need to call the funeral home, but there's been an emergency." He told her about being stun gunned and Harper's abduction.

She put her hand to her mouth. "There's no sign of her?" Her lingering gaze rested on Scott, who straightened.

"No, nothing."

He squinted in the dim light at the diamond-and-opal bracelet glittering on her wrist. He took her by the hand and pulled her closer. It was an exact match for the one that had been found in Judy's hand when she was murdered.

Willow pulled her hand away. "What's wrong?"

"Where'd you get that bracelet?"

"It was Grandma's. This was one of the pieces Mom gave me. Isn't it beautiful?"

Grandma? She'd been gone about ten years, so he couldn't ask her about it. How odd there were two identical bracelets out there.

"Do you know how she came to have it or its history?"

"Not much. Mom said there were three of them in existence. Grandma and two of her best friends had them made in 1969, I think it was."

So there were three of them. "Any idea who had the other two?"

Willow frowned and thought for a long moment. "I don't know if Mom ever said. She might remember though. She's always interested in genealogy. Is it important?"

"It might be a clue to who has Harper."

His sister looked deeply into his eyes, then nodded. "You really care about her, don't you?"

"Yes." His voice was hoarse. "We have to find her, save her."

Her pregnancy didn't matter anymore. He could love a child that wasn't his, and there was plenty of love to go around.

"Let me call Mom. She's more likely to cooperate if I ask."

That was an understatement. Ridge walked away to give her privacy. Scott came with him. "What do you know about your grandmother?"

"She came from money. Her dad owned a bunch of imported automobile sales stores all over the state. She went to a finishing school in England and married my grandfather when she was twenty-five. He was in the oil business."

"This plays into the clue we had that Judy's beau was from a wealthy family and so was his fiancée."

He watched his sister's body language and deduced she

was getting something from their mother. She was jotting down something on a notepad.

When she ended the call, she came toward them with a satisfied smile. "She said one of Grandma's friends is dead— Alice Goodwin. But the other one is still alive. Her name is Elizabeth Kennedy. She used to be Elizabeth Marshall before she was married, and her dad was Grandpa's partner."

"I've met her and her family. At least her husband and her son." Ridge looked at Scott. "It seems a long shot but it's all we've got. Can we talk to her?"

Scott checked the time. "It's only seven. I'll call it in and get the address. That's Tom's wife, right?"

"Yes."

The frail old man hadn't seemed as though he would live long, and Ridge hated to go busting in on a harebrained idea, but there was nowhere else to look, and he had to try something. Maybe Elizabeth would know something about how that bracelet came to be in Judy's possession.

While Scott walked off to call and get the Kennedys' address, Ridge walked his sister to her car. "Thanks for helping me, Willow. Be careful. I don't want anything to happen to you."

She tipped her head back and studied him. "Harper's changed you. You're softer somehow. Your defenses are on the ground."

"She's special. If we make it through this . . ." He stopped and swallowed down the lump forming in his throat. "I hope you take the time to get to know her. She didn't grow up with a silver spoon in her mouth like we did, but she's got grit and integrity. I was too ready to believe the worst about her, and I was wrong. It opened my eyes to how quick we embrace bitterness and lay blame when we shouldn't be making snap judgments about people. She's the one who told me I should give you the money. How about that?"

Willow blinked and took a step back. "I want to get to know her, too, Ridge. I'm grateful for a fresh start with you." Her lip quivered, and her eyes filled with tears. "I haven't been the best sister. I'm going to do better." She stood on tiptoe and brushed her lips across his cheek. "Let me know when you find her."

He laid his hand on Willow's shoulder. "I will."

She got in the car, and he shut the door behind her, then watched her taillights as she turned the corner. Harper had changed so much in his life. He had to find her and tell her what she meant to him.

37

August 1970

Who could resist Annabelle's blonde curls? Judy had dressed her daughter in a pink dress with lacy socks and white shoes. The bonnet on her head was the cutest thing she'd ever seen. "Daddy's other woman will be sure to back away when she sees you."

She lifted her daughter from the backseat "nest" she'd made for her with a crib mattress filling the space. Annabelle had played quietly with her Raggedy Ann doll and the other toys in the back during the long drive from Weeki Wachee to Clearwater.

Judy's stomach fluttered as she stared at the mansion in front of her. It had to cost the earth. Her orange shift dress had seemed so stylish and hip when she put it on this morning, but she realized with a sharp sense of dismay that this woman would likely have the top European fashions at her fingertips. Maybe she shouldn't have worn these white go-go boots. They felt too trendy and cheap now.

She pushed away the butterflies in her belly and carried Annabelle to the front door. She pressed the doorbell firmly and waited. No one came to the door. Had his fiancée seen her through the window and recognized her? Surely not.

She'd turned to go back to the car when she heard music playing. She followed the sound around to the back where the massive yard sloped down to the beautiful blue of Clearwater Bay. Seagulls squawked down on the dock, and the music nearly drowned out the sound of the waves.

She found her rival, dressed in a navy-blue polka-dot bathing suit, lying on a blanket in the yard. The Beatles sang "Lady Madonna" and the tune blasted from a transistor radio. The scent of Coppertone suntan oil hung heavy in the air and overlaid the salty breeze. Judy took in the woman's lovely shape with her taut and perfect stomach. A stomach that had never carried a baby. How did she compete with this woman's beauty and money? She'd felt the same way the first time they met. Judy's figure was hardly perfect any longer.

She dropped her gaze to her daughter's beautiful face. Annabelle was her ace in the hole. "Excuse me."

The woman lifted her head, and she quickly sat up and reached for a beach towel. She rose and wrapped herself in it. "I never thought to see you again." Her words were flat and hostile. "Do you want the money now?"

Judy shifted Annabelle to the other arm. "This is Annabelle."

The woman's gaze dismissed them both. "What do you want?"

"I want you to do the right thing and let him go. He loves us, you know. He's going to break the engagement to you, but you could make it easy on him."

"And why would I want to do that? He doesn't have the guts to leave me and all I can offer him."

"He's already introduced me to his father and told him he's

going to break up with you," Judy lied. "He wanted his father to meet his grandchild. If I were you, I'd want to save face and break the engagement myself. Then no one could say I'd been thrown over."

The woman's lids flickered, and the color ebbed from her face. "I don't believe you."

Judy shrugged. "Ask him yourself. He loves Annabelle, and he wants to make this right."

She forced herself not to look away. Not to show any fear. She had to give the performance of her life for Annabelle. Her beautiful daughter deserved more than a father who flitted in and out of her life. She deserved nice clothes and a beautiful home like this one. She deserved everything, and Judy was determined to get it for her. Even if she had to lie, cheat, or steal.

This standoff had to end. Her rival wrapped the towel more tightly around herself. "The wedding is in two weeks. I can't break it off now. I'd have to send back all the gifts that have been pouring in. My parents would be out all the money they've spent. You say I could save face, but I'd actually be blamed for causing a lot of trouble." She lifted a brow. "And I think you're lying."

Judy raised her chin. "Try me and find out."

"You can see yourself out, I'm sure. We're done here."

Judy knew fear when she smelled it. The two locked glares and squared off. Judy was sure she had won when her rival lowered her gaze and headed for the house.

~

Ridge connected the USB drive to his dad's huge-screen television in the media room and grabbed the remote to turn it on. "How many movies do we have here?"

Scott sat in one of the leather chairs in the home theater. "I think there were five."

This room had been a favorite spot over the years. He'd often shared a bowl of popcorn with his dad while they watched a movie or golf. Ridge could almost catch a hint of butter in the air, and though he knew it was his imagination, his eyes blurred with moisture.

He pushed back the memories to focus. Harper was counting on them. They had to figure this out quickly. The darkness outside was a reminder that she'd already been gone much too long. Was she even still alive?

He had to hold on to hope.

Ridge started the first film, and the grainy video started. It was in color, which surprised him. Judy must have had a decent camera for that decade. She smiled at the camera and waved. She was holding a tiny baby girl, presumably Annabelle, and Ridge saw Scott's soft smile at his mother's appearance.

"She was blonde even as a baby," Scott said. "Look at all those curls. Mom will like seeing this."

The movie played to the end, and Ridge started the next one. Judy was swimming with a manatee, and the movie recorded them through the glass at the mermaid auditorium. She seemed so carefree and happy with her dark-red hair floating around her in the water. The manatee bumped against her in a gentle nudge, and she rubbed its head.

"I wonder who is taking these movies?" Scott asked.

"Maybe Grace. We could ask her."

They watched a third movie with Annabelle rolling on the floor. A man's hand moved into view.

"Look at that ring," Scott said. "It's a navy ring. I'll bet that's my grandfather's hand."

There were a lot of navy rings out there, and it would be impossible to identify this one. These videos looked to be a bust, but there were two more. Ridge started the fourth one.

This one was of Annabelle sitting up with a small Raggedy Ann doll. This time a man stepped into view and scooped her up. His back was to the camera.

"I know that guy, but I can't place him. Turn around," Ridge said.

The guy backed out of view without showing his face.

"One more." Ridge started the last bit of footage.

The movie showed Judy sitting outside in the sunshine in front of some kind of spinning wheel. She was making a fine golden thread.

Ridge settled on a chair beside Scott. "I think that's byssus she's working with. Harper will want to watch this. That's a very thin thread, which must be how she managed to make such beautiful sea silk."

The camera zoomed in on more byssus lying on racks. Sliced lemons floated in bowls on a nearby table with byssus strands in the water.

"What's that for?" Scott asked.

"Sea silk is made by soaking the byssus in lemon juice, then letting it dry in the sun. It lightens it to that golden color."

This wasn't telling them much so far. He started to fast-forward through it, then paused as a woman came into view behind Judy. The woman was out of focus, but he could make out her dark hair and slim build.

He froze the video. "Who's that?"

"It's too fuzzy to really see her face." Scott pulled out his phone and pulled up a number. "Hey, can you go to the first video where the woman steps into view in the distance and see if you can enhance that for me? Email it to me when you're done." He ended the call and leaned forward in his chair. "Let it play. Maybe something will jump out at us."

Ridge started the video again.

The woman strolled through the background, then stopped and picked up something. Ridge froze the video again and studied it. "I think she's got a pen shell."

Could they be about to witness the actual murder? Ridge pressed Play again, but as the woman started toward Judy, Judy rose and moved straight to the camera. The video ended.

Ridge shut off the television. "She must have had it on a tripod."

"I think this might have been just before the murder," Scott said. "If she'd let it play, we might have seen it."

"If so, the murderer was a woman, which is a surprise."

"Could be the guy's fiancée, and she took Judy out before she could steal him away."

Ridge hadn't considered the possibility that the murderer might be a woman. "Remember when Kelly said a woman approached Lisa when she was at the beach with the boyfriend? She basically warned her off by telling her the guy she was with was dangerous and that she should investigate the murder of a mermaid. What if that was the fiancée trying to get Lisa to break it off with him?"

"It makes sense." Scott's phone dinged, and he turned it on. "The enhanced picture is here."

The picture came into view, and Ridge leaned over to study it with him. "I still can't make out the woman's face."

He'd been hoping for a better picture because he still felt he might know this woman. She'd be older now, of course, but he couldn't call up anything.

That's it then. No help from the videos.

38

The Kennedy mansion was one of those places you never forgot. Ridge had seen it during a home show once about ten years ago when he'd gone with his father, though he hadn't met the owners until the other night at the fund-raiser. The old-world style with its stucco and green tile roof felt like stepping back in time. The mansion sat on a large three-acre lot overlooking Clearwater Bay, and he could see the moon and stars glittering on the water. If he remembered right, the home had ten bedrooms, a couple of pools, a tennis court, and a basketball court.

The lavish boathouse held a yacht and two smaller boats, and a massive dock led down to the water. While Ridge could afford something like this if he wanted it, he couldn't imagine wandering around a thirteen-thousand-square-foot mausoleum. It would take a housekeeping army to keep it clean.

Scott spoke to the gate guard who let them in immediately. The wide brick drive wound through lush vegetation illuminated with lights. The drive curved back on itself in a circle driveway in front of massive steps and a circular porch.

"Nice digs," Scott said.

The lights came on in the front of the house as they got

out and approached the twelve-foot-high double doors. Ridge pressed the doorbell, and a young woman dressed in black slacks and a demure white blouse admitted them and led them across marble floors to a large living area. The fireplace took up a whole wall, and flames danced in its depths, chasing away the chill from the heavy rain.

Elizabeth Kennedy, dressed in a black dress and heels, rose and came toward them with her hand extended. "How nice to see you again, Ridge." Her smile faltered when her gaze fell on Scott who was holding out his badge. "Is this an official visit, Detective?"

Scott smiled and put his badge away. "Let's call it friendly. It's about an investigation, and we thought maybe you could help us." He nodded to Ridge.

Ridge had retrieved the bracelet from Harper's purse, and he pulled it from his pocket. "I wondered if you recognized this bracelet."

Her eyes went wide. "I haven't thought of that piece in forever. Mine is somewhere in my massive jewelry box."

"Could we see it?" Scott asked.

"Of course. Is this one your grandma's, Ridge? Or is it Alice's?"

So she'd known he was Laura Nicholson's grandson when they'd met at the fund-raiser. Why hadn't she mentioned it then?

"We don't know," he said. "It was found clutched in a murder victim's hand. This piece of evidence has just come to light. If you have yours and my sister has my grandmother's, this one must have belonged to Alice. What can you tell me about her?"

"I'll get mine for you." Elizabeth moved toward the door.

It wasn't until a shadow moved in the corner that Ridge realized Tom Kennedy was in the room. A faint hum came from his wheelchair as he turned it toward them, blocking Elizabeth's path. "What's this all about, Ridge?"

His voice quavered with weakness and age, and as he moved into the light, Ridge saw his yellow pallor. A blanket lay on his lap, and his hand trembled as he reached out toward Ridge.

Ridge took his hand and felt him quivering. It was a wonder he wasn't in the hospital. "You both met Harper Taylor at the fund-raiser."

"The beautiful artist, yes," Elizabeth said.

"She's been abducted, and we're trying to find her."

The old man let out a moan, and his wife hurried to his side. "Let me get your medicine." She fumbled through a basket of pill bottles and popped one open, then slipped a pill into her husband's mouth. "Maybe you should go lie down, Tom."

"No, no," he muttered.

Elizabeth turned back to them. "I don't understand why a bracelet found a long time ago would have anything to do with Harper."

"Quite frankly, neither do we," Scott said. "When she was taken, we decided to retrace everything we know, starting with the DNA test linking her to my mother."

Elizabeth's eyebrows winged up. "Your mother?"

"It was my grandmother, my mom's mother, who was murdered in 1970. Her name was Judy Russo."

Elizabeth stilled. "I don't think I know that name."

"DNA?" The wheelchair hummed again as Tom maneuvered it closer to them. "This is very confusing."

"I agree. Both my mom and Harper took a DNA test and found out they're half sisters. The day she found out about the connection, Harper was attacked while diving. Yesterday, my mother was abducted from her kitchen, but she was released when she told the kidnappers she was supposed to start cancer treatment. There have been several unsettling incidents ever since the two women found out they were related."

There was something in the tenseness of the old man's demeanor that Ridge didn't understand. "Someone in a gray Cadillac forced Harper's Jeep off the road today. I was stun-gunned and Harper was abducted in broad daylight on I-275. We haven't been able to find her."

"This is terrible. I'm so sorry." Tom wheeled around abruptly and moved from the room. "I'm not feeling well. I'd like to rest now. I'm sorry this has happened to Harper, and I hope you find her soon."

"I hope so too. She's pregnant." He hoped that news might make them more willing to help, but the man continued to move away.

The tires hissed along the marble floors, and Tom disappeared from sight around the hallway corner.

Elizabeth's heels clicked on the marble, and she moved to a wet bar on one wall. "Would you like a drink? I think I need one after this terrible story."

"No, thank you, ma'am," both men said in unison.

"What about Alice Goodwin?" Ridge asked. "What can you tell us about her? Did she have a boyfriend in the navy who nearly broke up with her?"

"Alice did marry a navy man, but there was never even a hint of scandal as far as I know. We stayed friends until her death, and I can assure you she would never have murdered anyone, not even a rival. She was a gentle soul. Too gentle, really. People rode roughshod over her, including her husband." She poured herself a glass of wine. "I wish I could help you, but I'm clueless on this."

Tom had seemed upset, but was it because of Harper's abduction or because he was ill? Ridge didn't see any way of getting to the truth.

He and Scott exited the house and got in the car. "They know something." Scott started the engine.

"I think so too. There's a son. Let's try talking to him. I've got his address."

———

Perspiration beaded on Harper's forehead, and she didn't feel well. She'd only eaten a couple of spoonfuls of her soup before she detected a strange taste under the peppers and tomatoes. She'd pushed it away, but had it been soon enough? Her limbs trembled, and she went to the bathroom. She sank to her knees in front of the toilet and stuck her finger down her throat until she was sure she'd vomited up every drop of the soup.

They'd drugged her soup. Or tried to poison her.

She rinsed her mouth and felt better. That strange floaty feeling was beginning to dissipate. She went back to the bedroom and stretched out on the bed. While it felt wrong to just lie here, she'd already exhausted every escape option. Rest might be the thing that flipped her between escape and confinement.

Or life and death.

What did it mean that the nurse had checked her out and taken her blood? Had she stumbled into some kind of organ-harvesting ring? She'd heard of things like that, but they'd seemed too far-fetched to be believable, but this was clearly about something medical.

And Ridge? Was he dead, or out there looking for her? She prayed he was all right and that he'd come busting through the door at any moment, but the sane part of her brain whispered it would be impossible. She'd been in the trunk for a long time, and Ridge would have no idea how to track her down. She doubted he'd gotten the license plate of the car—not when he'd been stunned. If he was even still alive.

Tears leaked from the corners of her eyes, and she sat up. She wouldn't lose hope. God saw her in this place. She had to hold on to faith.

She heard a faint disturbance on the other side of the door— banging and someone shouting. She vaulted from the bed and rushed to press her ear against the door.

"Sir, please step away from the door." Her captor's words were measured but respectful.

"Get out of my way!"

Harper stepped away when the dead bolt clicked. The door opened, and a man in a wheelchair looked up at her. He was familiar, but it took several moments to place him.

Tom Kennedy. She'd met him at the fund-raiser that felt like a million years ago. He appeared frailer, and he had a scary yellowish pallor. His hands trembled on the arms of his wheelchair, and his blue eyes were rheumy.

"Mr. Kennedy?"

He beckoned to her with a shaky hand. "Come with me. I'm busting you out of here. There will be time for explanations later."

He didn't have to urge her. She shot through the door and past her captor, who was on the phone and gesturing wildly.

He dropped the phone and reached out to grab her arm. Mr. Kennedy screeched and fiddled with the controls on the wheelchair. The chair jerked forward and slammed into the younger man's leg.

He yelped and the grip on Harper's arm loosened enough for her to pull free. The old man backed up and hit her captor's leg again.

The big man danced away from the wheelchair. "You old coot, what's wrong with you?" When Harper stepped toward the door, he grabbed her arm again.

The old man set his jaw. "I'm taking her out of here. My chauffeur is waiting in the car. We're leaving now."

"No you aren't." The big guy gestured to the nurse who appeared through another doorway.

She held several needles. "We've been given the go-ahead to prep them."

"No!" Mr. Kennedy moved his chair toward the exit and fumbled with the doorknob.

The nurse approached with a needle. "There, there, Mr. Kennedy. You're going to be feeling much better very soon."

He held out his hand. "Stay away from me!" He fiddled with the controls, and the chair rammed into the nurse. Several syringes went flying and broke. Their contents spilled onto the concrete floor.

The nurse cursed under her breath, then narrowed her eyes and approached him again. Before he could protest further, she slipped the needle into his arm and pressed the plunger. "I'm sorry, sir. It's for the best."

His eyelids began to flutter. "No, no, not her. Please, let her go." His words slurred, and his head fell back.

The nurse went to the operating table. "Bring her over here. I thought she'd be out by now. She must not have eaten the soup."

Harper had been right—the soup was drugged. She tried to escape the man's grip, but he dragged her toward the oper- ating table. "What's going on? Please let me go."

"Sorry, sweetheart." He didn't sound sorry—he sounded gleeful.

"You said something about the doctor helping your little boy. Is he sick?"

His eyelids flickered. "He needs a kidney transplant. Maybe yours will work for him." He dragged her to the side of the table. "Get on it."

"No." She yanked on her arm again.

"Have it your own way." He swept her into his arms and plunked her down on the table.

She immediately scrambled to the other side to slide off, but he held her fast as the nurse approached with an injection. Harper's chest squeezed at the sight of the needle, but she couldn't go anywhere with the big man's painful grip holding her in place.

"Why are you doing this to me? What's happening?"

"The old guy needs your liver. Sorry." The nurse plunged the needle into Harper's arm.

She wrenched away and the needle popped out, leaving some of the liquid in the syringe. Enough entered her body that warmth began to spread up her neck, and her mind went fuzzy.

She sagged and closed her eyes. Liver? But she couldn't survive without a liver.

39

It was all going to come out her way. Judy smiled and smoothed the fine fabric hanging on a rack in the yard. Lightened by the lemon juice, the sea silk shimmered in the sunlight. Her radio playing "(Sittin' On) the Dock of the Bay" added to her sense of satisfaction.

Huey dropped his arm around her. "It's beautiful, Judy. I think this is going to make us rich. Once people see it, it's going to be a status symbol to own something made from sea silk, just like it was in ancient times. It's so unique. I can't believe you figured out how to make such a fine fabric." He picked up a piece and squeezed it in his fist. "It compresses to nothing."

She'd read every ancient reference to sea silk, and the final product she'd come up with seemed to mimic all the texts. "Once we have the business established, you can break your engagement."

He hugged her. "I was so certain this would free me that I already told her, honey. She wasn't happy, but she accepted it. She only asked that I not tell anyone for a couple of weeks until she could make plans to go to Paris. She didn't want to be here to be around all the questions."

She threw her arms around his neck. "Oh, Huey! I'm so happy. I'll work hard, and we'll be free of her money. You'll see."

He dropped a lingering kiss onto her lips, then stepped back. "I have to get to work. Where's Annabelle?"

"With Grace and Silvia. I wanted to concentrate on finishing up the fabric, and Grace offered to take her."

"I'll stop by later tonight to see her. Love you."

"Love you too."

She watched him walk off across the grass to his car, a new Plymouth Road Runner his fiancée had bought him for his birthday. One day they'd be able to afford things like that themselves. He'd no longer feel he had to stay with that woman because of money. She'd understood he had ambitions, and his fiancée's wealthy family could provide so much opportunity for him, but money wasn't everything. Annabelle had wrapped her little fingers around his heart, and he'd been unable to resist her dimpled smile.

She rubbed the ache in the back of her neck and stretched out her back. Birds chirped, and the cicadas took up the chorus too. She had one more basket of byssus to wash and spin into thread, and then she could rest. She went back to her cabin and began to gather the byssus from the pen shells.

When she heard the door behind her, she thought Huey had come back, and she turned with a welcoming smile. It died on her lips when she saw *her.* "What are you doing here?"

Liz's eyes looked crazed. "Why couldn't you leave him alone? He loved me before you came along."

"I didn't seek him out. He pursued me, and it just happened. I never meant to hurt you, but I love him."

Liz advanced a few feet. "Please, let's end this. I can give you two hundred thousand dollars. That's enough to keep you in style for a very long time. You'll have everything you need for the baby, and you'll never even need to work. You can stay home and take care of her."

The money wasn't even tempting. "Annabelle would rather have her daddy than pretty clothes. And we don't need your money. I'm going to make us rich with my sea silk technique."

Liz's eyes narrowed. She picked up a pen shell and turned it over in her hands. "So that's why he's willing to walk away. It's all about money, not love."

"That's not true!"

Why couldn't this woman just let them be? She was beautiful and wealthy. She didn't need Huey, not like Judy did. Not like Annabelle needed him.

Judy turned her back on the woman and bent to her task again. "I don't have time to argue with you. You need to accept the circumstances and move on with your life. Huey said you understood and were going away to Paris."

"Quit calling him Huey! It's ridiculous."

Judy realized Liz's voice was closer, and she looked up to see the woman rushing at her with the pointed end of a pen shell aimed at her head. She threw her hand up and grabbed at something shiny on the woman's arm, but it was too late.

Annabelle's sweet face flashed into her mind before the blow crushed into her and blotted out everything.

———

Ridge and Scott sat in the car outside Eric Kennedy's more modest home. Though in a pricey neighborhood, the beautiful

Spanish-style home was a fifth of the size of his parents' lavish estate. They'd been here over an hour, but no lights were on inside the house, and no one had answered the door.

Ridge moved restlessly. "Time is running out. We could try his office. He's running for city council." His mouth tasted like stale coffee, and he uncapped his water bottle to take a swig.

Scott shook his head. "I had a car go by there, and it's dark too. Let's wait a few more minutes. If he still doesn't come home, we'll go back to the Kennedy place and try again with the senior Mr. Kennedy."

Ridge's phone played, and he saw Brown and Sons Jewelers on the screen. "Mr. Brown, do you have information for me?"

"I spoke with my father, and he identified the bracelets as being commissioned by Thomas Kennedy as a gift for his fiancée and her bridesmaids. I hope that's helpful."

"It is. Please give him my thanks."

"Will do."

Ridge put his phone away and told Scott the news. "So we're definitely on the right track."

Car lights came down the street, and Ridge leaned forward and prayed it was Eric. The car drove by slowly, then turned into Eric's drive. Ridge's pulse quickened. It was a gray Cadillac. The garage door rose, and the car drove inside.

"Let's go." Ridge threw open his door and got out.

Scott was right beside him, and they both rushed the garage before the door descended.

"Mr. Kennedy," Scott called. "I'm a police detective, and I have an urgent matter to discuss with you."

Eric shut his door and turned toward them. He was dressed in khaki slacks and a polo shirt as if he'd just come from the golf course.

Irritation flashed across his face before he went expressionless. "What's this all about?"

Where to start? Ridge wasn't quite ready to assume the Kennedys had arranged for Harper's abduction, but he suspected they knew something that could help them. He kept quiet and let Scott take the lead.

"Sorry to bother you so late," Scott said in a calming, even tone. "We're looking for Harper Taylor, and we're aware of an altercation between you and her."

Brilliant move. Scott knew his interrogation techniques. Ridge prayed the man would reveal something.

"Altercation? There's no animosity between the two of us. I merely asked her to move her bivalve beds. No crime in that. I haven't seen her since the fund-raising party." Eric's gaze went to Ridge. "You were there too. I'm sure you noticed our exchange was friendly."

"Yes, I remember. Your parents were there too."

Eric nodded. "It's not likely my father will see another party. His liver continues to fail."

"I'm sorry to hear that. Is there anything the doctors can do?" Scott asked.

Eric shrugged. "A liver transplant is about all the hope we have, but he's hard to match. A relative would be best, but he has a rare blood type, and no one is lining up to offer up part of their liver." His wry grin didn't reach his eyes. "I'd give him part of mine, but I've already got some liver issues."

A relative.

It all clicked into place as he remembered seeing the ads for Eric's campaign. "Your grandfather was a US senator, right?"

Eric nodded again. "My mom's father, yes."

And Annabelle's father had been engaged to a woman

whose dad was a senator. Had they stumbled onto the identity of Harper's father?

Who needed a liver.

The blood drained from his head at what this might mean. "Your mom is a doctor of some kind."

"A transplant surgeon. She's exhausted every possible way of helping Dad, but there isn't much she can do."

Scott was looking at Ridge with a quizzical expression. He still didn't get it.

Ridge wet his lips. "Which hospital does your mom use?"

Though she wouldn't be harvesting Harper's liver in a hospital. She'd likely take her somewhere and render her unconscious, then take the harvested liver to her husband. Was there any chance Eric knew this? Ridge studied the man's face and decided he probably didn't know anything about this organ search.

Had it been Tom Kennedy's idea or Elizabeth's?

"She's certified at any hospital," Eric said. "These are strange questions. What's this all about?"

"Do your parents have any other property other than the big mansion on the bay?"

Eric's frown deepened. "I've said all I intend to. None of your questions have anything to do with Harper."

"I suspect one or both of your parents have taken Harper in order to harvest her liver for your father. I think she's your half sister."

Ridge watched the words register on the man's face. Disbelief flickered in his eyes, and he took a step back. "That's an absurd claim."

"If we're right, there isn't much time to spare, and you'll be held culpable in her death. She was abducted in a gray Cadillac. Where did you take her?" Ridge demanded.

Eric went pale. "I've been golfing all day. You can call the course. My car was handed over to the valet. The golf course will confirm I had nothing to do with this."

"Where might they have taken her?"

Eric blinked at Scott. "Th-There's a small building out in the woods. I can tell you how to get there."

Scott pulled out a notepad. "Go."

Eric rattled off directions down country roads and small highways. The location was about thirty minutes away. "But I think you're wrong." His voice lacked conviction.

"Let's go." Scott turned and raced for the car.

Ridge threw himself into the car and slammed the door. "Is there anyone who can reach them sooner?"

Scott stomped on the gas pedal, and the car took off with a squeal of tires. "No. We're closer than anyone in Orlando, and the only officers out there might be a sheriff or deputy. It would take longer to tell them about this and get someone on the way than for us to drive there. I'll call on the way." He switched on the siren and lights. "I can make it in twenty minutes."

Ridge felt like adding his own scream to the siren's as they raced off into the night. It might already be too late.

40

She was cold, so cold.

Harper strained to open her eyes. She heard the distant murmuring of voices, and she moved her hand. The sting of some kind of antiseptic burned her nose.

"She's waking up. Get another syringe."

The woman's voice was familiar. Harper forced one eye open and winced at the blinding light above. It hurt her eyes and made her head pound. Nausea churned in her stomach.

Don't go back to sleep. If she slept now, she'd never awaken, and her baby would die with her. With monumental effort Harper opened her eyes and looked up into the eyes above the doctor's mask. She knew those eyes.

Elizabeth Kennedy. And she was holding a scalpel.

"Why are you doing this?" Harper pushed the words past dry lips, but they came out in a whisper.

Elizabeth's eyes widened. "Get more drugs," she snapped at the nurse. "She should never have awakened."

"I don't have another syringe," the nurse said. "When your husband attacked me, he broke several of them."

"I don't want to take her liver while she's staring at me!"

293

Take her liver.

Harper rolled her head back and forth. "No, no. You can't do this."

"I'm sorry, Harper." But Elizabeth didn't look sorry. The brown eyes above the mask were stony and determined.

Harper's head was clearing more by the minute. She could move her hands again, and she was beginning to feel her feet. If she could just get off this table, she might be able to walk. Only Elizabeth and the nurse were in the room. The big man was gone and so was Mr. Kennedy.

Maybe she could keep Elizabeth distracted. "Where's your husband? I don't think he wants you to do this. And why me?"

"He needs a liver from a relative. I've been looking for you and your sister for a year. I ran Tom's DNA but adjusted his settings so he wouldn't show up as a result. However, I monitored results showing up for him, and voilà. There you were. You and Annabelle, just as I thought. I always knew you were out there somewhere."

Harper pitched her voice weaker than she felt as strength continued to course back into her limbs. "You killed Judy. Tom was going to leave you for her, wasn't he?"

"Silly twit thought she could take what belonged to me."

"And my mother. You had her brake lines cut. Why punish the women when Tom was the one with the wandering eye?"

"All men are like that. They can't stay faithful to a woman."

Ridge would. "That's a false generalization. I know many men who are steadfast and love one woman." Could she anger the woman enough to throw her off balance? "Maybe it was you all along. Tom saw into your heart and found it dark."

"That's not true! I loved him. None of this would have happened if he'd stayed true. But this will prove to him how much

I love him. He's upset now, but he'll thank me when he feels how much stronger he is with a new liver. Then he'll love me as much as I love him."

The woman's obsession had cost two women their lives, and Harper wasn't sure she'd be able to escape with Elizabeth looming over her with the scalpel poised to plunge into her body and steal her life.

She glanced at the nurse on the other side. She didn't have a weapon, so Harper's best chance was to roll off the table on that side. There was a tray of other scalpels and tools next to the nurse, too, so she could try to grab a weapon.

Harper tensed for her move. "What if he doesn't forgive you? All this might show him you were the one who killed the two women he really loved."

"I'm sure he already suspects that. He'll never leave me though." She raised the scalpel.

Now or never. Harper coiled every ounce of strength she possessed into her muscles and rolled violently to the left. She swung her leg over the edge of the table and came off it. Her legs weren't as strong as she'd hoped, and she stumbled into the stainless-steel tray table holding the operating tools. The tools went flying and clattered to the ground as she fell there herself. A scalpel was by her right hand, and she snatched it up as she got to her feet.

She held it out in front of her as the nurse came her way. "Stay away. I can gut you like I do a fish."

The graphic warning stopped the nurse for a moment until she gave a pretty smile. "You don't have the courage."

"That's where you're wrong. You're not taking my liver. I'm pregnant, and I'll do anything to protect my baby. I'm shocked you'd help this madwoman."

The nurse circled her and the smile never left. "And you're not stealing the money she's paying me. I hate the operating room, and I'll have the funds for a new life."

She feinted toward Harper, and Harper slashed the woman's wrist with the scalpel. Blood dripped to the concrete floor.

"You cut me!" The woman clapped her hand over the cut.

"Oh for heaven's sake, must I do everything myself?" Elizabeth came around the operating table. "Put that scalpel down, Harper. I'm much stronger than I look, and I'm an expert at using one of these."

Harper waved the scalpel in a menacing arc. "It's not much different from a fillet knife. I've gotten the hang of it."

Her heart pounded in her chest as she waited for Elizabeth to make her move. If the nurse came back with a scalpel, too, it would be two against one, but Harper didn't have anything to lose. She'd go down fighting.

Ridge peered through the sweep of headlights for the driveway. "There's the turn. Switch off the lights. We don't want to tip them off."

Scott slowed the car and killed the lights. The world ahead plunged into darkness with no streetlights or security lamps in the area. The car scraped a high spot as he turned it into the narrow drive, overgrown with weeds and grass.

Ridge unfastened his seat belt and leaned forward. "There's a light in that building. A couple of cars are there, too, including a gray Caddy. Looks like there's a chauffeur inside."

A shadow moved to the right of the building, and a man moved toward the front of the building. In the light shining out the front window, Ridge spotted a glint of metal. "I think he's got a gun."

"I'm calling for backup." Scott grabbed his phone and called in the request. "I don't think he's seen us yet."

"Let's back up out of the drive and walk in so he doesn't spot us. Maybe we can get the jump on him."

"I think he'll see us. I'll switch off the inside lights, and we'll slip out." Scott reached for the dash and fiddled with the controls. "Leave the door open so there's no noise."

Ridge opened his door and stepped into the weeds beside the drive. Noiselessly, Scott joined him. It was a dark night with the last of the storm clouds blotting out the moon and stars. He thought he heard someone running toward them and tensed with his fists up before he realized it was the wind rustling through the pines and oaks.

Scott pointed for him to go one way while he went the other, and Ridge nodded. Scott pulled out his gun and crept forward through the weeds. The man in front of the building patted his shirt pocket, then withdrew something. A flicker of flame showed him lighting a cigarette, and a curl of smoke drifted above his head. A few moments later Ridge caught the scent.

Good. He was distracted and might not notice them creeping up on him. Ridge moved to the left of the building with as little noise as possible. The shadow that was Scott moved to the right, and the guard didn't seem to notice until he froze and tipped his head as though listening.

Ridge tensed. Was that a scream from inside the building? His heart kicked in his chest, and he crept to his side of the building even though he couldn't see the guard any longer. The small window was high off the ground, and he had to stand on his toes to peer in the window. He spotted Harper right off. She was backed into a corner by two women, though she waved a scalpel. He didn't recognize the younger woman, but he recognized the doctor as Elizabeth.

He had to get inside. This window was too small, but maybe there was another way in. Scott could handle the guard. Ridge crept around to the back, but there was no door there or on the other side. They'd have to take out the guard and go through the front door. He sidled along the right side of the building until he nearly bumped into Scott.

"We have to get in. Now," he whispered. "I'll create a diversion, and you take him down."

Scott nodded, and Ridge looked around for a large rock. There. He grabbed one out from under an oak tree, then heaved it into the woods with all his might. He quickly seized a large tree branch and held it ready like a bat.

The guard's steps thundered their way, and they quickened as he neared the tree line. "Who's there? Show yourself or I'll shoot."

Scott brought up his gun. "Police! Get your hands up!"

Ridge coiled his muscles when the guard uttered an expletive and whirled with his gun in his hand. Ridge stepped past Scott and swung the branch with all his might. It connected with the guard's wrist, and his gun went flying. The guard glanced from Ridge to Scott, then took off at a quick run and disappeared into the forest.

"I'll go after him," Scott said. "You get Harper."

Ridge bounded for the door and threw it open. The women approaching Harper must have thought the guard had come to help them because they didn't stop stalking toward Harper.

"This is over! The police are here and more are coming."

The nurse's scalpel clattered to the floor, and she turned to face him with a dismayed expression. "It was all her fault." She pointed at Elizabeth.

Elizabeth turned with the scalpel still in her hand. "No, no, you can't stop this. It's too important. Tom will die without her liver. I have to save him."

She whirled back toward Harper with the scalpel raised, and Ridge vaulted toward her. He hit her in the back, and they both flew two feet before they hit the wall. Elizabeth was twisted under him. He tried to get up and bring her with him, but her eyes narrowed and she struggled to jab him in the neck with the scalpel.

The blade slid into his neck, and blood ran down his skin to his chest. She raised the scalpel to stab him again.

"No!" Harper moved quickly to grab the older woman's wrist. She twisted Elizabeth's hand until the scalpel clattered onto the concrete floor.

Elizabeth sagged and tears leaked from her eyes. "You've ruined everything—you've sentenced Tom to death." She ripped off the surgical mask and huddled in a ball in the corner while she continued to wail.

Ridge had never seen a better sight than Harper as she moved toward him. Her face was white and her hair was in disarray, but she'd never looked more beautiful.

"We need to stop the bleeding." She grabbed gauze from a stainless-steel tray and pressed it against his neck. "It's not too bad."

"I'm not hurt much." He took her in his arms, and she nestled against his chest as though she'd been made for that exact spot. And maybe she was. "I thought I'd lost you," he murmured against her sweet-smelling hair. "Thank God you're all right."

His embrace tightened around her, and she wrapped her arms around him as though she'd never let him go. And he hoped she never would.

41

Hospital personnel had whisked Harper off to be checked out the minute the ambulance brought her in. Ridge had been sent in another direction to get stitches, and as a nurse wheeled Harper to an exam room, she saw Mr. Kennedy brought in by stretcher from another ambulance. His color was nearly orange as they rushed past with him to another room.

His wife was nowhere to be found since she'd been taken into custody as police cars poured onto the property. Harper tried to listen to determine what was going on, and her pulse stuttered when she heard one of the nurses say he wasn't going to make it. His liver had failed.

Once her blood had been drawn and she felt less wobbly, Harper slid off the exam table and opened her door. His exam room across the hall stood open, and she saw him on a table hooked to equipment. His eyelids fluttered, so at least she knew he was alive. This might be the only opportunity she had to talk to her father.

Her father.

It felt surreal to know his face and name after all these years. She cast a glance down both directions of the hall, then darted out of her room and into his. She pulled the door shut behind her and approached him.

She touched his hand. "Mr. Kennedy."

His eyes opened, and he looked up at her. A smile lifted the corners of his lips, and a cough wracked his body. His breath wheezed through his chest, and his color was awful. She didn't know how he could look so bad and still be living.

"Hello, Mr. Kennedy. I-I'm your daughter. Harper."

His shaky hand reached up and touched a wisp of her hair. "Beautiful like your mother. So sorry, little girl. Should have left Liz a long time ago. Never meant for her to hurt you."

"Did you know she killed Judy and my mother?"

He wheezed again, and a coughing spasm left him gasping. He blinked watery blue eyes. "Thought maybe. Didn't want to know though."

The door opened, and a nurse stepped inside. "What are you doing in here? The doctor is looking for you."

"This is my father. I wanted to see him for a minute."

The nurse fixed her with a disapproving stare. "You can come back later. The doctor is in your room."

"I'll be back." She went across the hall to join the doctor.

"There you are. I have your test results. You're a very lucky lady. The drug administered to you would likely have killed you if you'd gotten even a little bit more of it. You say Dr. Kennedy planned to take your liver and give it to her husband?"

"That's right. He's my father, and he needs a new liver from a relative because of certain parameters in his body according to her."

"She had to have realized he couldn't survive the surgery. He's much too weak."

"I could tell he's in bad shape. How long is he expected to live?"

"I'm afraid I can't tell you that. His son is on his way, and perhaps he will tell you what he knows. He and Dr. Kennedy are the only ones I'm authorized to share information with."

"Of course." She hesitated. "As I mentioned when I was brought in, I'm pregnant. Would this drug harm my baby?"

He winced. "It does increase the risk of miscarriage. Have you had any spotting or cramps?"

She put her hand on her stomach. "No, I've been feeling fine."

"How far along are you?"

"I had an embryo transfer over two weeks ago."

"So we'd call that a four-week gestation. That's too early for an ultrasound to check for a heartbeat." He touched her shoulder. "Try not to worry and check with your obstetrician in a couple of weeks. An ultrasound should set your mind at ease."

"I'll do that, thanks. Can I see my father again?"

He hesitated, then gave a slow nod. "It might be a good idea."

Her chest squeezed because she realized what he was saying. There wasn't much time left. She followed him out of the room and across to her father's room.

Eric stood beside his father and had his hand on Tom's shoulder. "Dad?"

The alarms began to go off, and the doctor leaped into action. Harper backed out of the room and stood there as Eric was shooed out as well and two nurses and another doctor flew in to assist. The door shut, and Harper backed away to lean against the wall.

Tears tracked down Eric's face. "He's not going to make it."

"I know," she whispered.

He looked at her then, really looked at her. "Is it true that Dad is your father?"

She nodded. "Your mother wanted to steal my liver to give to your dad. He has another daughter as well." She told him about Annabelle and what had happened to her.

Eric clasped his hands together and paced the floor, shaking his head. "I can't believe Mom would do this."

Harper hesitated. This was all going to come out. "It appears likely she killed my mother and Annabelle's mother as well. She was determined not to lose your dad." And this guy was her half brother. It was hard to wrap her head around.

Eric winced. "I was their only child, and I often felt like an intruder. Mom loved him beyond all reason. I went into politics and thought maybe she'd finally be proud of me. I shouldn't have bothered." His gaze bored into her. "I vandalized your pen shell beds. I'm sorry for that. Causes like the Native American burial grounds get me fired up. I'd like to make amends."

"It's okay. I'm going to move them."

"I'd like to help."

"And I'll accept your help. Thank you."

Elizabeth might never be convicted of the murders, but she'd go to jail for Harper's attempted murder, and Eric's life would never be the same. Elizabeth and her cohorts had been arrested, but Harper couldn't help worrying about her kidnapper's little boy. What would happen to him?

Harper heard Ridge call her name and turned to see him walking toward her down the hall. A white bandage was on his throat, but he looked good—really good.

She went to him, and he opened his arms. They had so

much to talk about, but right now she just wanted his arms around her.

⌒

The two days since Harper had been rescued were hectic for Ridge with arrangements for his father's funeral. He stood just inside the door half an hour before the mourners were due to arrive. He hadn't wanted to see his father's body, so it would be closed casket. His dad would have wanted it that way too.

Flowers filled the large church, and the cloying scent made his head ache. Or maybe it was the pain in his heart when he thought about his dad.

He scratched at the stitches on his neck, then tugged at the tie strangling him. His gaze followed Harper as she approached the closed casket and touched the spray of roses atop it.

This would be a hard day for all of them. His sister would be here any moment, and he hoped Willow stayed as soft to Harper as she'd seemed to be the other night.

They still hadn't talked about the future. He couldn't find the words yet while he was dealing with his dad's murder. Elizabeth had arranged for Dad's murder because of the investigation into Harper's parentage. The private eye had called back and confirmed he'd told Dad the details. It was all going to come out, and Elizabeth had been desperate to prevent it.

So many people dead because of one woman's obsession. Even if she'd taken Harper's liver, her husband would have died. Tom had never come out of liver failure the night of the rescue, and Eric was planning his father's funeral as well. Elizabeth would likely never get out of prison.

Harper walked back to join him by the door. She looked beautiful with her dark-red hair in an updo. She wore an aqua dress that deepened the color of her eyes and showed off her long legs. But those eyes were shadowed with pain, and he knew she missed Dad as much as he did. He'd been a rock for her, and she had to feel adrift.

He took her hand. "You finally found your dad only to lose him. I'm sorry."

Her fingers tightened around his. "He wasn't much of a father, not even to Eric, I think. And he suspected his wife had killed his mistresses, yet he'd never done anything about it. He didn't even leave her. Oliver had more strength in his little finger than Tom did in his whole body." She looked up at him with tears shimmering in her eyes. "We're always going to miss Oliver. I keep wanting to call him and tell him something, and then I remember he's gone."

"Me too." He swallowed down the lump in his throat. "We haven't talked, and we need to."

"But not today." Her gaze went back to the casket. "Today is about Oliver. He left you an awesome legacy of courage. And me too. I wouldn't be the same person if Oliver hadn't rescued me."

Ridge still hadn't let go of her hand, and he raised it to his lips. "I'm glad he did too. And I'm sorry I didn't appreciate him more. I want to emulate the way he loved other people. He was always thinking of others. I get way too busy and don't even notice. He wasn't perfect, but who is?"

Her gaze returned to him, and she nodded. "I hope we can continue his legacy."

"I have some ideas about that I want to talk to you about when this is over."

"Okay." She glanced over his shoulder toward the door. "Your sister is here. Your mom too."

He turned and waved to them. Maybe the first place to change would be with his own family. He needed to turn the other cheek and learn to love past slights and disagreements.

42

Though Ridge had said he wanted to talk to Harper, there had been no time in the past two weeks. She had found a place to move her mollusk beds, far from the burial grounds. It felt like the right thing to do in case she was intruding on history. She was beginning to have some morning sickness, but as long as she made sure she had plenty of protein, she wasn't miserable.

The flutters in her stomach as she sat in the waiting room weren't from morning sickness. Today she'd get a glimpse of her baby and make sure everything was all right after her ordeal. She'd been tense and worried about it since she'd been given the anesthetic, but there'd been no sign of any problems. That wasn't foolproof though. Her baby could have died, and she just hadn't miscarried yet. She'd heard stories that kept her from relaxing.

Other women were waiting, too, some wearing tense expressions and others laughing and kidding with their husbands. She wasn't the only woman here by herself, but she wished she wasn't facing this alone. If Sara had been available, Harper would have asked her to come with, but her friend was getting the final fitting on her wedding dress today.

She caught sight of a familiar shock of dark hair passing the plate-glass window. Ridge? She half rose as he walked into the office, then sank back down as he came toward her. She drank in the sight of him in a royal-blue shirt and jeans.

"What are you doing here?" she whispered as he sat beside her.

He clasped her hand in his. "I didn't want you to do this alone."

"How'd you know where I was?"

"Sara, of course. You should have told me."

"It's been a busy time, and I didn't want to bother you." While he'd been sweet and kind to her, they hadn't had a private conversation about what he was thinking. Did he see a future with her, or was he just being a friend?

A nurse called her name, and Harper fumbled to her feet. Ridge followed her through the inner door and back to the ultrasound room.

The tech greeted them with a smile and directed her to climb onto the table. She pointed out a chair to Ridge. "Feel free to pull that wherever you want it so you can see the screen, too, Daddy."

Harper gulped, but it didn't seem the right time to contradict the tech as she directed Harper to disrobe from the waist down. She gulped again and looked at Ridge, who quickly backed out of the room with the tech. This might be a bit embarrassing.

She yanked off her shorts and pulled the paper sheet over her. "I'm ready," she called.

Ridge came into the room first, and the tech followed him. He leaned down and whispered in her ear, "Don't be embarrassed. I'll watch the screen, and I won't look your way."

Her face went hot, but she managed to mouth *thank you*

before the tech moved into place. She lifted the sheet. "Let's see what we've got here." She began to move the ultrasound wand around.

Harper squinted at the screen, which was just black-and-white blobs to her. She didn't know what she was looking for.

"There's your baby." The tech pointed out a black space that held a small circular C-shape. "And there's the heartbeat! See that fast little flicker? Everything looks good." She hit a button. "I'm printing it off for you."

Tears flooded Harper's eyes, and she pulled the sheet back up. Her gaze never left that tiny baby nestled comfortably in her womb.

She was going to be a mother. It seemed almost impossible to believe. Ridge's warm brown eyes were smiling with his lips, and he was watching the screen as well.

"Can you tell the gender yet?" he asked.

"No, it's much too soon," the tech said. "She needs to be at least sixteen weeks before we can tell that. But everything seems fine. You appear to be about six weeks along." She handed Harper a handful of paper towels. "You can clean off the gel with these and get dressed. Congratulations."

Ridge winked at Harper and followed the tech from the room. Still in a daze, Harper cleaned off the gel and pulled on her shorts and sandals. When she exited the room, she found Ridge standing in the hall by the door. He was staring at the printout of the baby.

He looked up when the door opened and handed her the picture. "There's your little one. It's hard to believe we got a glimpse of life like that. I'm glad I was here."

"So am I."

He hadn't said *our* little one, and a heaviness descended on her shoulders. If he loved her and wanted to be part of her life, wouldn't he have said something by now?

It was a gorgeous day for a wedding. Harper couldn't imagine a more perfect setting for this much-anticipated day. White chiffon covered the wedding arch and fluttered in the gentle breeze off the ocean. It was a perfect sixty-nine degrees, about average for late February. The wedding had been beautiful, and the reception was in full swing with guests partaking of cake and drinks. She'd met old friends of Sara's from Hope Beach, but the names all ran together. She remembered Elin, whom she'd heard a lot about, and there was a Libby and Amy she thought. They'd come with smiles and husbands and children in tow.

Harper smoothed the silky turquoise material of the maid of honor dress over her hips and sipped her punch. Laughter rose over the sound of the gulls and the waves, and she released a sigh of satisfaction. Sara had finally married her Josh, and Harper loved looking at the two them, hands clasped and so obviously in love.

Ridge stood with a group of Coast Guard men off to one side. From the bits of conversation she heard, they appeared to be talking about football.

She put down her punch and kicked off her shoes to walk along the beach. She needed to decide what she was going to do. Her houseboat wasn't big enough for a baby, and besides, it hardly seemed safe once the little one began crawling and toddling around. That meant she needed to find a house. Thanks to Oliver's generosity she could afford one.

Ridge's deep voice broke into her thoughts. "Mind if I join you?"

She stopped and turned. "Of course not, though I didn't want to pull you away from your important discussion about passes."

His smile flashed, and he took her hand. "You look beautiful today, but you were so somber just now. Is everything okay?"

She relished the feel of his strong hand enfolding hers. "I'm fine. Just thinking about the need to move from my boat."

"I'd thought about that too. It's not the place to raise a baby."

At least he'd thought about her and the baby. She hadn't been sure he had spared her a thought, though she knew he'd been swamped with details of Oliver's businesses. So many things had been screaming for his attention, and though she'd thought about stopping by several times and telling him how she felt, she hadn't wanted to run the risk of rejection.

She couldn't bear it right now.

"I know what you did for that little boy. You're a good man, Ridge Jackson. How did you hear about him?"

"Scott heard about it after he arrested his dad. The boy's only five. I had to do something. He got a new kidney yesterday. You approve?"

She smiled up at him. "You're amazing."

He stopped and pulled her around to face him. "With so much death, it didn't seem the right time to tell you how I feel about you, Harper, but seeing how happy Josh and Sara are, I realized we don't know what tomorrow will bring. We didn't expect my dad to die in his sixties. Life is unpredictable, and if something happened to you . . ." His voice grew choked.

What was he saying? It felt as though her feet might float

right off the ground. She searched his brown eyes for some kind of reassurance.

He held her gaze with serious intent. "I love you, Harper. I love your deep commitment to family and the way you love other people. I love the care you took of my dad and the way you throw yourself so fiercely into everything you do. I love the way you didn't let your past define you and you managed to work past your trust issues. I want to spend the rest of my life with you. I want to be a father to this baby and to all the other babies we might have together. I see a future filled with love and joy. If you'll have me."

He reached into his pocket and withdrew a small velvet box, then dropped to one knee. When he opened the box, the most beautiful rose-gold ring she'd ever seen winked in the sunlight. Tiny stones circled the large black pearl in the center.

"Is that the pearl we found in the bivalve?" she whispered.

He nodded. "I wanted your ring to remind us both of all that binds us together. Harper, will you marry me?"

Her throat was so tight she couldn't speak so she nodded instead. Tears spilled from her lashes and ran down her cheeks as she finally found she could whisper, "I love you, Ridge. So much."

He pulled the ring from its nest and slipped it on her finger. "I had to guess on the size. You wouldn't believe all the jewelry stores I had to visit to track down that pearl."

"It feels perfect." She held it out in the sunlight and admired it.

He rose and pulled her into his arms to the sound of thunderous applause and catcalls. She peeked around his shoulder to see everyone from the wedding had crowded around them. Sara was crying, and maybe there was even a glimmer of a tear in Josh's eye.

Harper hid her face against the rough fabric of Ridge's jacket. Family could be made up of friends, too, but she'd been too focused on finding her father to appreciate the blessings she already had in her friends. She had the best future she could imagine looking back at her.

She raised her face for his kiss, and Ridge brushed her lips with his. "I'll do a better job of this when we're alone," he whispered as he pulled her closer into his embrace.

Every time she looked at this ring she would remember the way he'd charged into danger for her. It would be a reminder of the storms they'd weathered hand in hand and how the remaining strands of truth from the past had reached out to draw them together. His arms would always be a forever home to her.

A NOTE FROM THE AUTHOR

Dear Reader,

Everywhere we look there are ads for DNA kits to trace your ancestry and family. While this kind of information is fascinating, the possible abuses are daunting as well. What will people do with new family information? It has the power for great connections but also for great hurt.

My daughter-in-law had her DNA test done and discovered family members that led to some closer-than-anticipated connections. I heard all kinds of dramatic stories. My mind always runs to murder mysteries, so that's where the germ of this story idea was born.

Have you had your DNA done? I'd love to hear any interesting stories you've run across! I love to hear from readers, and I hope you enjoy this twisted tale.

Love,

Colleen Coble

colleen@colleencoble.com

ACKNOWLEDGMENTS

My great thanks to Jochen Gerber, Invertebrates Collections Manager at the Chicago Field Museum! Your help with pen shells and sea silk was invaluable as well as all the information you gave me about malacology. I loved the behind-the-scenes look at the Field Museum!

Special thanks to Felicitas Maeder from the Naturhistorisches Museum in Switzerland. She's the foremost authority on sea silk, and her research was so interesting and valuable! While I might have loved to really believe that all the references to byssus in history were about sea silk, her meticulous research proved that idea wrong. Thanks so much, Felicitas!

And special thanks to Michelle Glandon for your help with the Dunedin details! All those pictures, videos, and descriptions inspired many scenes. Thanks so much!

I'm so blessed to belong to the terrific HarperCollins Christian Publishing dream team! I've been with my great fiction team for seventeen years, and we've grown closer and closer over the years.

Our fiction publisher and editor, Amanda Bostic, is as dear to me as a daughter. She really gets suspense and has been my friend from the moment I met her all those years ago. Fabulous cover guru Kristen Ingebretson works hard to create the perfect cover—and does. My amazing fiction family: Becky Monds,

Acknowledgments

Allison Carter, Jodi Hughes, Paul Fisher, Matt Bray, Kimberly Carlton, Laura Wheeler, Jocelyn Bailey, and Savannah Summers all contribute so much to my career. You are all rock stars! I wish I could name all the great folks at HCCP who work on selling my books through different venues. I'm truly blessed!

Julee Schwarzburg is a dream editor to work with. She smooths out all my rough spots and makes me look better than I am. I'm so thankful for her touch on my books!

My agent, Karen Solem, has helped shape my career in many ways, and that includes kicking an idea to the curb when necessary. We are about to celebrate twenty years together! And my critique partner of over twenty years, Denise Hunter, is the best sounding board ever. Thanks, friends!

I'm so grateful for my husband, Dave, who carts me around from city to city, washes towels, and chases down dinner without complaint. My kids—Dave, Kara (and now Donna and Mark)—love and support me in every way possible, and my little granddaughter, Alexa, makes every day a joy. She's so grown up now, and having her spend the night is more fun than I can tell you. Our little grandson Elijah is twenty-seven months old now, and his baby brother, Silas, is eight months old. We try to split our time between them, but I'm constantly missing someone.

Most important, I give my thanks to God, who has opened such amazing doors for me and makes the journey a golden one.

DISCUSSION QUESTIONS

1. Ridge disliked Harper for taking advantage of his dad. Why is it harder to forgive someone for hurting someone we love?
2. Harper has always longed for family. What do you think of her decision to adopt an embryo?
3. Have you ever had your DNA done? If so, were there any surprises?
4. Ridge had relationship issues with his mother and sister. What was at the root of it?
5. Oliver helped salvage Harper's life. Have you ever stepped out in a major way to help a stranger?
6. Harper kept the truth of her pregnancy secret from Ridge for too long. Why is it hard to tell the truth sometimes?
7. Ridge decided to share the inheritance with his sister. Why or why not do you think this was the right decision?
8. Do you agree with Harper about how we can create our own family among friends?

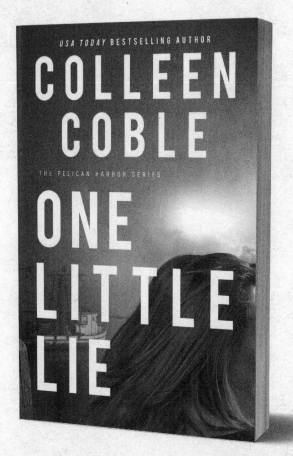

Don't miss Colleen Coble's Lavender Tides series set amid the gorgeous lavender fields of Washington state—but the beauty masks deadly secrets.

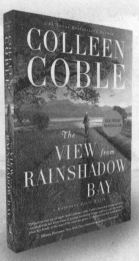

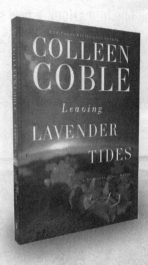

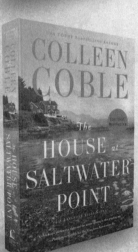